Written by Ben Coleman

Copyright © 2025 Ben Coleman

All rights reserved. This book or any portion thereof may not be reproduced or used in any manner whatsoever without express written permission of the publisher, except for the use of brief quotations in a book review.

ISBN 9798286819157
Independently published

MEET THE SQUAD

Captain Clean
Clifford Cane
(The leader)

HyJean
Jean Wilkes
(The genius)

Faucet
Nelson Spigot
(The superpower)

Flush
Will Armitage
(The part-timer)

Sgt. Suds
Mick Goldman
(The muscle)

Mary
(The administrator)

SANITARY SQUAD

PIPES OF WAR

Filtham. A city just outside London, but far enough that they didn't have to increase the prices of their hot beverages to trick unsuspecting tourists. It was a small city; historically unimportant, but a few famous writers and sports people had been born there – before quickly moving to London when they realised it was much nicer and had better coffee. The city of Filtham seemed to live up to its name, with barely a see-through window in sight along the well-littered streets. No matter how much people cleaned, it always seemed to revert back to a less than welcoming state. But one place that was cleaner than most was the shopping centre. Filtham Shopping Centre was the heart of the city. Partly because it had a wide range of shops and restaurants to offer retail and nourishment, but also because there were plenty of regular beatings going on. This was mainly due to drunken parties who had wandered over from local bars at night when Filtham City Football Club (or "FC squared" as the locals referred to it, which in turn led to rival fans nicknaming it "FC scared") lost a match – which was unfortunately quite a regular occurrence. But aside from the occasional hooliganism, it was a fairly ordinary shopping centre. Trendy clothes shops, expensive electronic shops, too many artisan coffee shops and not enough escalators. Least important were the toilets – unless you were desperate, in which case they suddenly became the most important place in the shopping centre. On the second floor, tucked away next to a women's clothes shop, were the public toilets. Inside, on one particular day, a man called Chad Baker zipped up his flies and did his usual little post-wee whistle. He was a young, handsome guy, dressed in trendy clothes. In years gone by, he would've been described as a yuppie, but these days people had other, less polite names they would use.

'See you out there,' he said to his equally despisable friend, who was still in the middle of relieving himself at the urinal. Chad made his way towards the door, heading back out into the crowded shopping centre to continue buying things he didn't need just because he could afford them. He eyed himself up in the mirror as he passed, admiring his reflection with a self-assured grin. However, as he turned to leave, a hand suddenly reached out and slammed against the door, pushing it shut. Slowly and silently, the hand reached down and turned the lock, trapping the three of them inside.

Chad stumbled back in surprise and watched as the mysterious doorman stepped out of the shadows. He was a tall, well-built man, who was muscular but still had a bit of a 'dad bod', dressed in a blue shirt and jeans, along with a pair of marigold gloves and a matching yellow bed sheet tied around his neck. But most surprising was his face, or rather the lack of one. His head was completely concealed in toilet paper, wrapped around like a modern-day mummy, with only a small gap showing his dark eyes, staring menacingly at Chad.

'Yurph durphum rursh yurh hurph,' mumbled the man.

'Wh-what?' asked Chad, a slight quiver in his voice as he took a step backwards.

'Yuph durph… hurph urmph,' he raised a gloved hand and pulled a bit of the toilet roll away from his face to reveal his mouth. 'You didn't wash your hands,' he said in a deep, gruff voice that sounded like he'd just swallowed a bag of gravel.

Chad stood up a bit straighter, some of his confidence returning after hearing the less than threatening accusation. 'Yeah, so what?' he scoffed.

'Don't you know there's a virus going around,' said the man. 'You're spreading your germs among all those people out there.'

'Who cares? I ain't got no virus,' said Chad, moving forward to try and push past the crazy man.

However, the crazy man stopped him and pushed him back with a surprisingly strong shove.

'You might have it and not know it!' he shouted angrily. 'You could pass it on to anyone! And even if you don't, you'll still be spreading around your germs! Now wash your hands!'

'Hey, leave him alone freak!' came a voice from behind. Chad's friend – who had been struggling to finish at the urinal while all this was going on – ran forward and took a swing at the man. Little did he know, the masked man was actually an expert in several martial arts. He dodged the swinging arm and threw his own punch at the kid's face, knocking him back down onto to the floor.

'Now wash your hands!' he repeated to Chad in his gravelly tone.

'Or what?' said Chad, still not deterred by the sight of his friend lying on the floor with blood trickling out from his nose.

'Or I'll…' but the man was interrupted by the sound of ringing. It was coming from his pocket. 'Aww man, not now.'

He reached into pocket and pulled out a pair of handcuffs. In a swift movement, he grabbed Chad and cuffed him to the tap. From his other pocket, he pulled out his phone and answered it.

'Hello… oh hi mum… my voice? … oh, uh, I have a sore throat … yeah,

I will… okay, I'll pick some up and drop them off later … okay, mum I've got to go now … no, I don't care about the woman next door, look I've got to go … okay, bye mum … yes, I… I love you too … bye.'

The man pocketed his phone and turned back to Chad, who had just been looking on in bemusement at the strangely ordinary phone call.

'Okay, so where were we?' the man asked.

'Well, you'd just punched my friend and then you cuffed me to this tap,' said Chad, as he returned to his worried state, as if they'd been rehearsing a play and briefly stopped for a drink.

'Oh yeah. Right, now are you going to wash your hands, or are we going to have to do this the hard way?'

Chad gulped. 'What's the hard way?'

'I cut off your hands and wash them myself.'

'Ha, with what?' asked Chad with a slightly nervous laugh.

The man pulled back his cape slowly to reveal what was clipped to the left side of his belt.

'A pack of wet wipes?' asked a confused Chad.

'Huh? Oh, sorry. New belt,' said Cap. He pulled back the cape on the other side to reveal a large pair of secateurs attached to his belt.

Chad let out a little squeal. 'I'll wash them! I'll wash them!'

He fumbled around and managed to turn on the tap that his wrist was still cuffed to. He rinsed his hands under the water, smiling nervously at the man, looking desperately for approval.

'With soap,' said the masked man sternly. 'All over.'

Chad nodded frantically. 'Of course,' he said, as he covered his hands in a ridiculous amount of soap and washed them as thoroughly as he could.

'Good. Now make sure you do that every time you finish in the toilet,' he said, talking as if Chad were a young schoolboy learning for the first time.

'I will, I promise,' said Chad, nodding furiously. 'C-can I go now?'

The toilet roll-covered stranger nodded his toilet paper-covered head and uncuffed Chad, who promptly ran out of the toilets. The masked man heard a groan and looked down at the floor, where the other young teen was still lying clutching his nose.

'Hey! You forgot your…' he called after Chad, but there was no way he'd hear him now. He just shrugged and muttered, 'Ah forget it.'

He pulled the toilet paper back over his mouth and headed for the door. As he was leaving, the kid on the floor sat up.

'Uh mister… who are you?' the boy asked.

'Irf cupfhuhn cruuhm,' mumbled the man.

'Huh?' he replied.

The man pulled the toilet roll away from his mouth and repeated, 'I'm Captain Clean.'

💧💧

Six years and a few weeks later.

It was early and so was he. Martin Daley paced the corridor, running through his presentation one last time. Today was the day he finally gave his pitch to the head of product development at LoTech, Filtham's largest technology company – "why settle for high tech when you can have LoTech" as their advert proudly boasted. Their products were expensive and solved problems that nobody knew even existed until LoTech told them they did. If you didn't have the latest LoTech computer, TV or stereo system, you were a nobody. Or at least that's what their adverts with the sexy young couples liked to make you believe.

Martin was a short man in his forties, and everything about him was round. His rotund belly, which had long since given in to his love of cake; his balding head, which certain tribes might have rubbed for good luck; and his bulbous nose that made it look like he was holding in a dozen sneezes. Martin had been working on his presentation for weeks and he knew that, if he pulled it off, he would get the promotion he so desperately wanted and felt he deserved. He checked his watch. 8:54am. He still had six minutes until the meeting. As he leaned against the wall and rehearsed his pitch for the 17th time that morning, a familiar face came around the corner. Victor Timm, his colleague and arch-nemesis. It was a bold term to describe someone, but Martin felt it applied. Victor was taller, slimmer and had more hair than Martin, but he didn't have a 10% discount at the local bakery like Martin did – he loved the tarts in that bakery, and liked their cakes too. He had joined the company at the same time as Martin and it hadn't been long before a rivalry was born. He was the sort that did very little and showed no respect, but somehow managed to succeed at everything. He won all his pitches, got all the bonuses and copped off with all the new girls at the Christmas party. And now he was trying to take Martin's promotion from him too.

'Oh, you're going for the job too?' said Victor, pretending like he hadn't found out a week before from Janet from HR while they were making out in the stationery cupboard.

'Yes,' said Martin, clutching his folder a little tighter but still trying to appear unphased.

'Well, good luck I guess,' he said with a smirk. 'You're gonna need it.'

'Damn straight I am!' said Martin in a strangely confident tone.

Victor was interviewing after Martin, so he went into the toilet to relieve himself first. After he'd done his business, he sauntered over to the taps. Rather than wash his hands, though, he checked himself out in the mirror and adjusted some individual strands of hair that were covered in a thick layer of gel. Had he not been so focussed on admiring his perfectly combed hair, he would've heard the faint crackle as a flaky crust started to grow at a rapid pace around the taps.

The counter began to shake a little, and cracks started forming, gradually growing out from the sink along the worktop. Victor continued to be oblivious to what was going on below him, far too interested in his own reflection to pay anything else in the world any attention. He smiled at himself in the mirror and gave a cheeky wink. At the precise moment the mirror caught his wink, the sink below him suddenly gave way, collapsing in on itself and pulling the taps down with it into the hole below.

The area in front of him exploded with jets of water, splashing up like someone on the ceiling was having a shower, and soaking the floor beneath him. Victor jumped back and let out a high-pitched scream. He panicked and made a run for the door, but the wet floor made him stumble and the collapsing ground around him pulled him down. He felt some kind of hand rise up and grab his leg, surprisingly light to the touch, but making a crunching sound as it gripped him. He screamed and shouted, crying out for help with high pitched squeals that evaporated any coolness he had.

Outside, Martin became alerted to the tumultuous fracas coming from inside the toilets. He wasn't usually one to put himself in any kind of danger, but knowing who was inside, he felt he had to at least check it out, if only to have something to hold over Victor later. He tried to open the door, but something was jamming it from the inside. He pushed and kicked it with all his strength – which wasn't much – and eventually the door gave way, pushing aside the rubble that was blocking its path.

Martin peered in just in time to see a grotesque, grainy claw pull Victor down into the hole where the sink had been. He stood aghast as Victor's screams slowly faded away. Martin stumbled backwards out of the toilets and fell into the corridor. He was terrified by what he'd seen and didn't know what to do.

At that moment, the meeting room door opened and one of the senior members of staff came out to get him.

'We're ready for you Martin,' said the interviewer.

'Wh… but… in the… Vic… and the…' he stuttered, still in shock.

'It's okay, there's nothing to worry about,' the man said, taking Martin's arm and guiding him into the boardroom. 'Everyone gets nervous before an interview.'

He led Martin inside and closed the door behind them.

Filtham Community Centre was a stone's throw away from the city centre – if the person throwing the stone was an Olympic javelin champion that had been exposed to radiation and gained super strength. It was a place where the people of the community could gather and enjoy themselves and revel in exercise for both the body and brain. The first and third floors were home to regular activities for children, the elderly and anyone else who didn't fall into either of those two categories. From coffee mornings and book clubs to martial arts and pottery, the community centre offered a little slice of joy and culture to the city. The second floor, however, was off limits to the public. It was said to be space that politicians and very important businesspeople used for private meetings, but this was merely a cover for something far more interesting.

In a small office on the second floor, Clifford Cane was sat at his desk, reading a book entitled "Microbial Choreography: Biofilm Formation and Communication in Bacterial Colonies" by the author I.M. Boring. Clifford was a middle-aged man, with short hair and no other real distinctive features. He was a tall and well-built, muscular but still with a bit of a 'dad bod'. Overall, his physical appearance was extraordinarily ordinary. Suddenly, a knock on the door disturbed the silence. A woman poked her head around the door. She was dressed smartly, with an outfit accentuated with purple skirt and boots, and matching gloves. Her top was white though, because dressing all in purple would have made her look like a walking aubergine. She wore a belt with several small spray bottles and plastic sample tubes attached to it, finished with a buckle in the shape of a circle with a water droplet over it. She had long brown hair and a kind face that had clearly been worn down by years of stressful work and frown lines on her forehead that were reserved for her boss.

'We've got another one Cliff,' she said.

Clifford looked up excitedly, happy for some action after a quiet few days. 'Where?' he asked.

'The LoTech building,' she told him. 'The police report says he witnessed a man disappear down a sink.'

'Is he still there?'

'No, he disappeared down a sink.'

'I mean the witness.'

'No, the police sent him home and passed his number on to a local psychiatrist.'

'Great, I'll pay him a visit.'

'The psychiatrist?'

'No, the sink man,' he grumbled.

'Ah, shame,' she muttered. 'I thought for a minute there you might get some help.'

'I don't need help,' said Clifford, standing up. 'I need answers. And tea, but that can wait.'

Clifford walked over to a machine on the wall and pushed a button on it. A small roll of what looked like toilet paper popped dropped down onto a little tray at the bottom. He took the roll and started wrapping the paper around the top half of his head.

You see, Clifford was better known as Captain Clean – or Cap to his friends, who were mainly his colleagues as he didn't have the time (or social skills) for friends. Captain Clean was the leader of the Sanitary Squad, a group of "grime fighting heroes", set up and funded by the council, that dealt mainly with sanitation themed crimes. For some reason, there seemed to be a lot of sanitation themed crimes going on in the city. Some people suspected it may have been in direct response to the Sanitary Squad forming, but nobody really said anything, as very little else happened in the city and it was something exciting to watch on the news instead of news stories about annoying celebrities cheating on each other with even more annoying celebrities.

The woman who had brought the news was Dr Jean Wilkes – known in the squad as HyJean – and she was the brains behind the group. She was gifted when it came to technology, science and pretty much anything that she put her brilliant mind to. She was a competent fighter, but her strength lay more in being a strong strategic thinker, often avoiding fights through more clever means. With several degrees and a wealth of experience working at some of the top scientific research institutes, she was arguably overqualified for the squad, but that didn't stop her. Since she'd mentioned in her interview that she owned a computer, she was also put in charge of monitoring the criminal activity in the city using a series of computers that lined one of the walls in the base – actually just one computer with several cheap monitors to make it look a bit more impressive. She was also frequently bombarded with questions about phones not working or broken coffee machines, because that's what happens when you use a computer for work, everyone thinks you're a technician who can fix any technical fault.

Like most of the squad's equipment, HyJean had developed the captain's toilet paper mask, making it out of a special material so that it was extra durable and waterproof. She'd also advised him to remove the bottom half so that he could be heard more clearly – a decision which she often regretted.

The captain was dressed in his usual blue shirt with blue jeans and yellow boots. He would've liked a professional uniform for his squad, but their budget from the council only allowed them the luxury of a few accessories to spice up their everyday clothes. His included a yellow cape made of a special stain-resistant waterproof micro-fibre cloth, leather marigold gloves and a belt that had a buckle with a water droplet insignia on it that matched HyJean's. This was the squad's logo, although the design was less by choice and more because he'd seen the belt buckles going cheap on a plumber's stall at a car boot sale and bought a load of them.

He then moved over to a row of sticks that were hung on the wall. Each had a different appendage on the end, including a toilet brush, a pair of plungers and a short mop. They looked like ordinary cleaning tools, but again, HyJean had modified them to make them infinitely more useful. The toilet brush had metal bristles that were very painful when smashed against your face – as the captain had accidentally found out the first time he used it – the plungers had enough suction for someone to easily climb a wall, and the mop could spin at an alarming speed that was enough to lift someone a few inches off the floor – something that rarely came in useful. Today, Captain Clean opted for the toilet brush, which he retracted and clipped to his belt. He probably wouldn't need it, but it made him feel safe and he thought it made him look cool. He thought wrongly. Nobody wearing yellow leather marigolds with toilet wrapped around their heads looks cool.

'What else do we know?' he asked as he made his way out of his office. 'What's their security like? Could someone have broken in?'

'I doubt it. Their security is top notch, as you'd expect,' she replied. 'Windows and doors are all alarmed, scanners at all entrances, and all their best tech is chipped so it can't leave the building without the boss's say so. Something that could do this wouldn't be easy to sneak in.'

'Interesting,' said the captain. 'You got the address?'

'Sort of,' she replied, handing him a small note. 'I've found out what street he lives on, but not which number. I'm afraid you'll have to do this one the old-fashioned way.'

'Thanks,' the captain sighed. 'While I'm out, see what else you can find in the media that might be of some use.'

On the way out, the captain passed a small office with an older, grey-haired woman sat inside, tapping at a computer that she barely knew how to use. Her desk piled high with papers, hiding the small plant that was so desperately craving sunlight. The woman was Mary Goldman, the squad's secretary in charge of admin. Being a council-funded operation, there was often a lot of paperwork (invoices for damages, purchase orders for new equipment, expenses, etc.) so Clifford had hired Mary to take care of it all.

'Can you cancel my 1 o'clock lunch appointment please Mary, I'm going out.'

'You haven't got a 1 o'clock lunch appointment,' she replied, turning to him and pressing her glasses back up the bridge of her nose.

'Really?' asked a bemused captain, 'I thought I did?'

'I cancelled it when I saw Jean going into your office.'

'You're far too good Mary.'

'I know,' Mary grinned as the captain left.

♦ ♦

Captain Clean stood at the top of Witnessal Street and wondered which side to start on. The police would have already visited Mr Daley, because they knew where everyone lived – they were nosey like that. The captain had asked for access to their databases several times, but apparently giving out personal data to strange people who run around in silly outfits wasn't something the commissioner was very keen to do. HyJean had suggested trying to hack their system to get the data, but the captain was insistent that they shouldn't do that as it was "probably illegal".

'Might as well start with number one,' Captain Clean said. He marched up to the first door on the left side of the road and knocked on it. While he waited, the captain noticed that the door knocker was quite dirty, so he pulled a cloth out from a little compartment on his belt and gave it a quick wipe. After a short wait, the door opened to reveal a rather jittery man who appeared to be 50 years old, although he'd actually been wearing the 50th birthday badge for over 2 years now. The resident of the house was surprised to find a strange-looking man polishing his door knocker.

'Oh, hello,' said Captain Clean, suddenly spotting the man at the door and hiding his cloth. 'Are you Martin?'

'No, I'm Brian,' replied Brian in a nervous tremor. 'Why? Who sent you? Is this to do with the courgettes again?'

'No, no. I'm with the council,' he explained, not mentioning the squad as this would likely frighten the man even more. 'I'm looking for a Mr Martin Daley. I don't suppose you know where he lives do you?'

'I don't know anything!' shouted the nervous Brian before slamming the door in the captain's face.

Cap made a little note in his notebook: 1 Witnessal Street, suspicious nutter.

He carried on down to 3 Witnessal Street and once again knocked on the door. This time a little girl, no more than 6 years old, opened the door.

'Hello little girl, does anybody called Martin live here?' he asked, not even making his voice sound friendlier, just talking to her like an adult.

'I'm not supposed to talk to strangers,' she replied, talking to him like he was an idiot.

'I'm not a stranger,' he said. 'I'm Captain Clean and I'm –'

'Your outfit is pretty strange,' she interrupted.

'No it's not, I'm a superhero.'

'Really? Can you fly?'

'Well… not per se.'

'What does that mean?'

'It's a fancy way of saying no.'

'Oh. Can you shoot lasers from your eyes?'

'No.'

'Can you run faster than a speeding bullet?'

'I don't think so, but I've never really tried.'

'So, what powers do you have?'

'Um… a thirst for justice and a brown belt in karate, ju jitsu and kick boxing.'

'My brother's got a black belt in karate.'

'Alright kid, it's not a competition.'

At this point, the girl's mother came to the door to see who her daughter had been talking to. She was not exactly pleased to see it was a man whose face was wrapped in toilet paper.

'Ah, hello madam,' said Captain Clean, 'I was just speaking to your daughter.'

'About what?' asked the worried mother, 'Who are you?'

'It's alright mum, I've got it,' said the girl. 'We don't know anyone called Martin, now clear off you dirty old perv!'

And with that the girl slammed the door in his face.

Captain Clean had to admit that he wasn't off to a great start, and his next few attempts didn't go too well either. But eventually, after knocking on 32 doors on the left side of the street, he did find someone who knew where Martin lived. As it transpired, Martin lived at number 2 Witnessal Street – the first house on the right side of the street. Oh, how the captain cursed when he found that out.

Martin was surprised to see a man who looked like he'd just come from a fancy-dress party standing on his doorstep. It hadn't been the first time, though. A few months prior, he'd opened the door to find a man dressed as a priest outside. One of the local lads had been to a fancy-dress party, gotten very drunk, become convinced he was a real priest and started knocking on doors asking if anyone needed him to perform an exorcism. Only one person did, and it went surprisingly well.

'Can I help you?' Martin asked as he looked the grime fighter up and down.

'Are you Martin Daley?' asked Captain Clean.

'Yes,' Martin replied.

'Thank god for that,' he sighed. 'I'm here to talk about your hand.'

'My hand?' Martin asked with a bemused look, instinctively feeling his left hand with his right as if it were about to fall off.

'Yes, the hand you saw snatch the guy in the toilets at work,' the captain explained. 'May I come in?'

'I… I suppose so,' Martin nodded, still rubbing his left hand just to be sure.

He invited the captain into his living room and went off to make him a cup of tea. The costumed hero sat on the sofa, looking somewhat out of place in the council house living room trying to avoid the small dog on the sofa next to him that was sniffing his gloves. He'd always held the view that pets – and animals in general – were highly unsanitary and not to be trusted. After a few minutes, Martin returned with the tea and a plate of biscuits. The captain would neither drink the tea nor eat the biscuits, as he could not be certain how clean Martin's kitchen was.

'Get off the sofa, you daft bugger,' Martin said as he entered the room.

'Oh, sorry' said the captain, quickly standing up.

'Not you, the dog,' Martin clarified.

Martin moved the dog away from the captain and sent him off to play in the garden. The captain sat back down and began his investigation.

'How are you feeling, Mr Daley?' he asked.

'I'm not too bad, thanks,' Martin said cheerily. 'How are you?'

'I'm hungry, Mr Daley,' the captain replied.

'Oh, would you like some biscuits?' he replied, moving to pick up the plate.

'No, Mr Daley,' said the captain, now leaning in more seriously. 'I'm hungry for the truth.'

'Oooh,' said Martin, who had been drawn into the theatrical nature of the costumed man's demeanour. 'If you don't mind me asking, who are you exactly? You're not a Jehovah's Witness are you?'

'My name is Captain Clean. I'm a grime fighter with a group called the Sanitary Squad – we investigate this sort of phemon… phemomom… phenonon… strange goings on,' he explained. So, what can you tell me about the victim?'

'Victor Timm? Oh, he's a smarmy git,' said Martin in a very matter of fact manner that clearly conveyed his dislike for the man. 'Thinks he's god's gift to women, always spends ages checking himself out in any mirror he's nearby. And he keeps using my stapler without asking!'

'Okay, thank you, but I meant more his physical appearance,' the captain clarified.

'Oh, well he's taller than me, slimmer than me, more smartly dressed than me,' he said with an air of contempt. 'And his hair's gelled back so slick you'd think an army of snails had slid over his head.'

'Very well,' said the captain, recognising that he wasn't going to get an unbiased opinion of the man. 'Tell me about what happened to Mr Timm when he went into the toilets.'

'Well,' said Martin, clearing his throat and sitting back to tell the story that he'd told police and journalists many times already. 'He went in to go for a slash and it was quite normal for about a minute, just the usual sounds you know.'

Martin paused and raised his eyebrows. The captain nodded to show that he was well acquainted with the sounds men usually make when they go to the toilet.

'Did he wash his hands while he was in there?' asked the captain.

'I don't think so, I didn't hear the tap running. I was listening in you see, trying to hear him practice his pitch – not that he did, he's too confident for stuff like that. Anyway, I just heard this crashing and screaming,' Martin continued, 'I went inside to have a look, and the sinks had been destroyed and he was being pulled down into a hole.'

'Was there anyone in the toilets before your colleague entered?'

'Not that I know of.'

'Did you see what the hand looked like?'

'Yes.'

There was a slight pause and the Captain sighed, 'Would you care to tell me?'

'Oh, sorry. Well, it was horrible. There were four fingers and a thumb, like a human hand, you know, but they were long and thin – like talons they were. And the skin was a dirty grey, and crusty, with dark yellow flaky scales. It was like something out of them alien films.'

'I doubt this is an alien invasion.'

'But that's what they always say, in the films, right before an alien invasion.'

'This isn't a film Mr Daley, it's real life.'

'They say that as well,' said Martin, getting more and more worked up.

'Mr Daley, there's nothing to worry about,' said the captain, trying to calm him down.

'That's always their last words right before they're killed!' He stood up and started pacing around, jittery at the thought of an impending alien invasion.

The captain picked up his cup of tea and flung its contents in Martin's face.

'Mr Daley, calm down!'

'Sorry, I'm a bit nervy when it comes to aliens,' he explained as he sat down. He wiped his tea-soaked face with a biscuit and then ate it. 'I was attacked by someone in an ET costume out trick or treating when I was young. Never liked them since.'

The captain continued to ask a few more questions, making notes as he did, then sat in thought for a moment. Martin drummed his fingers on the chair, a little unsure what was happening and whether to interrupt the captain's musings to offer him more tea.

'One last question Mr Daley, has there been any other unusual activity in the building recently?'

'I don't think so. I mean, the printer kept jamming last Tuesday, but I don't think that's got anything to do with it.'

'No, I don't think so either,' the captain said as he stood up to leave. 'Thank you, that's all for now.'

'Are you sure you wouldn't like a biscuit?' asked Martin.

'Give mine to the dog,' the captain replied.

'But he doesn't like rich tea.'

'Then he will enjoy it just as much as I would.'

💧💧

When Captain Clean arrived back at the base, he was greeted by Sergeant Suds; a man several years older than the captain, but much more muscular. He was mostly bald, and wore a military green outfit of cargo pants, vest and heavy black boots. Mick Goldman, as he was known outside of work, was married to Mary, but had joined the squad a few months before her. He had originally signed up to the army, but a mistake on his form meant he'd signed up to be a cleaner rather than a soldier. He spent a few years there, cleaning the barracks and longing for more action. This was also where he'd earned the nickname Sergeant Suds from the soldiers who he'd become friends with. When he left the army, he joined the squad and used the skills he'd learned in the army to help fight grime. HyJean had even created him a special gun that fired soap at various consistencies, allowing him to fire a watery slime if he needed to slip someone up, or a thick, sticky ooze if he wanted to trap someone.

Suds had been out in the morning, dealing with a rather deranged man, who had branded himself the Dust Devil, that had been running around the city with a homemade gun that created mini tornados.

'How did you get on?' asked Captain Clean.

'Wasn't too much trouble. I was able to disrupt the airflow with my soap and after that it was just a case of punching him real hard,' he replied as he removed his fake grey goatee beard, which he wore partly as a disguise and partly because he'd never been able to grow an actual beard and liked how he looked with the fake facial hair.

'Excellent work, although I do wish you'd tone down the violence a little; it's not great for our image,' the captain replied. As he looked up, he noticed a small trail of soil on the floor that Suds had left.

'Mick! Your boots,' he said, jumping up and running over to the sergeant. He pushed him against the wall and bent down, tugging furiously at the black, heavy boots.

'Hey! What are you doing?' Suds asked as he tried to retain his balance.

'You've got dirt on them!' the captain replied as though he were alerting him to an oncoming tornado.

'It's fine, it's just a bit of soil is all,' Suds replied, pushing the captain off him and taking his own boots off. 'Relax will you, a bit of soil isn't going to kill anyone.'

'You never know,' the captain replied. 'Do you know how many soil-related deaths there are every year?'

'No. Do you?' Suds replied, raising an eyebrow. He knew the captain wouldn't know the answer. He never did. He would often try to hype things up and threaten people with stats but rarely knew the answers himself. And if he did, his memory was so bad that he'd likely forget them anyway.

'That's beside the point,' said the captain, with his usual deflection. 'Anyway, clear up that mess and ask Jean to spray your boots later. I've told you before, if you buy new shoes, they need to be sprayed.'

The spray in question was a special concoction that HyJean had invented that made the soles of their footwear completely stain resistant, meaning that any water, mud or the other kind of unpleasant animal-related substance people sometimes step in would simply slide off. It didn't keep them one hundred percent clean, but it was sufficient enough to keep the floors of the base dirt-free to Captain Clean's satisfactory standard.

While Suds wandered off in his socks to get the dustpan and brush, the captain headed over to the furthest wall of the base where HyJean was sat at a set of computers. She had clearly had a busy afternoon, as there were four mugs of coffee on her desk. Her colleagues were able to measure how busy or stressed HyJean was by how many mugs were on her desk and how neatly or randomly they were arranged. A couple of mugs in a neat row was a fairly quiet morning, but half a dozen mugs spread around the desk was a hectic one.

'What did he say?' HyJean asked the captain without even looking around.

'Not a lot, pretty much what was in the report,' he replied, before recounting their conversation to HyJean. 'Though I did find it odd that he said the hand was crusty and flaky, like an alien hand.'

'Interesting,' she said, and it was interesting enough for her to look around this time. 'I wonder what it could be. Did he say what colour?'

'He said a dirty grey – although all grey is dirty to me – with yellow flakes or scales,' said the captain.

'Interesting twice over,' said HyJean, turning back to the computers. 'Anyway, I've got a few things to show you.'

The captain stood watching as HyJean rolled around on her swivel chair presenting her findings.

'There's been a few reports of toilets being trashed and they all correlate with people going missing. The victims are generally people in high powered jobs in specific industries, such as engineering and mechanics, so my guess is this person's building something and is kidnapping people with expertise.'

She rolled the chair over to the next computer and continued.

'This isn't the first time it's happened at LoTech, but the first time it was kept hush, with the police writing it off as an act of vandalism.'

She rolled over to another computer at the other end of the desk, like she was a dancer gliding across the floor and stopping with grace.

'There have also been several tweets with people complaining about strange noises coming from underground, but the council have checked the sewers and there's nothing odd down there.'

'Interesting,' said the captain. 'Jean, I think we should start by checking out the LoTech building, see what we can find.'

'Okay, but can we go after lunch? I'm starving,' asked HyJean.

The captain agreed. He'd not eaten either and there was even the tiniest part of him that was slightly regretting not taking one of Martin Daley's biscuits, so he sent Mary to the local café to get some sandwiches for the rest of the squad while he had one he'd prepared at home. Captain Clean rarely ate food he hadn't prepared himself, as he didn't trust the hygiene levels of kitchens he couldn't see, and it had become embarrassing being repeatedly thrown out of restaurants for insisting on inspecting the kitchens.

♦ ♦

With their bellies full, Captain Clean and HyJean now stood outside the LoTech building. The entrance was blocked off, with police cars, policemen and intrigued people who were not affiliated with the police all looking on at the crime scene through mobile phone screens, hoping to catch a bit of gossip to tell their friends later. It's a sad fact that with the rise of technology, people's reactions to situations have gone from concern for the wellbeing and safety of others to concern for how many views their footage of it will get on social media. And while victims may be immortalised on film, this does not provide them any comfort. Unless their situation is embarrassing and they get hold of the video and send it off to a TV show that shows clips of people in funny situations, in which case they could earn a bit of money.

'How are we going to get in?' asked HyJean.

'Is there a back entrance?' asked the captain.

'I don't know, I've never been here before.'

'Then where do you buy all our equipment?'

'From a shop, like any normal person.'

'Fine, then I'll need you to create some sort of distraction so I can sneak in.'

'Hold on, why are you going in?' asked HyJean, sounding a bit cheesed off.

'To investigate,' explained the captain.

'No offence, but as the resident scientist, I think I'd be better off going in,' she replied. 'I can analyse the wreckage and take any samples I might need.'

'Offence taken, and I'm still going in,' said the captain firmly. 'Now help me create a distraction.'

HyJean thought for a moment and then had an idea.

'Okay, take your mask and cape off and go into the crowd,' she told him. 'Make out like you've spotted something and start shouting to get people's attention. Then I'll jump out and pretend to fight it off, while you slip into the building.'

'Good idea,' said the captain, taking off his cape and mask sticking them under his shirt, making it look like he had a large pot belly. 'I think I can do that. I did go to RADA.'

'Really?' asked HyJean.

'Yeah, a few years ago, but it was shut when I got there.'

Captain Clean slipped into the crowd and began his theatrics. He pointed in the opposite direction down the road and started shouting. 'Oh my goodness, look! There is a giant robot heading this way! Somebody stop it!'

As he'd hoped, everybody turned to see where the imaginary giant robot was. Not-as-he'd-hoped, HyJean then snuck inside the building, leaving a desperate Captain Clean to try and explain to disgruntled onlookers why there was no giant robot down the street.

'Idiot,' HyJean muttered as she entered the building and swiftly made her way up to the 6th floor, where she'd read the incident had happened. Rather than try to sneak around and keep hidden, she just confidently walked straight to the toilets, where she saw a familiar face. At the door was a short, portly police officer with a scraggly ginger beard.

'Officer Down!' called out HyJean.

'What? No! Where?' the police officer cried, jumping to the floor and pulling out his gun.

'Put the gun down, Sid, I'm talking to you,' HyJean said with a roll of her eyes. She offered a hand to help him up. 'Come on, get up.'

'Oh, sorry,' said Officer Down. He chuckled as he stood back up and put his gun away. 'Easy mistake. Still, I'm sure I'll get used to it once I've been in the job a while.'

'You've been saying that for the past 2 years.'

'Oh? Has it been that long? Well, doesn't time cry... uh, fly.'

Officer Sidney Down wasn't the best that Filtham City Police Department had to offer – ranking somewhere just above the water cooler – but somehow, he'd managed to keep his job on the force long enough to be in charge of a walkie talkie. He was a nervous man and was often prone to getting his words mixed up, much to the amusement of the other officers.

'Hm, yes,' she said, shrugging off his remark. 'Anyway, I'm here to inspect the crime scene.'

'But you can't, nobody's allowed in. Chief's orders,' he explained, puffing his chest out a little to seem important.

'He's given me clearance, that's why I'm up here,' HyJean said coolly. 'Ask him yourself if you don't believe me.'

'Okay. Sorry love, nothing personal, just more than my job's worth,' he said as he pulled out a pair of handcuffs and put them to his ear. 'Oops, wrong socket… uh, pocket.'

He chuckled as he put the handcuffs back and pulled out his walkie talkie from the other pocket, but as he switched it on, a prepared HyJean discretely flipped a switch on a nifty little device in her pocket that scrambled the signal to his walkie talkie.

'I can't get hold of him, I'll have to go down and ask him,' said the policeman. 'Just wait here until I get back. And don't touch any elephants… uh, evidence.'

Once he'd left to find his boss, HyJean, ignoring the officer's orders, continued into the toilets. Her footsteps squelched and crunch as she made her way across the water and rubble that covered the floor.

'Thanks officer,' she said as she entered the room, fooling the policemen inside into thinking she'd been given permission. 'Alright then lads, let's take a look.'

Unsure what to do in the presence of a costumed lady, one of the policemen saluted, but the other one nudged him and told him to put his hand down. HyJean crouched down and inspected the great hole. She noted that, unusually, there were two sets of pipes leading up, one small pipe and another that was considerably wider than the other – almost big enough to fit a small human. She shone her light down and took a closer look at the larger pipe, which was lined with the remnants of a dirty yellow, crusty substance.

'That looks like… limescale,' she muttered to herself as she out a small scalpel and chipped off a bit into a little plastic bag. 'I wonder how that got there.'

'The plumber was surprised by that too,' said one of the policemen.

'Hm?' asked HyJean.

'They had a plumber out here to take a look,' he explained. 'And he said there shouldn't be any limescale in the pipes because they're not connected to the main water supply.'

'He didn't know what it was connected to,' added his colleague. 'We reckon there's a monster in the sewers.'

'Like a mutant snake, slithering up to grab people,' said the other, clearly enjoying theorising what was down there.

'If it was connected to the sewers, it'd be part of the sewage pipework, by the toilets,' HyJean pointed out. 'So why build extra pipes next to the water supply pipes?'

As the two men contemplated their theories with this new information, HyJean heard a faint but familiar voice coming down the corridor.

'I think that's enough for now,' she said, gathering her things and quickly exiting the toilets, running around the corner at the opposite end of the corridor to avoid being seen by the approaching policeman, who had now learnt that she didn't have permission to enter the scene at all.

'Where is she?' asked Officer Down.

'Who?' asked one of the policemen in the toilets.

'The Sanitary Squad woman who was just in here,' said Officer Down in an exasperated tone that people usually used with him.

'Oh, she's gone,' said the policeman.

'I think she got everything she needed though,' added the other policeman.

'You idiots, she wasn't supposed to be in here,' explained Officer Down.

'Really?' said the first policeman. 'But she seemed so nice.'

'Look, none of you mention this to the beef… uh, the chief,' said Officer Down. 'If he asks, we got rid of her straight away. Okay?'

The two policemen agreed to keep it quiet and went back to staring at the hole, pretending they knew what they were doing, when in actuality they were just passing time until they could go back down and declare their findings to be inconclusive.

HyJean, meanwhile, had made it to a stairwell and found a board that showed what was on each floor of the building. Scanning it, she saw that the CEO's office was on the next floor up. She doubted that he'd be there now, but it was still worth a look around. She climbed the stairs and made her way to the office. The lights were off in the corridor and there was an air of silence, making it feel creepy and dramatic. Things always seem creepier in the dark, even when you're in a familiar place. Our minds conjure up images of murderers jumping out on us with knives or ghosts watching us, even though the doors are locked and ghosts are just images projected by our brain to try and fill in missing information in the presence of something inexplicable. Still, HyJean found herself focusing on the one spec of light bleeding out from the bottom of a door at the end of the corridor. As she got closer, she crept slower, listening to the faint sobbing noises coming from inside the room. This made her feel a little safer, as knife-wielding murders and ghosts don't usually spend their time crying in locked rooms. Although, if films are to be believed, ghosts often sit around crying – and why shouldn't they, they're dead. The sign on the door read "Peter Lotech, CEO" so she knew she was in the right place. The door was slightly ajar, so she tentatively pushed it open and entered.

'Are you okay?' she asked softly.

This startled the crying man, who jumped in his chair and knocked over the glass of water he'd been nursing. He stumbled to his feet with a look that was more nervous than angry. 'Who are you? How did you get in here? What do you want?'

'My name is HyJean and I'm here to help,' she said calmly, taking out a cloth from her utility belt and cleaning up the spilled water, as if this somehow proved that she was not a threat. Peter watched, a little confused, as she stood the glass up and put her surprisingly absorbent cloth away.

'You're not with the police?' the CEO asked.

'It's that obvious?' she said with a slight chuckle. 'No, I'm with the Sanitary Squad. We're a group of grime fighters, funded by the government, and we've been asked to look into this matter by one of your employees, Martin Daley. It's kind of our speciality.'

Peter slumped down into his chair, seemingly already defeated and not in a mood to protest HyJean's presence. 'Well, I guess it doesn't matter now, the whole city seems to know what's going on this time,' he sighed. 'I just don't know what to do. An employee goes missing and nobody's got the foggiest idea how it happened, except for one guy who keeps rambling on about alien hands. I've had to shut the building down and the staff are all terrified. This could be the end of us.'

'Mr Lotech, you said "this time",' asked HyJean. 'This has happened before, hasn't it?'

'What? No,' said Peter, looking more nervous than ever. 'No, I just... I meant this time as in this time of day.'

'Look, Mr Lotech, if this has happened before, I need to know,' said HyJean, clearly not buying his ridiculous story. 'It could help us figure out what's going on and prevent it happening again.'

'But... I...' he stuttered, before sighing heavily once again. 'You said you're not with the police?'

'No, but you can trust me,' said HyJean. 'We won't tell anyone anything. That's not why we're here.'

'Fine, then yes, it happened before,' said the CEO, taking out a bottle of whiskey and pouring himself some. He offered it to HyJean, but she refused. 'A few weeks back, the same thing happened. We had some issues with the water, so it was turned off. Nobody was supposed to be using the facilities on site, but a woman went into one of the toilets and was kidnapped in the same way. Since we were already doing maintenance on the toilets, we closed it off until it was repaired and the police said they'd look into it. They haven't come back to us with anything and they just put her down as a missing person.'

'I see,' said HyJean, pausing to take in the whole story, piecing it together in her mind. 'So, a woman goes missing and you just covered it up?'

'I didn't… what could I do?' said Peter with a pitiful look of shame on his face. 'I didn't want to scare my employees. I mean how do you explain that someone went into a toilet and disappeared?'

'That's precisely what I'm going to try and work out,' said HyJean, making her way over to the door. She gave him one final look, but this time it wasn't of compassion or friendliness; it was a look of disgust. 'And let's just hope your two employees are still alive.'

💧💧

As HyJean and Captain Clean arrived back at the base, they were greeted by Mary, who had news. In this respect, she was a bit like a newsreader. Although in every other respect, she wasn't. She had never been on television, rarely wore a suit and was not reading the news she had off an autocue. Unlike newsreaders, she was able to remember the news she had. So, in this respect, she was better than a newsreader.

'Captain, I'm glad you're back. I've just had a call from a Dr Scope at the hospital,' she informed them. 'She's asked if you can go see her urgently. They've had a patient in with some very unusual symptoms that she thinks you might be able to advise on.'

'Okay,' said the captain. 'Jean, you'd best come too. You're much better at this sort of stuff.'

'What, talking to women?' came a voice from behind.

The voice belonged to Will Armitage, better known as Flush. He's the final member of the Sanitary Squad and has not featured until now because he was busy – not busy fighting grime, but rather doing another job entirely. You see, Flush was only a part time hero, as he also had another part-time job, though none of the squad knew what it was he did. When he joined the squad, he specifically requested that his other job be kept separate and refused to share any details about it, having seen in films what happens when superheroes and their daytime jobs collided. Captain Clean reluctantly agreed, though would still randomly ask him questions about it from time to time to try and catch him out. Flush was a good few years younger than most of the squad and saw himself as the cool one of the group. He wore a trendier outfit that consisted of dark teal trousers, matching teal sneakers and a white polo shirt with a teal collar, topped off with a mask and a spiky blonde wig that covered his naturally brown hair – designed to protect his identity that little bit more. His weapon of choice was an extendable whip that had been fashioned to look like an old toilet chain.

'Ah Will, just in time,' said the captain. 'We've got a little trip we need you to go on.'

'Ooh nice, where am I going today?' he said, rubbing his hands together with an excited smile. He was mainly doing this sarcastically, as their excursions were rarely nice places like a pool or a bar, but he still lived in hope.

'The library,' grinned the captain.

Flush's face fell. 'The library?'

'Yes, it's a place where they store books,' said HyJean.

'I know what a library is!' he groaned. 'I checked a book out a few weeks ago as it happens.'

'How's that going by the way?' asked Suds. 'Have you found Wally yet?'

'Shut up! I read proper books I do. Christopher Dickens, T.S. Lewis.'

'A.A. Milne?' suggested HyJean.

'Ah no, that's a trick one!' said Flush. 'He's not an author. He's the guy who invented the car breakdown service.'

'Anyway!' interrupted the captain. 'I need you to go to the library and find the original plans for the LoTech building. HyJean found out they have two sets of pipework and nobody there seems to know why. If we can find out what the second pipe is doing there and where it leads, we might have a clue as to where to find our kidnapper.'

'Mick, you'd better go with him,' said HyJean, adding with a grin, 'in case there's any long words to read.'

Suds chuckled, while Flush rolled his eyes. They gathered their things and promptly left for the library. Meanwhile, Captain Clean put his mask back on and HyJean set up a script on her computer to alert her of any mentions of sewers or toilet-related disappearances on social media.

'Right,' said the captain when he was ready, 'if you're ready to go I'll give The Driver a call.'

As grime fighting heroes, the squad often had to travel across the city to investigate various incidents. Since they couldn't afford their own car and the council were not willing to fund transport, they relied heavily on public transport or walking to grime scenes. For the longer trips, they used a regular taxi driver, although he wasn't a "regular" regular taxi driver. He was more of an "irregular" regular taxi driver.

The Driver, as he was simply known, was a young Indian man who had modified his car to drive at incredible speeds, faster than any formula one car. Despite his laid-back attitude, he was also an expert driver, so he could dodge traffic perfectly and had a remote control that his hacker brother had made to change the traffic lights at his will. The council had given him permission to use his extraordinary driving abilities to chauffer the Sanitary Squad around the city, as long as he drove normally at all other times. Which he did. Mostly.

'Hi, yeah, we need a lift,' said Captain Clean down the phone as they stood outside the community centre.

'I'll be there before you can say kaleidoscope,' said The Driver.

'Kaleidoscope?' the captain said in a puzzled tone.

As soon as he had finished saying the word, a car whooshed into the car park and pulled up with a loud screech. A window rolled down and The Driver said, 'Sorry I'm late.'

Captain Clean and HyJean set off in the taxi for the hospital, leaving Mary alone in her little office. Mary liked that she got to stay in the base on her own, because it meant she could play her music over the speakers. Today she opted for a bit of Black Sabbath.

Filtham Hospital was one of those buildings that looked small from the outside, but seemed massive inside. With endless winding corridors, staircases and wards that led off to other private rooms, it was like someone had built an Ikea inside the TARDIS. It was also one of the few immaculately clean places in the city, although Captain Clean often argued the opposite. No matter how many hygiene certificates they received, he still found something to complain about. The staff had gotten so fed up of him complaining that they just started ignoring him, which was fine by the captain, as he wasn't very sociable anyway. But there was one doctor that he had known for many years and was friendly with.

'Steffi, good to see you,' said the captain as he entered the patient's room, heading straight for the antibacterial gel on the wall. He had used every single gel dispenser on the way in, partly to keep his hands clean, but mainly to check they were all working properly after his complaints following his previous visit.

'Thanks for coming, Captain,' said Doctor Steffi Scope as she handed him a clipboard with the patient notes on. 'I've never seen anything like this before.'

'I believe it's called a clipboard,' said the captain, gesturing to the clipboard. 'It's used for holding pieces of paper in place.'

'I meant this,' Steffi said, tutting as she closed the door behind them and drew back the curtain, revealing the patient lying sedated on the bed. He was a young man whose entire body seemed to be leaking. There were several buckets around his bed catching the water, and more around the room that were full.

'He was brought in a few days ago. His name is Nelson Spigot,' Doctor Scope explained. 'We don't know much about him. According to the police report, he's an orphan from America, moved here about a year ago. No registered address or employment history. As for his condition, his body is secreting impossible amounts of water. At first we thought it was sweat, but the tests all say it's just pure H2O. We tried to draw bloods, but every time we did, the only thing that came out was water. We've done all kinds of scans, but this is beyond anything I learnt at medical school or watched on TV. I thought, since you and your team deal with a lot of… weird things, you might be able to help.'

The captain looked at HyJean who was staring at the patient with a mixture of awe and bemusement. After a minute alone to discuss it, HyJean told the doctor that they would take the case, but they would need to take the patient back to their base where they had more suitable equipment and facilities.

'We'd like to take him away to run some tests in our base,' explained HyJean.

'Take him away?' Doctor Scope replied.

'Thank you,' said the captain. 'That was easier than I expected.'

'No, I mean you can't take him away,' the doctor explained. 'We'd need to fill out lots of paperwork and get consent from the patient.'

'I don't think he'll mind; will you son?' said the captain, patting the now awake Nelson's arm. The patient responded with an indistinguishable gargled groan and the captain smiled. 'See, he loves the idea.'

'I'm still not sure, let me speak with my boss,' said Doctor Scope.

After explaining the situation and the squad's credentials to the senior doctors, it was agreed that they could take him - mainly because they didn't have a clue what else to do with him. Captain Clean and HyJean took Nelson back to their base, transporting him in a metal bathtub in the ambulance to contain the water. As they carried the bathtub through the ground floor of the community centre, the head of the receptionist peered up over her desk.

'Afternoon Captain,' she said with a well-rehearsed friendly smile.

'Yes, it is,' the captain replied, barely acknowledging her.

'What's up with him then?' the receptionist asked, gesturing to the unconscious water-soaked man in the bathtub.

The weird world of the squad would often pass through the community centre reception - a lot of which could have gotten them kicked out for breaking regulations - but fortunately the staff were very naïve and would believe any old excuse, and HyJean was now an expert at excuses.

'Uh, it's a charity thing,' HyJean lied. 'He's doing a sponsored tour of the city in a bathtub.'

'Ooh, well do let us know the details and I'll get the girls to do a whip round.'

'Will do. Thanks, Carol.'

In the base, a Nelson lay on a table in the shower room, where the water could run into the drains. It wasn't the most ideal place for a medical examination, but it was practical and – like every inch of the base – it was clean. However, as Jean turned to prepare her equipment, he slowly slid down the table and landed on the floor with a wet thud. Jean span around with a start. She offered to help Nelson up onto the table, but he insisted on doing it himself. He wearily dragged himself up and climbed on to the table as Jean continued to gather her equipment. However, before he could settle on the table, Nelson once again slid down the table and returned to the floor.

'Yeah, I might need some help actually,' he admitted.

After a few attempts, Jean eventually tied him down to keep him on the table. Nelson didn't say much about it, as the water pouring from his mouth made it difficult to speak and he was now in pain from falling.

When Jean started her tests, he said even less, because he was once again sedated. After hours of tests and experiments, Jean explained the situation to the captain and then woke Nelson to explain it to him.

'Okay, so based on the test results, you originally suffered from hyperhidrosis, which meant you sweated a lot anyway, but somehow it has been accelerated to an incredible rate. There were also a lot of unknown chemicals in your body which have diluted your blood to pure water. However, there are modified versions of the cells and minerals that blood usually contains, so your heart thinks this is normal and it's managing to pump the water around your body as if it were blood and it's performing all the same functions.'

'Okay, I didn't really understand any of that,' admitted Nelson. 'But you haven't said, why am I leaking all this water?'

'Um, well that's the thing see… I've no idea,' HyJean shrugged. 'I've done loads of tests and I've got a few theories, but it's just… impossible. It defies all the laws of physics and, to be honest, it's got me stumped.'

'Oh… okay,' said Nelson with a tone of disappointment in his voice. There was a long awkward silence, which he then broke. 'Can you help me?'

'I think so, yes,' said HyJean with a smile. 'You see, while I couldn't find out what's causing it, I was able to find a way to control it. If you'll allow me to demonstrate?'

She gestured to one of Nelson's arms and he nodded. She lifted it up into the air, watching as the droplets of water slowly dripped from it.

'So, your arm is leaking, but if I apply a little pressure,' she explained as she wrapped her hand around his wrist and squeezed gently. As it dangled there in the air, they all watched and were surprised to see the dripping stop. 'It stops the leaking. Not throughout your body, it seems to be localised to this arm. But I'm betting if we put something around both your wrists and ankles, it would cover your whole body and cancel the signal.'

'Really? Well, it's worth a try,' said Nelson, showing the hint of a smile for the first time since they'd met him.

'Excellent. And also… I still need to do a few more tests on you to check it will work, but I think I may be able to build a device that can control your leaking,' HyJean continued. After a little pause, she added, 'Control it enough to make you able produce water at will.'

'Why would I want to do that?' he asked.

'Well, that's what we wanted to talk to you about,' said the captain as he pulled up a wet chair and sat down beside the table with a squelch. He'd removed his mask so as not to intimidate the patient. 'From what Jean has told me, this cannot be fixed completely, but it can be controlled. If it is, you may be able to use it to your advantage.'

'What do you mean?'

'Well Nelson… we'd like you to join our squad.'

'What, are you guys like a pop group or something?'

'No, we fight grime.'

'Crime?'

'No, grime, as in sanitation themed crime. We ensure the city is safe and clean. There is evil out there, Nelson; criminals and psychopaths who want to bring down this city, creating chemical weapons and spreading viruses to wreak havoc.'

'Wait, what? How come none of this is in the news?' asked a startled Nelson.

'We try to keep a low profile,' the captain explained.

'Ha!' came a laugh from the other side of the base. It was laughed by Mary, who was currently typing up the seventh invoice that month for repairs to broken windows caused by the team.

'But we could really use someone like you on the team,' the captain continued. 'Sure, we've got technology and enthusiasm, but you've got actual super-powers. Jean reckons she can create something that will enable you to increase the volume of water and fire it like a jet. This doesn't have to be a burden, Nelson, you could do some real good.'

'Wait, so what you're saying is, you want me to become a superhero?' asked Nelson, sounding a little bemused.

'Well… yes,' said HyJean. 'But it's your decision and you need to think about it for a while, as there's a lot of danger and responsibility involved in –'

'Hell yeah!' Nelson cheered. 'Of course I'll do it.'

'Really?' asked a surprised HyJean.

'Lady, you had me at hyperhidrosis.'

'Excellent,' said the captain.

'Wait,' said Nelson as a thought suddenly occurred to him. 'I don't have to wear toilet roll on my head, do I?'

'No, that's my thing' said Captain Clean. 'Although you will have to have a shave; beards are terribly unhygienic.'

♦ ♦

Meanwhile, in the public library, Flush and Suds - or Will and Mick, since they were dressed in their everyday attire so as not to attract any attention - waited at the reception desk for the librarian to return.

'I just don't like libraries,' whispered Will. 'They creep me out.'

'Really?' asked a surprised Mick. 'I know people don't like hospitals and cemeteries, but libraries?'

'Everyone's got to be so quiet here and it's all dark and dusty,' he explained. 'And they're letting you borrow books for free, what's that all about? Nobody gives you stuff for free these days. And did you see that librarian?'

'What about her?'

'She was so polite and happy, she's got to be hiding something.'

'Oh come on, she's just being friendly.'

'No she's not, she's –'

'Shh, here she comes.'

The librarian reappeared behind the desk wearing a smile that made Will furrow his brow in suspicion. She was a young woman, dressed smartly with glasses that made her look as intelligent as she was, and blonde hair that she wore in a bun. A name badge on her jumper – which she had seemingly made herself in an effort to make her appear less formal, decorated with drawings of hearts and flowers – identified her as Lily. She proudly presented two books: one quite old looking and the other much newer.

'Here you go sirs, The LoTech Story and An Architectural History of Filtham City. Are you going to check them out or would you like me to find you a table where you can read them?'

'We'd like to check them out please,' replied Mick.

'Certainly sir,' Lily nodded. 'Do you have your library card?'

'Oh, um…' Mick fumbled around, checking his pockets for his wallet, but to no avail. He turned to Will. 'Have you got yours?'

'Mick, I hate libraries. Why would I have a library card?'

'I'm afraid I can't let you take the books without a card,' said the librarian.

'Damnit, we'll have to go and come back,' Will sighed.

'Is there anything you can do?' asked Mick. 'The city is in terrible danger and our colleagues need to see these urgently. We don't really have time to go and come back. Please?'

Mick's polite plea seemed to trigger something in the librarian. She gestured for them to lean in close. 'I probably shouldn't do this, but if you can bring them back by the end of the day, I'll let you take them without scanning them.'

'Yes! That's bostin, thanks love,' said Will.

'You're a lifesaver,' said Mick, adding, 'possibly quite literally.'

Lily the librarian glanced around the room and handed them the books. She just hoped they'd bring them back. She'd done this several times before and gotten into quite a lot of trouble for it. The last time had been a man who'd borrowed a book about ancient Egypt, and when he'd failed to bring it back, Lily had tried to convince her boss that there was no such book. It didn't work, due to the pure coincidence that it was her boss that had written the book. She was suspended without pay for three weeks and eventually allowed to return. Meanwhile, the man who'd borrowed the book had travelled to Egypt and was now being worshiped as a modern-day pharaoh.

💧💧

Back in the base, HyJean and Mick studied the two books, looking for any clues that might lead them toward some answers. Meanwhile, Flush had noticed some water trickling out from the door to the shower room and wandered over. He inched the door open and peered inside.

'Uh guys, there's a man in here and I think he's really upset about something.'

'Oh, no, that's a patient from the hospital, we're looking after him,' said HyJean. 'Don't go in there, he's sleeping.'

'Well, it looks like he's having a wet dream,' Will said with a smirk.

Captain Clean explained to his colleagues about their trip to the hospital and the prospect of Nelson joining the squad.

'But who is he?' asked Suds.

'He's uh…' the captain started, suddenly realising that they knew very little about the American stranger that was currently lying in their shower room. 'We don't know. But he seems like a nice guy.'

'Well, at least now Mick won't be the biggest drip on the team,' joked Flush.

But before Suds could respond, HyJean cried out, 'I've got it!'

The squad all gathered around her as she showed them a page she'd found in An Architectural History of Filtham City.

'There's an old reservoir right under the LoTech building. It was damaged during the war, so they drained it and built a new reservoir a few miles away. This one was abandoned, but the LoTech building was built decades later, so whoever built it must've known about the old reservoir. But why connect the building to the reservoir if it's out of use?'

'I think I can answer that,' explained Suds. 'The architect of the LoTech building was one Jeremy Staines.'

'I don't like him already,' Captain Clean muttered.

'You're right not to,' said Suds. 'I looked him up and he made the news. Not long after the building was built, there were reports of technology going missing. Turns out a group of them were smuggling things out and selling them to competitors, and Staines was involved from the start. Nobody knew how it was done, but they discovered he'd added in those pipes so that they could send stuff down into a secret underground location – I'm guessing the reservoir – to avoid being caught.'

'Of course! The technology can't leave the building,' said HyJean. 'But if it goes under the building, it wouldn't pass any security scanners and would technically still be in the building.'

'Then they'd have time to figure out how to remove the chip so they could sell it,' added Suds.

'How did they catch them?' asked the captain.

'One of them put it down the wrong pipe and when the plumbers came out, they found the other pipes,' Suds explained. 'They blocked the pipes, but it seems like whoever's doing this has found a way to unblock them.'

'And now they're using the pipes to kidnap people,' Flush added as he caught up with what was going on.

'But Cap said the guy saw a hand,' Suds pointed out. 'How would someone get up the pipes and be strong enough to drag someone else down?'

'That's a good question,' said the captain. 'And one which we're going to find the answer to. Jean, is there an entrance to the reservoir?'

'Um, hang on,' she said, flicking through the pages. 'Yes, there's two, one either end. The nearest one is Reservoir Road.'

'Well, that figures. I always wondered why it was called that. Makes a lot more sense now,' said the captain turning to Suds. 'I suggest you take that one then.'

'Me?' he protested.

'Yes, we need to investigate the reservoir, but Jean and I have to look after our new friend.'

'Actually, I'm alright on my own if you want to go,' said HyJean.

'No, no. I need to stay and oversee his progress,' said the captain quickly, secretly keen to avoid the dirty walls and water of the underground. 'Suds, you can take Will with you though.'

'Oh bostin,' said Flush sarcastically. 'I'll get my wellies then, shall I?'

💧💧

Underneath the streets of Filtham, Flush and Sergeant Suds made their way along the dark, dank tunnels of the secret underground reservoir. Their boots sloshed and squelched as they waded through the puddles of brown water that had dripped in through the cracks above. Rats scuttled by to check out the trespassers, eyeing them up for any valuables or cheesy comestibles. It was difficult to see much down there, but luckily Flush had brought a flashlight – or a "flushlight" as he insisted on calling it. They had very few self-branded tools and he couldn't resist the wordplay. He aimed it straight ahead and the light bounced off the curved walls and glistened on the dirty water, illuminating the endless damp corridor ahead.

'Jeez, it smells like my Nan's armpits down here,' said Flush.

'Did you smell her armpits often?' asked Suds.

'Well, she used to get us in headlocks all the time,' Flush explained. 'She was a tough old bird, big wrestling fan.'

As they turned a corner, Flush's light caught a rat that stared up at them. A surprised Suds quickly aimed his gun and fired it at the poor creature, soaking it in a big blob of pink goo.

'Dude, it's just a rat!' Flush pointed out.

'Oh, well… can never be too careful,' Suds said with a shrug as Flush reached down and wiped some of the goo away to free the startled rat, which ran off into the darkness.

They continued down the slimy, wet path and as they made their way around a bend, they suddenly saw something that shocked them as much as they'd shocked the rat. A man dressed in a white lab coat lay slumped against the wall, battered and bruised. His clothes were torn, and he had unusually large scratches on his face. But he didn't look upset about it. In fact, he showed no signs of life at all.

'That's an odd place to take a nap,' said Flush.

'I don't think he's sleeping,' said Suds as he took a closer look. 'I think he's dead.'

'Oh bugger, I hope not,' Flush replied. 'I'll check his pulse.'

Flush knelt down on the cold, watery floor and felt the man's wrist.

'Nothing,' he said, shaking his head with a mournful expression.

'Are you sure,' asked Suds.

'I dunno. Hang on, you hold this arm and I'll try the other one,' he said, handing Suds the detached limb he'd just been feeling. Suds looked at the severed arm with a mix of surprise and disgust.

'We've got a pulse!' cried Flush as he felt the man's other arm. 'He's still alive!'

'Phew. Quick, try and wake him up.'

'Hello! Mister, can you hear me?' asked Flush, tapping his cheek and shaking him roughly. But the man still lay motionless.

'Wait a minute, he's a man of science,' said Suds, before shouting, 'The theory of evolution has just been proven wrong!'

The man suddenly shot up with a startled gasp. He looked up at the two heroes that stood before him and muttered something in a panicked mumble.

'Calm down sir, we're here to help,' said Suds.

The man continued to mumble and stutter, scuttling about where he lay. He looked like a fish out of water, flopping about and babbling incoherently.

'Jeez, for a scientist he's not very literate is he,' said Flush.

The man suddenly started cowering as a dark shadow cast over him. He pointed up toward them.

'Alright,' said Flush, 'I know Suds is ugly, but he's not that bad.'

'N… n… no!' he stuttered and gestured to behind where they were standing. 'It's him!'

Flush and Suds turned around and to their surprise, they saw a giant creature – definitely humanoid in shape, but at least eight feet tall and skinnier than any fashion model. His bare, grey skin was rough and had little patches of a dark, mustard yellow in places. His face was grotesquely disformed, with a toothy sneer that made his face look like it was melting.

In a state of panic, Sergeant Suds whipped out what he thought was his gun, but was actually the man's dismembered arm, and pointed it towards the creature.

'Stay back,' he shouted, 'I'm armed!'

The creature lifted one of his own skinny arms, with long bony fingers that looked more like talons, and in one foul swoop, he sent the two heroes flying, bouncing off the wall and down into the murky waters. They lay motionless, just as the lab coated man had mere minutes ago.

💧 💧

On the second floor of the community centre, HyJean was busy working away, still running tests on her patient. As she took samples of Nelson's blood – or whatever it was – and analysed it on the computer, she smiled to herself. It wasn't often she had an unconscious but handsome, naked man lying on a table for her. Although she was married, she still couldn't help but engage in a bit of fun flirting with her unconscious, undeniably good-looking patient.

'Well Mr Spigot, there's nothing wrong with your abs I see,' she giggled.

'Thanks doc,' Nelson said with a smile without opening his eyes.

HyJean jumped and let out a little squeal as she stumbled back and ran out of the room. Nelson chuckled to himself as he lay on the table in his half-conscious, hazy state and drifted back off to sleep.

💧 💧

'Morning cocker,' said a cheery Flush, who'd clearly been awake for a while.

'Hm? What? Where are we?' asked a dazed Suds, looking around.

They were in a little alcove in a different part of the reservoir, both sat on chairs and tied to a large pipe that ran along the wall. It was better lit, and they could see there were computers dotted around the room outside, with people in tattered white lab coats operating them. Others were at desks, tinkering with little bits of metal components, or standing by a large, square, metal machine in the middle of the room, pressing buttons and taking notes. The people didn't look like they were there willingly. They whimpered and shook as they typed away and worked, like slaves, only better dressed.

'Slender Man over there captured us and tied us up,' Flush explained, gesturing to the giant grey monster who was pacing around. 'He's not very good at tying knots though. I wriggled free of mine a while ago, but I didn't want to leave you.'

'Thanks,' Suds said as he shuffled his hands and wriggled free of his own rope. 'You seem surprisingly calm about all this.'

'Not the first time I've woken up tied up in a stranger's home,' Flush said with a knowing grin. 'Right, shall we run?'

'No, wait. Let's see if we can get him talking first,' said Suds. 'Might as well try and find out what he's up to while we're here.'

'Good idea, leave this to me. I've got a way with people.'

'He doesn't look like people,' Suds said wearily.

Flush turned his attention to the creature who was now fiddling with the big machine.

'Excuse me mate!' Flush called, attracting the creature's attention. 'Alright mucker, how you doing? Looking very smart today, you're putting me to shame.'

The creature turned his head to them slowly. He looked confused and angry at being interrupted.

'Cut the flannel,' whispered Suds.

'Right, yes,' said Flush. 'So, my friend Suds and I - this is Suds here, say hello Suds.'

'Hello,' said Suds with a little wave, before suddenly realising he'd shown his untied hand and quickly whipping it behind his back in the hopes that the creature hadn't noticed.

'Ahem, so uh... my friend and I were wondering - we've got a little bet on whether you're human,' Flush continued. 'I think you are, but he reckons you're an alien. You're not an alien, are you?'

The creature slowly walked over to them, with long, heavy strides. Each step made a splash on the damp floor, echoing around the room. As he walked, his long, thin hands swung lazily by his side like two great pendulums.

'No. I am human,' he said with a raspy but imposing voice. He sounded like he'd been wanting to tell his story for some time and was finally grateful for someone that was interested, 'I was like you. A normal guy. They experimented on me in a lab, grew limescale on my body and injected me with things, made me into this. A monster. But I will have my revenge.'

'Right, I see, interesting,' said Flush. 'And how exactly will you get your revenge, if you don't mind me asking?'

The creature looked Flush straight in the eyes and its face contorted in an attempt to portray a sinister grin. Flush couldn't help but think it looked more like he was constipated.

'They brought me down here and abandoned me when their experiment failed. But I have been gathering people to construct this,' he said, pointing to the large machine in the middle of the room.

'Oh yes, that's a lovely bit of kit that,' said Flush.

'Very nice,' added Suds. 'But what does it do?'

'You will see soon enough. That is if you don't drown with the rest of the city.'

'Oh dear,' said Flush.

'That doesn't sound too good,' said Suds.

The creature gave a slightly breathy but very sinister cackle, leaning into both of them. They cowered back a little, which was more to do with the disgusting breath and flecks of spit that came from his mouth as he laughed than any kind of fear.

'Now silence, I must continue my work,' he said, turning to one of his workers. 'Sedate them.'

One of the white coated men came over and with an apologetic shrug he sprayed something in their eyes which made them suddenly feel very drowsy.

💧💧

Suds groggily opened his eyes, his head aching and his vision blurry. As the room came into focus, he turned to address his fellow grime fighter. However, to his surprise, he found himself quite alone. At first, he panicked, thinking Limescale had taken Flush, but then he spotted a note stuck to the chair next to him, which he took off and read.

GONE TO GET THE OTHERS.
BACK SOON.
X

Meanwhile, back in the base, Flush was busy telling Captain Clean and HyJean what had happened over a bowl of cereal, which he had felt necessary to prepare before he filled them in, since he hadn't eaten in a while.

'So let me get this straight. This tall, grey man… creature, thing is capturing scientists to build some sort of machine and Mick is still trapped inside the reservoir?' asked Captain Clean.

'Yep,' said Flush. 'That's about the size of it.'

'What did he look like?' asked HyJean.

'He was a bit dazed when I left him, but I think he's alright,' Flush said as he munched on his cereal.

'Not Mick! The monster man,' the captain groaned.

'Oh! Sorry. He was like… a giant stick insect that had mated with an out-of-date Twiglet. Actually, I got a photo of him on the way out for Jargle, look,' said Flush, pulling up the photo on the phone to show the others.

'Lovely,' said HyJean with a grimace as the haunting face stared back at her.

'What on Earth is Jargle?' asked the captain.

'It's the latest social media app,' Flush explained. 'You post photos and add fun little captions.'

'You put a photo of a creature from the underground reservoir on your social media account?!' asked the captain.

'Of course not,' said Flush, with a slight pause before adding. 'I put it on the squad's account.'

'We have a Jargle account?' the captain asked Jean. He was rubbish with technology and did not see the point in social media, so he always relied on HyJean to fill him in with the latest news and online social movements.

'Apparently,' she shrugged. She was not surprised that this had happened, as Flush was always coming up with new ideas for the squad and the captain seemed to have very little interest in them, which would lead to Flush doing them anyway and the captain not being bothered to do anything about it.

'Anyway,' continued Flush, 'our followers chose the name Limescale as their favourite, so I think we should start calling him that.'

'What do you mean, chose?' asked the captain.

'Well, while I was on the bus coming back, I put a few suggestions on there. Sink Smasher, The Piper and Limescale. Y'know, 'cause Jean found all that limescale in the pipes.'

'I think they might be onto something,' said HyJean, who had been studying the photo closely. 'It was definitely limescale in the pipes, and it looks like he's covered in the same stuff.'

'So, he's covering himself in limescale? Or some kind of limescale suit?' asked the captain.

'No, I think it's part of him,' HyJean replied, zooming in on the photo. 'Look, there's no join, it looks organic.'

'Oh! Maybe that's how he's getting up through the pipes,' suggested Flush, as he started to piece together the parts of the puzzle in his head. 'Controlling the limescale, making it spread and using it to pull people down.'

'That seems a bit farfetched,' said the captain.

'Yes, but Martin Daley said that the victim didn't wash his hands before he was taken,' said HyJean, with a sudden burst of energy at the emerging realisation. 'I think Flush is right. It's all starting to make sense now.'

'Does it?' asked Flush.

'Yes, this… Limescale,' she said, making sure to do air quotes when she said the name to show she thought it was a silly idea to name the villain, 'he's been coming up the pipes in various places and taking people. The limescale – the stuff, not the creature – can grow up the pipe and snatch people. Think about it, the first time it happened, the water had been turned off. The second time, he didn't wash his hands and probably stayed at the sink a little too long. Mr Daley said that the victim liked to check himself out in the mirror. Maybe the water was keeping it at bay.'

'Yeah, if the pipes were connected at some point along the way, then the water would've made it harder for the limescale to grow,' added Flush.

'Another perfect example why you should always wash your hands,' said the captain. 'If this man had washed his hands, he might still be alive.'

'He is still alive,' Flush pointed out. 'Limescale's got him working down in the reservoir.'

'Right, yes, of course,' said the captain, now pacing around overexcitedly. 'So, what is Limescale planning?'

'I don't really know, he didn't tell us anything useful,' admitted Flush.

'Well, what did he say?' HyJean pressed.

'He did say he was going to use this machine of his to flood the city.'

'I think that's pretty useful information,' HyJean said, a little frustrated.

'This is serious,' said the captain in a slightly worried tone. 'We have to stop him.'

'And rescue Suds and the kidnapped people,' added HyJean.

'Yes, I suppose we can do that as well,' agreed the captain. 'Right, we'll do a two-pronged attack. I'll go down on the north side and try to distract him, while you two go down on the south side and rescue Suds and the others.'

'What about the drip?' Flush said, gesturing towards the shower room.

'He'll be okay for a few hours,' said HyJean, who was walking off to her own room to clip some useful sprays and things onto her utility belt. 'I've got some extra-strong tranquiliser. We should be able to use that to take Limescale down.'

'Okay, cool. I'll just finish this and then we'll get off,' Flush said, gesturing to his half-full bowl of cereal.

Captain Clean grabbed the bowl and threw it in a nearby bin. Flush sat shocked and pouted a little like a spoilt child who'd just had his favourite toy taken away.

'There, you're finished,' the captain said. 'Now come on.'

💧💧

'Urgh, it's filthy down here. Someone should really come down and clean this place up,' said Captain Clean as he made his way through the dark, murky tunnels. He winced as he took each step, wading through a stream of what looked like sewage water. He shone his torch ahead, the light bouncing off the curved walls and glistening on the dirty water, illuminating the corridor ahead. As the captain moved further down, the light caught one of the reservoir rats, which looked startled and scuttled away, like it was expecting to be pelted by a blob of pink goo in the same way that they had heard their ratty friend had been attacked earlier that day. The captain let out a little squeal at the sight of the rat and was glad that nobody was around to witness it.

Meanwhile, HyJean and Flush were making their way through their own tunnel, Flush leading the way as he confidently lied about remembering which way he'd come when he had escaped. In truth, he'd been so busy running away that he hadn't bothered to remember the path he took. Eventually they passed a wall that he recognised, which was surprising, given how similar everywhere looked.

'Right, it's just down there,' Flush said, pointing to a corner where flickering lights reflected off the walls. As they crept closer, they heard the faint hum of machinery and noises of people working.

'Okay, let's wait here. Cap said he'll text me when he's in position,' HyJean said. They waited for a while, and sure enough, less than a minute later, her phone vibrated with a text message from the captain. There were no words, just one worried looking emoji.

'Is that the signal?' asked Flush.

'Must be,' HyJean shrugged. 'Let's go.'

They cautiously poked their heads around the corner and scanned the room. There was no sign of Limescale, just several dishevelled people nervously working at the computers. Captain Clean must have drawn him out, they thought. HyJean gave a nod and Flush quickly and quietly made his way over to where Sergeant Suds was being held, while she headed to the nearest person working at a computer - who just so happened to be Victor Timm.

'Shh, we're here to help,' whispered HyJean, holding up a finger to gesture for him to keep quiet.

'Oh, thank god,' whispered Victor nervously. 'I haven't a clue what I'm doing with this, I'm just tapping away and hoping he doesn't notice.'

'It's okay, Captain Clean is distracting Limescale while we help everyone escape,' she explained. 'You go and I'll get the others.'

Victor Timm thanked her and joyously left his cold, damp prison. On the other side of the room, Flush was busy untying his friend, whose hands had been tied tighter after being sedated.

'Why did you go without me?' asked a disgruntled Sergeant Suds.

'Well, you were sleeping and you looked comfy, so I didn't want to wake you,' said Flush. 'Anyway, how've you been?'

'Oh, just fine thanks,' Suds replied sarcastically. 'Aside from the freezing cold draft, the starvation and the constant threat of being killed by a giant raging monster, it's been just spiffing.'

'Alright, I said I was sorry.'

'No you didn't!'

'Okay, well I'm sorry. Now keep your voice down.'

As Flush worked on the ungiving knot, there came a tumultuous grumble that echoed around the reservoir.

'Blimey, you really are hungry,' said Flush.

'You!' bellowed the familiar booming voice of Limescale.

'You said that without moving your lips,' said Flush, still looking at Suds. 'How did you do that voice?'

As a look of panic grew on Suds' face and an eerie shadow loomed over him, Flush gulped at the sudden realisation.

'You are trying to escape,' Limescale continued.

Flush turned around and, despite being terrified, tried not to be intimidated by the towering, flaky figure. 'Actually, I've already gone and come back, mate. Did you not miss me?'

Evidently, Limescale did not take kindly to being taunted, and once again his large, vine-like arm swooped down on them. Flush dived out of the way and Suds' chair was knocked over, with Suds still partly tied to it. Flush grabbed the chair that he had once been tied to and swung it at the rampaging monster, adding a cry of, 'Take a seat!'

It was not quite as good a weapon as he had hoped. The chair smashed into pieces and barely had any effect on Limescale.

'Well, that worked,' groaned Suds, lying sideways on the floor.

Back in the main part of the reservoir, HyJean was alerted to the noise coming from across the room. Hoping the boys could keep Limescale distracted for a while, she looked around to find the captain, who she assumed must have been helping the kidnapped victims or sabotaging the machine. However, she quickly learnt that Captain Clean was actually nowhere to be seen. She tried calling him on the phone, but there was no signal.

'Typical,' she muttered to herself, before heading over to join in the fight.

By the time she got there, Suds had gotten free of his restraints and had recovered his soap gun, which Limescale had carelessly left nearby. Flicking it to the highest setting, Suds fired it at Limescale's grotesque face. With relative ease, the creature just wiped the pink goo off his face and flung it at Suds, who dodged it. However, it did give HyJean a window of opportunity to attack. She pulled out a spray bottle and started spraying it all over Limescale, who roared loudly as his body began to sizzle and burn, bits of his flaky skin peeling off and falling away.

'What was that stuff?' shouted Flush as he dodged Limescales flailing arms.

'Non-ionic surfactants!' HyJean replied.

'I repeat, what was that stuff?' Flush shouted back, a little more irritably.

'It's used to get rid of limescale,' she explained. 'It should weaken him at least.'

As Limescale's body continued to shed itself of the limescale, flakes peeling off and drifting to the floor like passengers jumping off a sinking ship, he became noticeably weaker – his movements slowed and his attacks had less power behind them. The grime fighters danced around, avoiding the swipes and jabs for a short while as their attacker weakened, until at last they nodded and attacked in unison. Flush whipped out his whip and swung it around Limescale's legs, expertly typing them together; Suds took a running jump and tackled him down onto the floor with a great thud; and HyJean stabbed him with the sedative she'd prepared. They pinned the creature down and watched as he wriggled and writhed, splashing about in the small puddles of dirty water like a fish at a rave, and then gradually settled until he lay still.

'That wasn't actually too difficult,' said Flush with a smile as he stood up and wiped his hands.

'I know,' agreed Suds. 'We must be getting better.'

As if on cue, there came the sound of splashing footsteps and Captain Clean ran into the room, panting as if he'd just finished running a marathon. With his adrenaline levels already high, Suds reacted instinctively and span around, throwing a punch at the captain's face and knocking him to the ground with a splash.

'Oh crap,' Suds said when he realised who it was he'd punched. He reached down and helped the captain up. 'Sorry Cap, didn't realise it was you.'

'No worries,' he said, using his cape to wipe his aching face. He gestured down at Limescale. 'You stopped him then?'

'We sure did,' said Flush proudly.

'And where have you been exactly?' asked HyJean.

'I uh… I got lost,' the Captain replied between pants, a little embarrassed.

'Why are you so dirty?' asked Suds.

'I was… in the sewers,' he mumbled.

'What?'

'I was in the sewers, okay!' he shouted. 'I went down the wrong manhole and ended up wandering about in the sewers.'

'Didn't you have your tracker app on?' asked HyJean, referring to an app she'd made for the squad that allowed them to see each other's whereabouts.

'I thought I could navigate myself,' the captain argued. 'Look, it doesn't matter, I'm here now. What's the situation?'

'We nearly got killed because you cocked up the plan,' said Flush.

'Very helpful, thank you Flush,' the captain replied.

'We've sedated Limescale, but we've no idea what this machine does,' explained HyJean, pointing to the big machine in the middle of the room, which had suddenly sprung to life, with lights flashing and gears grinding. The computer monitors were also in a frenzy, with graphs and text flashing all over the screen.

While the others checked out the machine, HyJean wandered over to one of the computers. It didn't make much sense to her, but suddenly the screen changed and several elements on it turned green, with "complete" notices indicating that the machine was now fully functioning and ready to do immeasurable damage.

'Um, guys. This doesn't look good,' HyJean said, calling them over.

'Oh bugger,' said Flush. 'What's it doing?'

'I've got no idea, I've never seen anything like this before,' said HyJean. 'But I'm guessing it's activated and ready to flood the city.'

'Yeah, that's definitely in the not good category,' said Suds.

'Right, let's figure this out,' said Captain Clean. 'HyJean, take a look at the computers, see if you can shut it down. Flush, try and wake Limescale, see if we can get some answers out of him. Suds, help get those last couple of guys out. I'll see if I can turn this thing off.'

HyJean rushed over to the row of computers, tapping at the keys, but after being abandoned for a while, the computers had gone into standby mode and required a password to get back in. HyJean typed RESERVOIR1 and hit enter. Nothing. RESERVOIR2. Nothing. RESERVOIR3. After a few more attempts at increasing numbered intervals, she suddenly had an idea. PASSWORD. It worked! She was in.

'When will they learn?' she muttered as she skimmed through everything on the screens and frantically began tapping and clicking to try and stop the process.

Meanwhile, Flush was busy slapping Limescale on the cheeks. 'Helloooo! This is your morning wakeup call! Come on you stupid great twig, wake up!' He leaned down and shouted into his ear, 'WAKE UP! WE NEED YOUR HELP! WAKE UP DAMN YOU!'

Due to his size and abilities, HyJean had used an extra strong tranquiliser, which was proving very effective, as Limescale lay perfectly still, not even flinching. While his colleagues were trying their best to find answers and get people to safety, Captain Clean was pacing around next to the machine. Back and forth, back and forth, muttering to himself.

'What do I do? What do I do?' he asked himself repeatedly. In a moment of frustration, he kicked the machine.

It clanked and whirred loudly and then… it stopped. The lights flickered off. The dials slumped down to zero. The whole machine fell silent, and the computers turned red and stated the machine was inactive.

'It's stopped,' said a bemused HyJean. 'But… how?'

'I found a way to uh… reroute the circuits to reverse the polarity of the…' the captain began.

'You kicked it didn't you?' she said with a frown.

'Yes,' he said with an embarrassed nod.

They had done it. They'd stopped the machine and saved the city from being flooded, as well as capturing the monster behind the evil plan.

'Nice work,' said Suds, as he joined them by the machine.

At which point Flush's efforts suddenly paid off and Limescale burst to life, roaring and thrashing about. Flush flew off him and tumbled onto the floor with a thud. The three remaining grime fighters ran over and HyJean managed to sedate Limescale again.

'We should call the police before he wakes up again. There's no signal here though,' said HyJean, turning to Captain Clean. 'You go and call them, if you can manage that, and we'll wait here.'

The captain took out his phone, but as he was about to leave, he paused. There was a noise. An echoey noise in the distance. He looked at HyJean. She had clearly heard it too and was looking around the room. The noise grew. It sounded like someone screaming. Then suddenly, Chief Inspector Dovedale came flying out of a large pipe hole in the ceiling that was coated with bits of limescale. He landed in the dirty water with a splash and a thud, causing the others to jump back a little in surprise. As he pulled himself up and brushed himself off, Dovedale looked around at the grime fighters.

'What are you lot doing here?' he asked. 'Where's the monster?'

The grime fighters all silently pointed to Limescale, who was still lying unconscious on the floor.

'Oh. I'd come down here to stop him,' said the inspector, sounding a little disappointed. 'We just figured out where the pipes lead.'

'We've already stopped him,' said HyJean, trying not to sound too smug, but inside she was blowing a triumphant raspberry at the Chief Inspector.

'That was a cool entrance though,' said Flush, leaning in and giving him a thumbs up. 'I definitely want a go of that.'

'Right, well I'll call my men and have him taken away then,' said Dovedale. 'We'll get this place sealed up too.'

'Aww, I was thinking we could use it as a new base,' said Flush. 'It'd be cool, like the Batcave.'

'Absolutely not, it's filthy down here,' said the captain sternly, holding up his hands in an X shape. 'And it's infested with rats.'

'Oh come on, they're not that bad,' said Suds, who had picked up one of the rats and held it out towards Captain Clean.

The captain squealed and cowered from it, shouting for Suds to put the filthy rodent down and get it away from him. But, in good spirits from their latest victory, Suds instead started chasing the captain around the old reservoir, teasing him with the rat while the others watched and laughed.

💧💧

The next day, the male members of the squad, along with Mary, were gathered in the base discussing their new recruit.

'Have you found out what happened to him?' asked Suds, gesturing to the room where Nelson had been kept.

'He remembered he was a volunteer test subject at some lab, but he can't remember much else,' said Captain Clean. 'Whatever they did to him, it seems to have affected his memory.'

'Wait, Limescale said some guys in a laboratory made him look like that,' said Flush. 'Maybe it's the same lab?'

'Maybe. I'll look into it,' said the captain. 'We also need to find him somewhere to stay temporarily.'

'He can stay with me,' said Flush keenly. 'I've always wanted a flatmate, and it'll keep the water bill down if he doesn't need to shower. Do you reckon his water is drinkable?'

'Don't ask him that, dear,' said Mary. 'The poor boy's been through enough, without you turning him into a walking water cooler.'

Before they could discuss it further, HyJean entered and gestured for them to be quiet.

'He's ready,' she said.

The squad all turned their attention to her direction, and she beckoned for Nelson to come into the room. As he entered, the squad were surprised to see that he was no longer leaking. Dressed in just a pair of trunks with a pair of metal gauntlets on his wrist and a nervous smile on his face. The rest of the squad gave a little cheer.

Captain Clean stood up and shook Nelson's hand, 'Good to see you so dry.'

'Yo, Nelson! You look bostin mate,' said Flush.

'Thanks,' said Nelson with an appreciative little nod.

'How do you feel?' asked Suds.

'Much better, thanks,' Nelson smiled.

'Now all he needs is an alias,' said Catain clean, sitting back down at the table.

'Why does he need a book of maps?' asked Flush.

'No, an alias,' said Suds. 'A name he'll go by as a grime fighter.'

'He's got a name,' said Flush. 'He's The Drip.'

'We're not calling him The Drip!' said the captain.

'What about Moist Man?' suggested Mary.

Flush burst out laughing at this suggestion and HyJean couldn't help but giggle too. Suds gently patted his wife's arm and said, 'No love, that sounds wrong.'

'What about something more literal, to do with turning the water on and off like a tap?' suggested HyJean.

'Hm, I like the idea, but The Tap doesn't sound very authoritative,' said the captain.

'Well in America, we don't call them taps, we call them faucets,' said Nelson.

'Faucet huh?' said the captain thoughtfully.

The squad all looked at each other and each of them smiled.

'What, is that like a rude word over here or something?' asked Nelson, confused by their reaction to the name.

'No,' said HyJean. 'No, it's not.'

'But it sounds like a perfect name for a grime fighter,' said Captain Clean.

'Really? You like it?' asked Nelson.

They all nodded in unison.

'Awesome,' he smiled. He punched the palm of his hand with his fist and in the coolest voice he could muster said, 'Well in that case… hi, I'm Faucet!'

A SPOT OF TROUBLE

Buzz. Buzz. Buzz.

As the sleeping Nelson Spigot stirred, a moist hand reached over and slammed down on the button on the top of the alarm clock. As he did so, the water caused it to spark, sending a shock wave right through him. His body jolted furiously for a single second and he let out a yelp of surprise.

'Aaargh! I'm up! I'm up!' Nelson cried, scrambling around and falling off the edge of the bed.

As he pulled himself up, he looked down at the bed and saw that it was soaked. He sighed and looked at the metal bracelets on his wrists. Having been experimented on in a lab, Nelson now had the extraordinary ability to produce large amounts of water from his body at will, which had been controlled by his fellow grime fighter, HyJean, using the metal bracelets with some technology embedded within them that was far too complicated for anyone without a degree in science or technology to explain. His spasm had caused the bracelets to briefly short, leading to him releasing a large burst of water which flooded the bed.

'Ah man, this ain't good,' he muttered to himself as he grabbed a towel from the back of the door and started dabbing the bed fruitlessly. His unique abilities were still new to him, and he was still working on trying to control them. Though the bracelets had helped significantly, he still found himself having the occasional unintentional mishap.

What made it worse was the bed wasn't his own. His other fellow grime fighter, Will Armitage - also known as Flush - had let Nelson stay in his spare room that he'd just been using to store his impressive comic book collection, with a fold-out sofa bed for him to sleep on. As Nelson pulled off his soaked pyjamas, there was a knock at the door.

'You alright in there, bud?' Will asked with a voice that sounded only half awake.

'Uh, yeah,' said Nelson, opening the door just enough to poke his head through. 'Look, I'm sorry man, but I had a bit of an accident and the bed's all wet.'

'Oh,' Will replied, with a slight pause. He shrugged and continued, 'Well that's alright. No need to be embarrassed. It's a common problem that a lot of people have. Probably brought on by your recent trauma.'

'What? No, I mean there's water all over the bed,' Nelson explained. 'I got a shock off of the alarm clock and it shorted these out and I leaked.'

He gestured to his bracelets and then opened the door to show Will the bed.

'Oh, I see!' Will chuckled as he wandered over to the kitchen area of his open-plan apartment. 'Ah, don't worry about that. I'll sort it after breakfast. I'm making toast, want some?'

'Sure, thanks,' Nelson called as he pulled on the wetsuit that Captain Clean had given him to try out as a potential uniform. Once he was dressed, he joined Will in the kitchen.

'Hey, I was wondering, is your water drinkable?' Will asked out of nowhere.

'I dunno,' Nelson replied, looking at his hand as if it would have some kind of warning label on it. 'Why?'

'I was just curious,' Flush shrugged.

There was an awkward silence as they waited for the toaster to ping. They both stood and stared at the cupboards on the wall, both secretly thinking the same thing but not daring to say it aloud. Finally, Nelson caved.

'Wanna try it?' he asked.

'Yeah man!' said Will without a moment's hesitation.

He grabbed two glasses from off the drying rack and put them on the counter. Faucet sprayed some water into both, just enough for a few mouthfuls. They picked the glasses up and looked at them intensely, eyeing up the liquid inside for any signs that they shouldn't drink it. Neither saw anything that caused them any alarm.

'Bottoms up,' Will said, clinking his glass on Nelson's.

They both took a swig at the same time, swished it around in their mouth and then swallowed. There was a momentary pause, during which a look of deep regret flashed across both of their faces.

'That answers that then,' said Nelson quietly.

'Yep,' Will nodded, looking at the glass. 'I don't think I'll have a top up, thanks.'

'It tasted… I don't know… there was almost a metallic tang to it,' said Nelson.

'I've never tasted badger wee,' said Will. 'But somehow I feel like it tastes like that.'

'Yeah, I know what you mean,' Nelson nodded.

'I just hope it doesn't mess up my insides and make me like you,' said Will. 'Probably should've thought about that before we drank it, to be honest.'

'Let us never speak of this again,' said Nelson, and as if on cue the toaster pinged and the toast popped up to give them something else to focus on.

◆ ◆

A short while later, Flush and Faucet arrived at the Filtham community centre. The receptionist, Carol, was surprised to see Faucet and stood up to greet him as they passed.

'Oh, hello,' she said. 'How did your sponsored bath thing go?'

'What sponsored bath thing?' Faucet asked.

'I thought you were being carried around the city in a bath tub for charity?' Carol replied, looking a little confused.

Faucet looked at Flush, who just shrugged. Faucet had no idea what was going on, but didn't want to seem rude.

'Oh, yeah, that,' he said, scratching the back of his neck as he thought of what to say. 'Uh, it went well, thanks. In fact, Captain Clean was so impressed he offered me a job working for him.'

'Sounds like the sort of thing he'd do,' Carol chuckled. 'So you're working here now?'

'Sure am,' Faucet said proudly, puffing his chest out like he was showing off an imaginary medal.

'Oh, how lovely,' said Carol. 'Well, I'm always here if you need anything, and I do the knit and natter on Fridays.'

'Okay, sounds good,' said Nelson. 'Well, I gotta go. First day and everything. But it was nice to meet you and I'm sure I'll see you round.'

'Yes, yes, don't let me keep you,' she said, almost pushing him away. 'Go on, have a nice first day.'

They made their way up the stairs and into the base on the second floor. Captain Clean was already waiting for them by the door. He often liked to make things needlessly dramatic, and would stand around waiting for as long as he needed to in order for his surprise to work. He once spent nearly two hours waiting by a door for someone to come in, only to find out from Carol that they'd already left for the night.

'Good morning, gentlemen,' the captain said as they entered. 'And what time do you call this?'

'It's nine o'clock, the time we start,' Flush replied, a little defensively.

'I know, I was just asking because the clock's stopped,' said the captain. 'Suds, fix it for us will you. And in the meantime, Faucet, I'd like you to take a seat.'

'This isn't going to work,' said HyJean for the seventh time, in that tone that people use when they think they know better (and usually do) as she wandered over.

'It will, trust me,' said Captain Clean defiantly. 'It's an old trick I picked up in Denmark.'

HyJean sipped a cup of tea and sat on the edge of the table, ready to witness Captain Clean's attempt to hypnotise their newest recruit. When Captain Clean and HyJean first met Nelson in the hospital, he had very little memory of anything prior to being in hospital, other than something to do with a lab. HyJean suspected this was a form of amnesia brought on by the trauma of the experiments that had been done on his body. They were keen to know what had happened to Nelson, and the captain thought he had a way of finding out.

'I'm going to slowly put you into a trance and when you're under we should be able to access your subconscious memories,' Captain Clean explained.

'Okay, Mr Cane, let's do it,' said Faucet. He was never quite sure if he should refer to his boss as Clifford, Mr Cane or Captain Clean, so he took the more formal approach and used his surname. He was polite like that. Faucet took a deep breath and relaxed, before quickly adding, 'Just keep away from any private memories or… mature content.'

The captain nodded and started the process, but rather than swinging the bath plug side to side like a pendulum, he instead held the plug perfectly still and began swaying his body left and right.

'You are feeling veeeepy,' he said in what he thought was a soothing voice, but actually came across quite sinister, with an unintended accent that made him sound like Count Dracula.

'Shouldn't it be the plug that's swinging?' asked Sergeant Suds from behind, sipping a cup of tea while he watched.

'This is a seeeecret variaaaaation that is much more effeeeective,' said Cap in the same breathy lilt, still staring directly at Faucet. 'Veeeeery sleepy… veeeeery sleepy.'

'He should just give him one of his pre-mission motivational speeches,' Flush muttered to HyJean, 'That'd send him right off.'

HyJean gave a little laugh back. She was the most sceptical of the captain's methods and was watching purely for entertainment value.

'When I make a bird noise, you will be under,' continued the captain, who then did a loud 'SQUAWK!'

The others jumped a little, but Faucet seemed to suddenly snap into a hypnotic state, staring straight ahead blankly with wide eyes and a totally emotionless expression, like a human statue who'd just had three rounds of botox.

'You are now under my spell,' said Captain Clean. 'To confirm, please state your name.'

'My name is Nelson Horatio Clarence Spigot,' said Faucet in a robotic, monotone voice.

'And where were you born?'

'I was born in Washington DC, United States.'

'Do you know the name of the person who experimented on you in the laboratory?'

'Yes.'

'Are you able to tell me the name?'

'Yes.'

A slight pause.

'Okay, tell me the name.'

'His name was…' Faucet said, with a long, dramatic pause, 'Sergeant Suds.'

Everyone let out a surprised gasp and turned around to Suds, who spat out his tea in shock.

'What?!' he cried, stuttering to try and explain himself to the baffled squad. 'I never… I didn't… I wasn't…'

'Nah, I'm just messing with ya,' Faucet chortled, quickly returning to his normal state and sitting back in his chair in a most satisfied manner. 'The hypnosis didn't work. But man, you should've seen the looks on your faces!'

💧💧

'Here's your order ma'am. I hope you enjoy your food and have a happy happy day.'

It was Wendell's first day working at Happy Happy Burger, the city's beloved fast-food restaurant. After studying for 5 years at medical school, his sudden change of mind about his career path was seemingly paying off. Now, as he stood wearing his customary burger-shaped hat, he felt like he was ready to take on the world… or at least Filtham's second largest branch of Happy Happy Burger.

The fast-food joint was not the best, nor was it the cleanest, but it was cheap, so it was popular. It was originally called Happy Burger, but the owner felt this wasn't positive enough, so as part of a very expensive rebrand, it was renamed Happy Happy Burger. The staff were mostly young post-graduates, desperate for a successful career but too lazy to get one. Wendell was no different. With his spotty face and square glasses, he looked like a stereotypical nerd - his naïvely optimistic outlook gleaming in the sparkle of his braces.

The morning had gone well, with a series of happy customers and an even happier manager. But things took an unexpected turn after one young girl took her Cheery Cheeseburger meal and a group of masked people in home-made costumes strode up to the counter. Wendell clung a little tighter to the till for support. He was new to the city and had not yet heard of its team of government-funded grime-fighting heroes. He struggled to maintain his professional manner as he sheepishly greeted the first of the costumed customers.

'Hello sir, what would you like today?' he muttered as confidently as he could manage.

Flush leaned in and spoke with a low, gruff voice, 'I'd like a city full of law abiding, respectful people with a side order of justice.'

'Um… wh… I uh…' stuttered Wendell as beads of sweat started to form on his brow.

'I'm just kidding,' laughed Flush, returning to his usual jovial state. 'A Happy Hamburger meal with fries and a strawberry milkshake please'

Wendell breathed a sigh of relief and gathered the items that made up the masked man's meal, including a little toy burger with arms and legs protruding from its burger body and a big smiling face on the front. He handed the meal to Flush and continued to serve HyJean and Suds, who had equally enthusiastically named meals. All the meals had positive, happy names, although the quality of the food generally left the customers with opposite feelings. But items such as "Bloated Beef Burger" or "Stomach-churning Chicken Nuggets" probably wouldn't have sold quite as well.

Faucet, meanwhile, was back at the base working through the physical training routine that Captain Clean had set him. The captain had never actually trained anyone from scratch before, so he mainly stole ideas from the film Rocky – not the punching meat bit, that was far too unhygienic - and mixed in some cleaning tutorials from YouTube to personalise it a bit.

Faucet didn't mind, he was just enjoying being part of the squad.

'Where's Cap?' asked HyJean once they'd all got their meals.

They looked around the restaurant and spotted Captain Clean in his trademark toilet roll mask, micro-fibre cape and marigold gloves on the other side of the restaurant. He was currently having an argument with one of the staff about the cleanliness of the tables. The girl was also in her late teens and was clearly not paid enough to care about giving each table a thorough clean between customers. Nevertheless, the captain started vigorously scrubbing a table with his sponge – he always carried one with him – and aggressively lecturing her on the importance of using anti-bacterial spray to make sure there was no leftover sauce or grease that could contaminate a customer's meal. The squad walked over to break up the lesson, with Suds calmly pulling the captain away while HyJean apologised to the girl, who by this point was on the verge of tears.

They all sat down in a booth and began eating their meals. Despite their job revolving around sanitation, most of the squad enjoyed eating at the unhealthy Happy Happy Burger. It felt like a bit of a break from their daily hygiene-focussed work. Captain Clean, however, did not share their feelings and was always reluctant to spend their lunchbreaks there. He'd even brought his own sandwich to avoid eating the poorly prepared food from the (he suspected) unclean kitchen. He was also picky about what foods he ate, preferring chicken or beef over any kind of pork, as pigs were notoriously dirty and he couldn't bear the thought of eating meat that had come from such an unclean animal. He laid a handkerchief out on the table and took out an anti-bacterial hand wipe from the dispenser on his belt.

'So, any news on Faucet's history?' the captain asked as he wiped his hands for an excessively long period.

'I'm afraid not,' said HyJean. 'I've searched the Washington records and there's nothing. It's like he doesn't exist.'

'And we're absolutely sure he does exist?' asked Flush.

'I'm pretty sure he does,' said HyJean sarcastically. 'I poked him quite a bit.'

'Have you spoken to the police?' asked Suds.

'I've emailed them, but you know what they're like. It'll take at least a couple of months until we hear back,' said HyJean, dipping a couple of fries into a little cup of something that looked not unlike ketchup.

'And what about the laboratories?' Captain Clean asked as he started on his chicken sandwich.

HyJean held her finger up, gesturing for the captain to wait a second while she finished what she was eating. She was polite like that. When she was finished, she answered, 'I've found a few laboratories in the city, but all of them seem pretty clean – figuratively, I mean. I can't say how clean they are literally.'

The captain was just about to reply with a plan when he suddenly felt a gentle tug on his cape.

'Excuse me mister. Can I have your autograph please?' came a young sounding voice behind him.

Captain Clean turned around to see a young boy who looked no older than seven, standing next to him, shyly holding a white napkin.

'No,' said the captain. 'Go away.'

HyJean kicked him under the table and cleared her throat whilst she gave him a reprimanding stare.

'Sorry,' the captain said in a politer tone, 'No, go away please.'

The boy sulked off and Captain Clean turned back to continue eating his meal.

'How could you do that?' fumed HyJean, 'That little boy considers you his hero and you just tell him to go away.'

'I said please,' said Captain Clean with a little embarrassed shrug.

'She's right Cap,' agreed Flush. 'That was a bit of a douchey move.'

'Go and apologise to him now,' HyJean insisted.

'But I'm eating!' he pleaded.

HyJean quickly leant over the table and grabbed his sponge off the table.

'Go, now!' she said in an authoritative voice. 'Or you won't get your sponge back.'

'Fine,' the captain sighed as he stood up like a schoolboy that had just been sent to the headmaster's office. He unwillingly went over to a table where a family were sitting.

'Sorry kid, here you go,' he said as he scribbled his name on a napkin and handed it to the young boy.

'Who are you?' asked the boy with a confused look on his face that matched those worn by the rest of his family.

'I'm Captain Clean, you just came and asked me for an autograph,' the captain replied, a little irritated.

'No I didn't.'

'Yes you did.'

'No, I really didn't.'

'Yes, you really did. Right over there,' insisted the captain, pointing over to their table. On second glance, he noticed HyJean was mouthing something and pointing to a different table where a familiar looking boy was sitting with his family. 'Okay, sorry to bother you.'

Captain Clean went to the correct table and gave the correct little boy the autograph. The boy got very excited and even the captain could see how much it meant to him. Although that didn't mean he wanted to make a habit of doing it.

♦ ♦

Meanwhile back in the base, Nelson was busy with his training. So far, the morning's routine had consisted of scrubbing a toilet and sink repeatedly with no real explanation. Now he was taking his anger and frustration out on an unfortunate punching bag. He'd drawn an angry looking face on it that grinned menacingly at him as he stood before it. He paced around on the spot, eyeing up the bag.

'Hey, you lookin' at me? You want a piece of this, huh bag guy? Well here it is!'

He ran forward to hit it, but slipped on a towel on the floor, lost his footing and fell face first onto the bag, bouncing back and falling to the ground. He groaned as he looked up and saw the bag grinning down at him, swinging gently like it was celebrating. He quickly stood up and brushed himself off.

'Oh, so that's how it's gonna be is it? Well in that case, have some foot!'

He threw his leg in the air and struck the bag a roundhouse kick. Sadly, it seemed to do more damage to his foot than the bag.

'Argh!' he cried. 'Right then, time to play dirty.'

He left the room and seconds later came running back in, screaming and brandishing a knife.

'Surprise attack!' he shouted as he jumped at the bag from behind and slashed it open.

The face slumped down into a sad expression as the sand poured out onto the floor and the fabric sagged down.

'Ha! Didn't see that coming did you?' he said, putting his arms on his hips proudly. He stood and watched the sand pouring out all over the floor, and his face slowly sank with a heavy sigh. 'Ah man, I gotta clear this up now.'

'So, we don't know anything at all about this guy, except his name and he's from America?' asked Sergeant Suds.

'Pretty much,' said HyJean with a shrug as she finished off her fries.

'Do you really think it's wise to let a total stranger join the squad, Cap?' Suds asked.

'Probably not,' the captain admitted. 'But we're better off keeping him around so we can help him figure out what's happened to him. Plus, you know, he's got superpowers, so we kinda need him.'

'I've got a question,' said Flush, who was playing with the little plastic burger mascot. 'Why is the burger happy? Does he not understand his only purpose in life is to be eaten?'

The others chuckled while the captain gave a dissatisfied look.

'Hey Flush,' said Suds. 'Don't you have work on Tuesdays?'

'Yeah, why?' he asked, not taking his eye off the toy.

'Well… today is Tuesday.'

Flush paused and looked up and suddenly realised he was late for work. He jumped up, climbed over the table and ran off. A few seconds later, he returned to pick up the remains of his burger.

'This is your fault,' he said, scowling at the toy burger and then once again he was gone.

Captain Clean was just about to take a sip of his bottle of water, but as he did so he noticed a young boy who had been waiting patiently with a hand-drawn comic book in his hand. The captain sighed.

'See, this is what happens when you do it once,' said the captain to the remainder of the gathered squad.

'Oh shut up,' said HyJean.

'Let's have a look son,' said Suds, taking the boy's comic and flicking through it to show the others.

'Wow, this is amazing,' said HyJean. 'You're so talented.'

'This is fantastic,' added Suds. 'Very creative.'

'My legs aren't that short,' Captain Clean grumbled. 'And the colours are all wrong.'

The squad all signed the cover of the comic and handed it back to the boy with more encouraging remarks and cheery smiles. The boy happily skipped off and the squad returned to their food and conversation. However, within seconds there was a cough behind them requesting their attention. The captain turned around and saw a dozen little boys and girls all queuing up in a line, holding napkins and drawings.

'Oh great,' Captain Clean sighed.

♦ ♦

'FAUCET!' came the booming voice of Captain Clean from the training room. Seconds later, Faucet came running in, breathless and worried as he looked at the captain staring at the deflated punching bag hanging from the ceiling.

'Hey Mr Cane, sorry about the punch bag,' he said sheepishly. 'Mary's ordered us a new one.'

'I don't care about that. Why is this place such a mess?' the captain asked.

Faucet looked around the room a little confused, as he couldn't see any mess at all. True, it had recently had a big pile of sand on it, but he'd swept it up and vacuumed twice to be sure.

'What do you mean? I swept up after I'd finished training and wiped the stuff down like you said.'

'The floor is filthy,' the captain replied, pointing to a spot on one of the mats. 'Look.'

Faucet bent down to look closely and noticed that about three grains of sand still on the wooded floor. He winced a little and clicked his fingers. 'Ah man, I thought I'd got it all.'

'Nelson, something you must learn is that no matter how clean you think the world is, there is always more to clean. It's our job to look for these grains of sand and pick them up when nobody else will.' The captain bent down and picked up the sand, holding it out in his hand as if he were a low-rate magician performing a mildly interesting magic trick at a child's birthday party. He was now in teaching mode and tried to continue the metaphor. 'These grains of sand represent all the bad in the world, and we are the… the uh… we're the crab on the beach of… of life. We move around sideways looking out for… no, the spade, we're the spade. And we gather the sand, which is the people, into the bucket of life, and try to mould them into a castle… a castle of good.'

Faucet stared blankly for a few seconds and then asked, 'What?'

'Never mind, just go,' the captain sighed. 'I'll finish off in here.'

'Okay, thanks Mr Cane. And sorry again about the sand,' Faucet nodded as he took the grains of sand from the captain's hand and sheepishly left the room. He tossed them in a nearby bin and sauntered over to HyJean and Suds who were sat at the central desk reading a magazine and a newspaper, respectively. 'Man, I've never seen someone get so worked up about a few grains of sand.'

'That's nothing,' said HyJean. 'One time I had a packet of crisps and he found crumbs on my desk. He flipped out so bad that downstairs called the police.'

'Yeah, I remember that,' said Suds. 'Was that the time they tranquilised him?'

'No, that was when we spilt the bag of rice in the kitchen.'

Faucet was starting to look a little concerned. 'Y… you guys are joking right?'

HyJean smiled, 'Yes, of course.'

'Phew,' Faucet sighed as he sat down. He looked over at the newspaper Sergeant Suds was reading, The Troubling Times, and an article, or rather the accompanying picture, on the front page caught his eye. 'Hey, I recognise that guy.'

Suds closed the paper to see who he was referring to. 'What, the flea circus guy?'

He gestured to a small article at the bottom of the paper about a man who had been found to be using robotic fleas in his flea circus rather than training real fleas.

'Huh? No, him, with the glasses,' Faucet said, pointing to the larger photo.

'Oh, that's Doctor Friedrich Ozone,' Suds explained. 'A local scientist and philanthropist.'

'I think… I think I know him,' Faucet said with a furrowed brow, like he was trying to coax a long-lost memory from his brain. 'I've seen him somewhere, I'm sure of it. I think he might be to do with the lab.'

'Really?' asked HyJean, putting her magazine down and sitting up intently at the revelation. 'I think we should tell Cap about this.'

'Tell Cap about what?' asked the captain himself as he came into the room.

'Faucet here recognises Doctor Ozone,' Suds explained. 'Thinks he's something to do with the lab that experimented on him.'

'Hm, seems unlikely. But we can go speak to him anyway,' said the captain. 'Come on, Faucet, let's see what we can find out. No time like the present. Except maybe the past, that was pretty good.'

Faucet got up and headed over to the door with Captain Clean, who didn't bother with his usual routine of arming himself with one of his upgraded toilet brushes.

'I think I'd better go with them,' said Suds as he stood up from the table. 'By the way, why did you say we were joking earlier? We did have to tranquilise Cap that time.'

'Well, we don't want to scare the boy off,' said HyJean. 'Besides, Cap's not that bad anymore.'

'Really? Yesterday he punched a guy because he didn't use a handkerchief when he sneezed.'

'That is pretty unhygienic.'

'The guy was a fireman hanging off the edge of a building!'

'Fair point.'

💧💧

As they walked across the foyer, the three grime fighters received many bemused looks from passers-by. Captain Clean and Sergeant Suds were used to it by now, as they often found themselves in their work attire in the most unlikely of places. Only the week before they'd been investigating a strip club called whilst in costume. To their frustration, they were mistaken for strippers, with several women stuffing bank notes into the captain's utility belt. It was an embarrassing, if prosperous, night, which both of them agreed to never talk about again. However, Faucet was new to the attention and felt a little embarrassed as the people looked at him and muttered to themselves.

They called the elevator, and when it arrived, they stepped inside, standing next to a young woman who was not wearing a white coat, so they guessed she wasn't a scientist. After a brief moment of awkward silence, the woman asked, 'Excuse me, but are you boys from Ruby Strippers?'

Faucet was surprised by the question, as it almost seemed like the woman recognised them. Both the captain and Suds gulped a little, hoping she wouldn't elaborate.

'No ma'am,' said Captain Clean proudly, 'we're grime fighters.'

'Oh,' she said. 'That's a shame.'

The rest of the vertical journey returned to the awkward silence, partly because the woman was wondering if she could get similar outfits for her husband and partly because Suds had farted in his moment of panic and didn't want to draw any attention to himself. After stopping to let the woman off, they continued riding upwards and Faucet finally broke the silence.

'So, who exactly is this Doctor Ozone guy?' he asked. 'What does he do?'

'He's a scientist, specialising in ecology - living organisms and their environment,' Cap explained as he started wiping the smudged fingerprints on the mirrored wall on the back of the lift that had been bugging him since they'd gotten in.

'He's also a notorious criminal,' Suds added, which piqued Faucet's attention.

'Really?' Faucet asked, keen to know more.

'No, Suds is wrong,' the captain, holding up his arms in an X shape to further illustrate his point. 'The rest of the squad seem to have something against him, but he's a perfectly upstanding citizen who's done a lot of good for this city. His research and new technologies have helped reduce carbon emissions, doubled our recycling output and made us one of the leading cities in renewable energy sources. He's a good man.'

'Cap, we literally stopped him from poisoning the whole city last week,' Suds pointed out in a frustrated tone that let Faucet know this was an often-repeated argument.

'I told you, that was a misunderstanding,' the captain sighed. 'He was the one distributing the antidote.'

'We distributed the antidote that Jean made!' Suds argued.

Their arguing was interrupted by a loud ding as they arrived at the top floor, where Dr Ozone's office was located. They left the argument in the lift to keep the newly cleaned mirror company, and the end of a short corridor, they came to a large set of doors, which Captain Clean knocked on. A door opened slightly, and a young woman answered. She had jet black hair with a single green streak and was dressed in similarly dark clothing. She was the sort who dressed like an emo but had very little interest in the music or behavioural quirks that came with the label.

'Yes?' she asked in a dreary voice, like a teenager who'd just been disturbed whilst listening to an album of sad music on repeat.

'We'd like to speak to Doctor Ozone, please,' Captain Clean said with a smile.

The girl looked back into the room and then back at them with a blank expression that gave away nothing. 'He's busy.'

She went to close the door, but Captain Clean, who was clearly used to this reaction, quickly wedged his foot between the door and the frame. The girl seemed to have some strength behind her, as the captain let out a little yelp as the door closed on his foot.

'It's rather urgent,' he said through a wince. 'He might have some information that could save a life.'

There was an audible sigh from behind the door and a voice with a distinct German accent spoke out.

'It is okay, Polly, let them-'

Before he could finish, Sergeant Suds' foot came smashing through the door. He'd grown impatient and decided to use brute strength to gain entrance, much to the surprise of everyone inside and outside the room.

'… in,' the doctor finished with an unamused roll of his eyes.

The grime fighters strode across the room, which had black walls lined with paintings that all shared a primarily blue colour palette. If Picasso had a blue period, this artist seemed to have had a blue lifetime. There was a section of the wall dedicated to framed degrees and newspaper clippings featuring photos of a wiry man with messy white hair and thick rimmed smiling. The room was relatively tidy, save for a large desk at the farthest end that was covered with papers and random metal objects that looked like they were parts of something bigger and more complex. Behind the desk was sat Doctor Ozone himself – a wiry man with messy white hair and thick rimmed glasses, which he adjusted as he stood up to greet them.

'Guten Tag, gentlemen,' he said, extending a hand for any of them to take. The captain seemed reluctant to touch a potentially unclean hand – even if it was a hand he greatly admired – and Suds was visibly turned off by the gesture, so Faucet leant forward and shook the hand. 'I don't believe we've met. I am Doctor Friedrich Ozone,' he said, before noticing his now moist hand and wiping it on his trousers. He gestured to the black and green haired girl standing next to them at the side of the desk, 'And this young Fräulein is my assistant and head of the pollution reduction department, Polly.'

Nelson looked at her and smiled, slightly smitten by her appearance, though she didn't return the smile.

'Now, how can I help you?' Doctor Ozone asked, turning back to face his visitors. 'I believe you said there was a life that needed saving?'

'Ah yes, well I may have embellished that a little,' said the captain, almost blushing under his toilet roll mask. He was quite the fan of the doctor and his work, so it felt like talking to a celebrity when he was in the doctor's presence. 'We'd like to ask you about our friend Nelson here. See, he was brought to us secreting water all over his body. We've discovered that all the blood in his body has been replaced by water, but still with all the essential properties of blood.'

'Interesting, very interesting,' Doctor Ozone said as he returned to his desk and sat down, gesturing for them to take a seat too.

'We've managed to control the water so that he can produce it from his body at will, but we have no idea how he came to be like this,' the captain continued as he sat down. 'The only thing he remembers is being experimented on in a laboratory. But earlier he recognised your face in the newspaper, so we thought maybe you might know something about him or his condition.'

The doctor paused for a moment, pondering over what he'd heard, before shaking his head. 'I'm afraid I cannot help you. As interesting as this all sounds, I do not know this Mr Spigot, nor any laboratory that would perform such… fascinating experiments.'

'Could you maybe get someone to have a look at him?' the captain asked. 'One of your team might be able to see how it was done.'

'My team are very busy with far more important work,' the doctor replied. 'But I will personally look into this matter for you, do not worry. I too find it most intriguing.'

'That would be superb, thank you doctor. We really appreciate your help, and I'm sorry for any inconvenience we've caused you today,' said Captain Clean as he made to stand up.

'Wait a minute,' said Suds as he suddenly realised something. 'If you don't know him, how do you know his last name is Spigot? We only called him Nelson.'

'Yes, that is what I said, Nelson,' Doctor Ozone said, brushing away the remark.

'No, you called him Mr Spigot,' Suds continued.

'Sergeant Suds, please, don't correct the doctor,' said the captain. 'The man clearly knows what he said, he's wearing a lab coat.'

Suds huffed and stood up, slamming his hands down on the desk and leaning in. The doctor remained calm and collected.

'He's clearly hiding something,' Suds said. 'Why can't you see it?'

'He's not hiding anything. He's a scientist trying to help the city,' Captain Clean argued. The doctor, meanwhile, sat and enjoyed the sight of the two grime fighters arguing, while Nelson sat awkwardly in the middle, his gaze firmly fixed on the doctor's assistant who had barely looked at him the whole time.

Suds let out a laugh and picked up an unusual looking gun off the messy desk. 'Really? By making weapons?'

'That is a hair dryer,' the doctor said in a lazy tone and a look that suggested he was lying but was confident they'd fall for it. Or at least one of them would.

Suds looked at it closer and spotted a little dial on the side. 'So why does it have a stun and a kill setting?'

'I have very tough hair,' he said dryly with the slightest hint of a smirk.

'Well then, you won't mind if I dry your hair right now,' Suds said as he pointed the device at the doctor, whose eyebrows raised slightly, but they were the only parts of him that moved.

Suds could tell by Polly's worried look that her boss was lying, but the explanation seemed to have won Captain Clean over. The captain stood up, snatched the gun out of Suds' hands and put it back on the desk.

'Look, there's an easy way to settle this,' he said, turning to Faucet. 'Nelson, do you recognise this man?'

Faucet looked at Dr Ozone sheepishly, then back at Captain Clean, then over at Sergeant Suds, then back to the captain. It was as if his eyes were watching an invisible tennis match that only he could see.

'I uh… well, I don't know,' he stuttered. He did recognise the doctor, but he didn't know where from. He also didn't know who to side with, since the captain was essentially his boss and the man who'd taken him in, but Suds seemed very certain that the doctor was evil. 'I mean I do recognise him, but I don't know if… I suppose he could've… but, I can't say.'

'Very enlightening,' Doctor Ozone said dryly. 'Gentlemen, consider this: I am a well-known and respected figure in this city. The boy has clearly heard of me and perhaps knows my recent projects in ecohydrology. It would be fitting, no?'

'There you go, see, a perfectly logical explanation,' the captain said to Suds. 'I told you this was a waste of time. I think we'd better leave the good doctor to get back to his work. Thank you for your help doctor, we'll see ourselves out. And send us a bill for the door.'

The captain wasted no time in leaving, marching out as boldly as he'd entered. Suds looked at the doctor, who just sat back relaxed and gave him a satisfied smile. Suds let out a defeated sigh, before unwillingly turning and following the captain out. Faucet, meanwhile, sat and waited in his chair, baffled by what was going on and waiting for someone to tell him what to do.

'I think you're supposed to go with them,' the doctor suggested.

'Oh right, thanks,' Faucet said, rising and quickly walking out after his two colleagues.

Polly closed the door behind them, bending down and looking through the big hole in the door that Suds' boot had made, watching their visitors slowly shrink as they walked down the corridor. She was about to move when suddenly an upside-down face appeared in front of her on the other side of the door. She jumped back a little startled.

'Hey, sorry,' said Faucet. 'Polly, was it? I just wondered if you fancied going for a drink later?'

Polly hummed and gave a flattered smile. She reached up and opened the door a little. As Faucet stepped forward to enter, she quickly slammed the door back shut, hitting him square in the face.

'I'll take that as a no then,' Faucet said, rubbing his nose and walking off down the corridor.

Polly chuckled to herself and walked off into another room to continue her current work on colourising carbon monoxide. Once she had left the room, Doctor Ozone picked up his phone and dialled. He waited for a moment for the person on the other end to answer. When they did, they said nothing.

'It's me,' he said in a very serious tone. 'He survived.'

There was a brief dramatic pause as the room filled with tension like a fart in an elevator, and Doctor Ozone waited to hear what reaction his big revelation would bring.

'Who survived? Who is this?' asked a voice on the other end. They sounded a little older than the doctor, but with a posh English accent.

'It's me, Doctor Ozone. Project Tap, the water guy, he somehow survived,' the doctor reminded him. 'The Sanitary Squad have him.'

'Does he remember anything?' the voice asked.

'It seems not, the clever one seemed to think it was my doing.'

'Good, let's keep it that way.'

The line cut off and the doctor put his phone down on the desk. He sat back in his chair and interlocked his fingers, staring into the distance. He looked down at weapon on his desk and laughed lightly to himself.

'Hairdryer,' he chuckled as he picked up the gun. 'He'll believe anything.'

He played with it until it accidentally went off in his hands, destroying a plant on the opposite side of the room. Polly poked her head around the door, looking at the plant-shaped scorch marks on the wall and then back at the doctor.

'Everything okay?' she asked.

'Yes, yes,' Doctor Ozone nodded, 'I mean to do that.'

♦ ♦

'Give it to me, I'll do it.'

'No, I can do it.'

'Just give -'

'No, get off, I'm doing it.'

It was late and Happy Happy Burger had not long closed for the night. Wendell had gone home to another streaming marathon of his top five Voyager-era Star Trek episodes and a dangerously bland microwave meal for one. His girlfriend preferred home-cooked foods, so she made her own dinner.

At the back of the fast-food restaurant, a pair of figures in masks were trying to pick the lock of the staff exit. The slightly taller one dressed all in black was a man called Gerry, known to the criminal underworld as The Blackhead. His partner was a younger woman with long, scarlet hair called Nell, known professionally as Pimple. They were swift, they were experienced, and they were married.

The two had met at a weapons expo a few years previously and had hit it off when Gerry was trying out a new crowbar and accidentally hit it off Nell's head. Luckily, she was testing a new metal helmet and only suffered mild embarrassment as the loud clang echoed around the hall.

They had bonded together over their uniquely disturbed skin. Both had unfortunate dermatological problems that meant their faces – and a lot of the rest of their bodies – were covered in spots, blemishes, blackheads, pimples, pustules, keloids, boils, and pretty much any other unattractive lump you could imagine. Their faces, which were thankfully often hidden under balaclavas, looked like a child's drawing of a plate of mouldy beans. But their facial imperfections had given the inspiration for their criminal aliases. They used their skin complaints as motivation to get back at the world and those that mocked them for it.

The two villains had had mildly successful individual careers as robbers, but now enjoyed working together to commit bigger robberies and other nefarious deeds. Although "enjoyed" may not be right word, as they were currently in the middle of one of their regular squabbles, which was about to be interrupted by a click as the door unlocked.

'Aha!' cried Blackhead as the lock gave a begrudging click. 'See, I told you I'd do it.'

'Oh yeah, after 5 minutes of picking,' argued his wife. 'You're hardly Harry Houdini.'

'Oh… shut up,' said Blackhead as he turned the handle and pushed open the door.

'Careful you don't cut yourself on that razor sharp wit,' Pimple smirked.

They crept into the room and over to the alarm system on the wall. They knew they had 10 seconds before the quiet beeping would stop and a loud wailing would alert the whole road to what they were up to.

'What's the 4-digit code?' whispered Blackhead.

'4, 6, 3, 5,' Pimple replied.

He tapped the numbers on the pad, but the beeping didn't stop. In fact, it got louder, and a little red light started flashing on the panel.

'Oh, for Christ's sake. Now what have you done?' Pimple groaned.

'Nothing, I put in what you said,' her husband replied. '4, 6, 3, 9.'

'I said 5! F-I-V-E, not 9!'

'You said 9!'

'I did not!'

'Well, it sounded like 9!'

'Well maybe if you listened properly, you'd get it right.'

'And maybe if you didn't wear a balaclava over your mouth, I could hear you properly.'

At which point their argument was interrupted by a loud wailing noise that was attempting to alert the whole road to what they were up to.

'Quick!' screamed Pimple. 'Make it stop!'

'What's the code again?!' cries Blackhead.

'I don't know!' she said in a panic. 'Try bash, bash, bash.'

'Right,' said Blackhead, as he whipped out a small metal hammer and bashed it on the alarm. It made a few distressed bleeping noises before it fell silent and the couple breathed a sigh of relief. There was a brief pause where they looked at each other, trying to be angry, but their fronts quickly broke like the alarm system in front of them and they both started laughing.

'That was close,' Pimple chuckled.

'I know,' Blackhead replied. 'Nearly ended up like that time in the jewellers.'

'Oh god, don't remind me,' said Pimple. 'I don't think I've ever run so fast.'

'But it was exciting though,' said Blackhead as he remembered the thrill of the escape.

'It always is with you,' said Pimple with a smile. It lingered for a few seconds, both of them remembering how it was to commit crimes alone and how much more fun it was to share it with someone, then a little spark came from the alarm and reminded them of their mission.

'C'mon, we've got work to do,' said Pimple, turning and leaving out the door they'd entered through. The two burglars returned to their van – which had been decorated with a black and red polka dot theme – and opened up the doors. Inside, a single, swinging lightbulb on the roof illuminated the spacious interior, revealing a large hose connected to a pumping machine that was connected to a large metal container with various switches and leavers on.

'Right, let's get this grease and go,' said Pimple, handing her husband the end of a hose that was connected to the machine. 'Think you can handle that?'

Blackhead stuck his tongue out playfully under his balaclava as he took the hose and headed into the main kitchen area of the restaurant, the hose unravelling as he went. He dropped it into one of the fryers and barked like a dog to signal his wife to turn it on. While the thick, beige liquid made its way down the pipe and into the container, Blackhead helped himself to some cold leftover fries and perched himself on top of the counter. After a few minutes, the grease was drained and they moved onto the next fryer. Soon, all three fryers were empty, and Pimple meowed to signal that the container in the van was full. Blackhead pulled the hose out of the fryer and returned to his wife.

'Here, I got you this,' he said, handing her a small plastic milkshake cup toy with little feet and an innocent smiley face, which he'd swiped from the counter.

'Aww, it's so cute!,' she said with a smile that almost matched the one on the toy. 'Thanks sweetie.'

They secured the containers and machine, packed the hose away and closed the van doors. Climbing into the front of the van, Pimple popped her new toy on the dashboard whilst her husband looked back at the restaurant they'd just looted.

'Should we lock it back up?' asked Blackhead, gesturing to the back door of the restaurant.

'Yeah, we best had,' said Pimple. 'Don't want anyone breaking in while their alarm's not working.'

💧💧

The next morning, HyJean was busy working away on a pair of metal bracelets in her office when there was a knock on the door and Faucet poked his head around.

'Hi Jean,' he said, before quickly adding. 'Sorry, I meant… I didn't mean… hello Jean.'

'Don't worry, the boys do that joke all the time,' HyJean chuckled. 'Come on in.'

'Captain Clean said you wanted to see me,' said Faucet as he entered, looking around at the office. It was a small room with a desk full of papers and "bits and bobs" that almost hid the laptop that HyJean had been busy tapping away at. On the wall was a notice board with more papers attached to it and a whiteboard with scribbled notes on.

'Yes, it's time to do the most fun part of being a hero,' HyJean said in a dry tone, turning to him and holding up a clipboard and pen. 'Paperwork!'

'Oh! Right, yes, of course,' said Faucet, sitting down in an old armchair that HyJean kept in the room for when she needed to relax or think about things. 'Fire away.'

'So, first of all, name?' HyJean asked.

'Nelson Spigot,' he replied confidently.

'It's good you remember that,' said HyJean as she made a note of his name. 'Some people with memory loss can forget even their name, which must be very difficult.'

'Well, to be honest, I did,' admitted Faucet. 'But I found it sewn into my underwear. It was either Nelson Spigot or Calvin Klein, but nobody else seemed to have any Nelson Spigot underwear.'

'I see,' HyJean nodded. 'What about age?'

'Ah, I'm not too sure about that one,' said Faucet. 'I've got no ID.'

'Well, how old do you feel?' HyJean asked, thinking it might give them some clue as to how old he was.

'Hmm, I think definitely in my late teens,' said Faucet, doing a little jogging motion with his arms as if to prove his fitness.

HyJean paused for a moment, staring at him silently, before returning to the form and quietly saying, 'I'll put mid-twenties.' She then moved onto a series of other questions. 'Address?'

'Don't know.'

'Phone number?'

'Don't know.'

'Email address?'

'I do not know.'

'National Insurance number?'

'No that, I do not.'

'Bank details?'

'My knowingness of that is non-existent.'

'Okay, well we'll need to set you up with a bank account so you can get paid,' HyJean explained.

'Sweet!' Faucet grinned. 'Is it a good wage?'

'What do you think?' HyJean scoffed. 'We work for the council, so it's pretty much minimum wage. And don't expect a rise anytime soon. The only rises we get are in stress levels. But we do get the odd bonus if we help out someone rich.'

'Fair enough. Not like I've got many expenses,' said Faucet with a shrug. 'I'm just excited to get started fighting crime.'

'Grime,' HyJean corrected him as she signed the bottom of the form and clicked her pen. 'We're not allowed to refer to what we do as fighting crime, creates all sorts of legal issues. But I don't see us as fighting criminals anyway, we're fighting against a bigger foe than that, uncleanliness.'

'Gee, you're really serious about that, huh?'

'Not as much as Cap, but we have been brought round to his way of thinking that a clean world is a better world,' HyJean nodded. 'And you'll have to think like that too if you want to fit into the squad. Hours are nine till five, but there may be some out of hours work if an emergency arises. You get weekends and bank holidays off.'

'Wait, there's no crime on weekends?' asked Faucet.

'Not much, the local criminals are surprisingly considerate like that. But Cap's always around to handle anything that does crop up, and Sergeant Suds are I are often on hand if he needs help,' she said as she put the form down and clasped her hands together. 'So, that's that done. You'll get a contract after your probationary period. That'll outline the usual details: you get thirty days holiday entitlement, there's no pension scheme, you're not allowed to tell anyone what we do here and if you ever try to kill us you'll be fired. Standard stuff. So, how did you get on with Doctor Ozone yesterday?'

'Ah, it didn't go great,' he sighed. 'The doctor didn't know anything, but he said he'll look into it for us, which was nice of him.'

'Hm, I can't imagine him doing that,' said HyJean. 'Knowing him, he probably just said that to keep Cap off his back.'

'Yeah, Mick seemed pretty doubtful too,' said Nelson. 'Doesn't seem to trust him at all.'

'And with good reason. But don't worry, I'm doing my own investigations into your situation,' she said with a reassuring nod.

'So, what's the deal with this Doctor Ozone guy? Mick thinks he's evil, but Mr Cane thinks he's good.'

'It's a bit of both,' she explained. 'He's a dangerous and complicated man. He's committed loads of crimes, mainly using other people to do his work so it can't be traced to him, but he's also done lots of good for the city and donates a lot to charity. Cap's completely oblivious to the bad side and we can never seem to get anything solid to take him down. So, we just have to keep an eye on him, stop his plans and try to convince Cap he's not a saint.'

'Right, gotcha,' Faucet nodded.

'Anyway, how's the training going?' she asked.

'Yeah, good. It's going well,' he nodded. 'If were ever attacked by an army of punch bags, I'll definitely be ready.'

HyJean chuckled as she tinkered with one of the bracelets. 'Well, these should be ready soon, so then the real fun will start.'

Faucet continued to study the wall of notes, while HyJean worked. For a moment there was silence, until HyJean suddenly remembered something that had happened a few days before. She put her tools down and turned around.

'By the way, I'm sorry about the other day,' said HyJean. 'Y'know, the... flirting. I was just messing about, I thought you were asleep.'

'Ah don't worry about it,' Faucet replied.

'It's just now that I'm married with a young boy, so I don't get to do much flirting anymore,' she explained.

'It's fine, honestly.'

HyJean gave a little relieved smile and continued her work.

'So does your husband know what you do?' asked Faucet.

'Yeah, I told him. I know you shouldn't, but it's easier than coming up with excuses why I come home bruised and worn out all the time.'

'That's fair enough. What does your boy think of it?'

'Oh, he loves it. He's not allowed to tell anyone about it. But I told him if he keeps it secret until he's 18 then he can join. Every night he asks me to tell him stories about fighting grime.'

'Aww, that's cute,' Faucet said with a smile. 'Hopefully he follows in his mother's footsteps.'

'God help him if he does,' said HyJean, giving a light chuckle. 'Now, I just need to calibrate the force indicator. But I need…' she trailed off as she searched her desk for the something she was missing. 'Ah, I know. MOP, I need you!'

It appeared as if HyJean was calling out to the air, and Faucet gave her a puzzled look, wondering if she had a habit of talking to inanimate objects, but she just gave a little smirk, as if something impressive was about to happen. A few seconds later, a little robot trundled into the room. It was a little smaller than a vacuum cleaner, with three appendages on its midsection that looked like arms. It was amateurly built, with lots of loose wires, mismatched buttons, a small screen on the front and a smiley face that had been drawn on to make it look friendly. Overall, it looked like a Dyson vacuum cleaner that had mated with the robot from the film Short Circuit. It rolled across the room on its tracks and stopped in front of HyJean, who grinned at Faucet.

'Woah!' exclaimed Faucet, shifting back in his seat in surprise. He stared own at the little robot with a mixture of amazement and confusion. 'What is that thing?'

'This is our mechanical office pet – MOP for short. I built him myself,' she replied proudly.

'Ha, you guys are crazy,' he said as he settled back in his seat and gave a little wave to the robot. 'Well, it's nice to meet you, MOP.'

'Yeah, he can't talk yet,' HyJean pointed out.

'Oh, okay. How about a high five?'

'You can try,' she said with a shrug.

Faucet held out his hand and the robot glided over to him, raised one of its metal limbs so clunkily that it looked like it was taking great effort. From a hole in the end of the arm, it sprayed a small amount of antibacterial gel onto Faucet's hand.

'He's still very much in the development stage,' admitted HyJean with a light giggle. 'MOP, can you bring me bring me the red hard drive for the computer please.'

The robot beeped and a little green light flashed on the screen. It drove back out into the main room of the base and over to the computer area to retrieve the hard drive.

'Oh, you have COMPUTER too?' Faucet said excitedly. 'What does that stand for? No wait, let me guess. Is it… Complete Organisational Machine… Providing… Uh… Users… Technical Evidence and… Resources?'

'Um, no. It's actually just a normal computer,' HyJean replied a little awkwardly. 'But I like that name though.'

💧💧

A while later, Sergeant Suds entered the base and found Captain Clean, HyJean and Faucet all sitting around the central table playing a game of scrabble. It was one of the things they liked to do in their downtime, though the rest of the squad disliked playing with Captain Clean as he refused to put a word down unless it was sanitation related, insisting that the game should in some way be related to their work to justify playing it.

'Hey guys, did you hear the news about Happy Happy Burger?' Suds asked.

'What, are they serving actual cow meat now?' HyJean said, not looking up from the board.

'No, they were robbed last night,' Suds said as he sat down next to Captain Clean, pointing to the captain's letters. 'You can do brush.'

'Seriously?' asked the captain.

'Yeah, you've got the B, R, S and H,' Suds began, pointing out the letters, but the captain brushed him away.

'No, I mean about Happy Happy Burger being robbed?' he clarified.

'Oh! Yeah, they broke in and stole all the grease from the fryers.'

'Well, we've all thought about doing that,' said Faucet, who was sat back in his chair with his arms folded, waiting for the captain to make his move.

'That's weird,' said HyJean, who left the game to go over to the computer and pull up some newspaper articles on the screen. 'That's the third fast food place this week that's been robbed.'

'Are there any patterns?' asked Captain Clean as he joined her at the computers, skimming through the articles. Once he'd left the table, Faucet put down some tiles to spell out "BOOBS" and giggled to himself.

'Well, the only thing they stole from each restaurant was a large quantity of grease,' she explained. 'But who could need all that grease?'

'A John Travolta tribute act?' suggested Faucet, who was now taking the opportunity to steal some better letters for the game.

'Or someone with a very weird fetish?' added Suds.

'Or maybe someone who wants to use the grease as a weapon,' reasoned Captain Clean. 'Suds, I think we should pay Happy Happy Burger a visit.'

'Hey, can you bring me back a burger?' asked Faucet. 'I'm starving,'.

'We're not going to get food,' said the captain sternly. 'HyJean are his bracelets ready?'

HyJean walked back over to the table and picked up three scrabble tiles which spelled out the word "YES", holding them up with a grin.

'Great, you can help him try them out then,' he said as he turned to leave.

'Do we have to call them bracelets?' asked Faucet. 'It makes it sound like I'm wearing jewellery, rather than a piece of really cool tech.'

'But that's what they are,' said the captain. 'The ones Wonder Woman wears are called bracelets.'

'Yeah, I know but... wait, is Wonder Woman real? Do you know her?' asked Faucet, getting a little over-excited.

'No, of course she's not real,' said the captain. 'If she were, do you think I'd still be working with this team?'

'Oh, that's charming,' said HyJean. 'Maybe I'd be too busy working with Batman.'

'Batman wears gauntlets,' Faucet pointed out.

'What's that got to do with anything?' asked the captain.

'Why can't mine be called gauntlets?' asked Faucet.

'To be fair, gauntlets are more a glove,' said HyJean. 'I think the more accurate term for these are bracers, like what archers wear.'

'See, just like I said, bracelets,' said the captain. 'Come on, let's go before he starts renaming the rest of his outfit.'

💧💧

'Chief Inspector Dovedale, what are you doing here?' asked Captain Clean as he entered the Happy Happy Burger manager's stuffy, dimly lit office.

Chief Inspector Dovedale was a tall man with a bushy moustache that undoubtedly held many secrets beneath it. His hair was thinning on top, so he often wore a battered fedora hat, which matched his long, brown coat. His ensemble was completed by a disgruntled look that seemed to permanently adorn his face. Many hard years in the force had culminated in him having to put up with "costumed weirdos" chasing "dirty freaks" around the city, which he did not enjoy one bit.

'I'm investigating a crime Mr Clean, it's what I'm paid to do,' came the chief inspector's sarcastic response.

'It's Captain Clean,' the captain pointed out, and by his tone it was evidently not for the first time.

'Until you provide me with evidence of your being awarded that title, I will not be using it,' Dovedale replied with a little huff for added emphasis.

'I was in the army y'know,' chipped in Sergeant Suds casually.

'Really?' asked Dovedale. 'Did you kill anyone?'

'No, but I washed a few dead bodies.'

'Right,' said Dovedale with a slightly perturbed frown that wondered why Suds had chosen to share this piece of information.

There was a young girl sat at the computer who looked like a female version of Wendell - in fact, it could almost have been him in a wig. She was frantically skimming through CCTV footage and suddenly piped up when she got to the footage of the break in. Captain Clean and Suds moved in for a closer look. The footage was dark, because it was night, and low quality, because the cameras were cheap. On the screen, two shadowy figures could just be made out picking the lock and entering the building.

'Well, that's bloody useless,' said the Chief Inspector, flapping his arms around. 'Can't see a flipping thing.'

'Do you have any other angles?' asked the captain. 'Perhaps showing them arriving or inside the restaurant?'

'No, sorry,' said the girl, in a voice that mimicked Wendell's, only in a slightly higher tone. 'The boss said one camera was more than enough and any more would be a waste of money.'

'Of course he did,' tutted Suds.

'Can we get a copy of this footage?' asked the captain. 'HyJean might be able to-'

'No!' said Chief Inspector Dovedale firmly. 'I've told you before, if you and your lot want to run around throwing soap at everything, that's fine, but you're not using official police resources.'

The captain paused, then let out a defeated sigh. 'Fine.'

He asked the girl to go through the footage again, so he could look closer and try to work out what was going on. With a nod from the Chief Inspector, she obliged and re-ran the footage. It looked the same as it had the first time, dark and blurry, with very few details visible. The captain asked a few more questions, and then the Chief Inspector stood forward holding his little notepad and addressed the room.

'Well, it seems to me that this crime was committed by two criminals who entered through the back door and disabled the alarm by smashing it,' he said. 'They stole all the grease and left without taking anything else. This would seem to suggest that they wanted the grease for something.'

'Hey up, the little grey hairs are working,' Suds whispered to Captain Clean.

'You're right,' the captain whispered back. 'Let's get out of here.'

As the two heroes slipped out of the restaurant, Suds seemed confused by the captain's apparent lack of frustration at not being allowed more involvement in the investigation. It was unlike him. Usually, once he'd been given an unsanitary matter to solve, he stopped at nothing and dedicated himself to solving the problem.

'You didn't seem that bothered when he said we couldn't have a copy of the footage,' said Suds.

'No need,' said the captain, holding up his phone with a self-assured grin. 'I filmed it on my phone.'

💧💧

'Okay, we're going to have to be quite quick changing these bracelets,' HyJean told Faucet.

The two grime fighters were in the shower room, ready to try out the new technologically enhanced bracelets that HyJean had recently finished developing. Like his current bracelets, they were made of metal, with a sleek finish, but these ones had more wires, power gauges and other tech built into the design to add extra functions. Faucet had his left arm resting on a table and HyJean had placed the new bracelets next to it, near enough for her to reach.

'Try and concentrate on holding the water in,' she instructed.

'Will that work?' Faucet asked.

'No idea. I just want to try and stay dry here,' she said with a raised brow. 'Okay, on 3?'

'Sure, go for it.'

'1… 2… 3…'

HyJean pressed the lock release on Faucet's existing bracelet with one hand and grabbed the new bracelet with the other. However, what she didn't count on was a large amount of water that had been building up in Faucet's wrist and now came gushing out and soaking her face. She fumbled about, trying to deflect the water and put the new bracelet on. Meanwhile, Faucet was panicking, fidgeting in his seat as his left arm flailed around and asking repeatedly what he should do. Obviously, HyJean didn't answer him because she didn't fancy her lungs being drowned with water. Faucet quickly remembered HyJean's advice and strained to try and hold in the water. With a look on his face reminiscent of a bad case of constipation, he tensed and relaxed his arm. He found the more he relaxed, the calmer it got, so he focused hard on relaxing. After a few seconds, it started to take effect and the water simmered down to a light spray, calm enough for HyJean to affix the new bracelet.

'Sorry about that,' said Faucet, with an embarrassed look as he just sat there in the same position with his arm resting on the table.

'It's fine,' said HyJean, although it wasn't fine at all. Her hair was soaking wet, her make-up was ruined, and her red eyes were stinging so much she could barely see.

'Wanna give it a minute before we do the other one?' Faucet asked.

HyJean nodded silently and slumped down onto one of the chairs, picking up a towel and drying her face and hair.

'Try… try that one out,' she said, rather breathlessly. 'Make a fist… tense your arm very slightly. The power of the spray will depend on how much tension there is.'

Faucet held out his arm and tightened a little too much. The sudden jet of water that came spurting out from his wrist and down his hand forced him to stumble backwards, swinging his arm around and spraying everything in the room with a powerful jet of water – including HyJean's face. She was pushed back in the chair, gargling as the water showered her face. Faucet quickly relaxed his hand and the water died down, eventually stopping.

'Well… I think it works,' said Faucet sheepishly.

'You think?' HyJean said as she wiped her face with the soaked towel.

♦ ♦

'I've enhanced it as much as I could, but it's still pretty poor quality,' said a now dry HyJean, her hair wrapped up in a fresh towel. Captain Clean, Sergeant Suds and Faucet gathered around the computer to look at the footage the captain had recorded. She played the video and paused it when the two criminals appeared on screen, the captain looked closer. He was sure that he recognised one of them. The one with the long, vivid red hair.

'That looks like the Scarlet Pimple,' he said, referring to Pimple's alias before she met her husband. 'We got her locked up a few years ago. But I don't know who the other person is.'

'Maybe it's her boyfriend, The Spot,' joked Faucet, little realising how close he was to the truth.

'If only we had the police files on her, we could find out more about her, track her down,' the captain groaned.

'We don't need the police files,' HyJean said, tapping away at her keyboard and pulling up a social media website on the screen. 'As I suspected, she's on Jargle. Nell Carbuncle, 45, lives in Filtham, married to Gerry Carbuncle. We can look at what she's posted and see what we can learn about her.'

The squad gathered around the screen as HyJean scrolled through the profile, skim reading the posts and photos she'd posted. There were a few photos of her in a bikini in her garden that HyJean scrolled past particularly quickly.

'There's nothing about grease on here. She painted her nails, had a meal at Greasy Pete's steak house, saw a goose at the park… aha! There's one from ten minutes ago saying she's going shopping at Filtham shopping centre.'

'Thank god for people's obsession with social media, huh?' Faucet said, a little surprised at how much information was available about a known criminal. 'It's almost like they want to be caught.'

'Good work, HyJean. Can you go to the shopping centre, tail her to find out what deadly weapons she's buying.'

'I'm not sure they sell flamethrowers in B&Q,' HyJean replied. 'But sure. I'll try and get a tracker onto her too so we can find their base of operations.'

'But just observing,' he warned, holding up his arms to make an X shape. 'No interfering.'

'Yes, obviously,' said HyJean, rolling her eyes. Although this was a rule that she considered quite flexible.

'How come she gets to go to shopping centres and I'm always going to sewers and abandoned warehouses?' Suds pointed out.

'Don't worry Suds, next time there's an attack at a local spa, it's all yours,' HyJean grinned.

HyJean quickly got ready and called the Driver, as she needed to get there sharpish to avoid missing Pimple.

'So, afternoon off for us then?' Faucet asked as he smiled and stretched, thinking what he could do with his free time.

'Certainly not, we've got training to do,' the captain replied.

'Aww man, not memorising cleaning products again,' Faucet groaned. 'I've had it up to here with hypochlorites and peroxides.'

'No, we're going upstairs, come on,' the captain said as he set off to the fire exit.

'Upstairs? But we're on the top floor,' Faucet said as he followed, a little confused.

'You're forgetting the roof,' the captain called back down.

'Good luck,' said Suds, patting Faucet on the shoulder as he left.

💧💧

HyJean made her way through yet another shop, looking for any sign of the red-haired criminal. She'd been through book shops, shoe shops, music shops and had even braved a charity shop, but there was no sign of Nell Carbuncle. She stopped for a while to treat herself to an iced latte at a coffee kiosk and ponder where her target might be. Then, finally, it occurred to her.

'Of course!' she cried, setting off up the escalators and into Oh Naturel, a beauty and cosmetics shop. As she suspected, in the middle of a shop by the skincare shelves stood Nell Carbuncle. She was someone who may have once looked quite pretty, but her face was now covered in spots of all shapes, colours and sizes, making her skin look like a sheet of ancient bubble wrap. HyJean made her way over, standing on the opposite side of the shelving unit. Captain Clean had said not to make contact, but she couldn't help herself. The opportunity was too perfect.

'Well well, if it isn't the Scarlet Pimple,' she said just loud enough for Nell to hear.

Nell gasped and looked up, surprised at the familiar voice. 'You? What are you doing here?'

'I'm just buying some…' she paused and picked up a random item from the shelf in front of her. 'Condoms… apparently. What about you?'

'I'm looking for the new AcneGo cream,' Nell replied through gritted teeth, almost loathing having to make small talk with the woman who'd helped put her away in prison. She knew HyJean was up to something, but hoped she didn't know about the grease scheme.

'I'd be careful if I were you, I've heard that cream can be quite… greasy,' HyJean said, raising one eyebrow.

Nell gulped, trying not to give anything away. She looked down at the shelf, trying to avert HyJean's gaze.

'You're not going to steal it, are you?' HyJean asked. 'That would be very wrong.'

'No. I don't do that stuff anymore,' Nell protested. 'Look, I did my time and now I'm a changed woman. You can't start harassing me while I'm out shopping.'

'Alright, alright. If you say you've changed, I believe you. Can't blame me for being cautious,' HyJean said, putting the pack of condoms down and pretending to browse. 'Especially with all this grease being stolen recently. I heard a couple of thieves stole it to bottle and sell as a fake health drink.'

'No, it's to dump it in Filtham river!' Nell said, and then instantly froze, realising what she'd said. The pair stared at each other, wide eyed for a few seconds, then Nell suddenly stuffed the cream she was holding in her pocket and made a bolt for the door. HyJean was quick on her tail and followed, but the pocketed cream set off the security alarm, alerting the guard, who only saw a masked woman fleeing the shop and assumed that HyJean was the thief.

'Hey, you! Stop!' he shouted as he sprinted after her. Now there were two chases happening at the same time, although HyJean didn't know she was also being pursued.

Nell had gotten a good head start and made her way down the escalator, pushing past the disgruntled shoppers. HyJean was far too polite for that sort of behaviour, so she asked them politely to move, but they assumed HyJean was the thief the security guard was shouting about and defiantly refused. HyJean stood and waited on the escalator, tutting and drumming her fingers frantically, but this gave Nell more time to get away. Finally, HyJean gave in and decided to try and jump down. Climbing over the railing, she dropped down onto the canopy of a sunglasses stall, which tore with her weight and made a big hole as she dropped through, knocking over several display stands and sending sunglasses flying everywhere.

'Sorry! I'll get that fixed!' she called out as she scrambled to her feet and ran after Nell.

The Scarlet Pimple was not as sprightly as she once was, so HyJean was able to catch up to her fairly quickly. Running down the row of shops, Nell tried everything she could to slow HyJean down. She ran through crowds, knocked plants over, jumped over benches, and at one point grabbed a tray of raisins and threw them on the floor in the hopes that HyJean would slip on them, which she didn't because raisins aren't particularly slippery. Eventually, Nell reached the end of the shops, only to discover that she'd taken a wrong turning and ended up at a dead end. Thinking on her feet, she dived into the nearest shop, a bookshop called Good Readz – the spelling had been changed to try and attract a younger audience, but it had not been successful and had instead alienated a lot of older readers.

HyJean followed her into the shop and scanned each aisle looking for Nell. Whilst she was looking, the security guard, who had finally caught up to them, appeared at the door and stood panting as he caught his breath.

'I'm getting too fat for this,' he sighed as he closed the door behind him.

As she walked down the aisle of cookery books, HyJean spotted a flash of familiar red hair in the next aisle. She ran around and raced after Nell, but the redhead reached the end of the aisle before her and pulled the bookshelf, causing it to topple and collapse onto HyJean. With a satisfied smirk, Nell made a run for the door, but seeing the security guard, she made a diversion and leapt out of a window instead. The glass shattered with a loud smash and glass rained down upon her as she fell out onto the pavement on the other side of the shop.

'Ow! Ow! Ow!' she cried as blood started to trickle out from several cuts on her body. She pulled herself up and painfully hobbled across the car park to her car.

Meanwhile, in the bookshop, the security guard lifted the fallen bookshelf back up, with some help from the owner of the shop.

'Urgh, thank you,' HyJean groaned as one of the shoppers helped her to her feet. 'Where did she go? I need to stop her.'

'You're not going anywhere,' said the security guard as he grabbed her by the arm. 'You're coming with me, you thieving scumbag.'

'I don't know which of those words to be more offended by,' HyJean scowled. 'But either way, I'm not the thief, she was.'

'Who was?' asked the guard, a little confused.

'The woman with the red hair who I just chased through the shopping centre!' HyJean exclaimed.

'I didn't see any woman,' he replied, brushing it off in disbelief. He turned to the shoppers and raised his hand to get their attention. 'Okay, listen up! Did anyone in here see a dodgy-looking red headed woman?'

The whole room was filled with nods and positive replies, followed by accurate descriptions and one declaration of love or the redhead.

'Okay, so maybe, just maybe, there might possibly have been another woman,' he admitted. 'But you've still got to come with me to answer some questions. I've got to be seen to be doing something or I'll get fired.'

♦ ♦

On the roof of the Filtham community centre, Captain Clean moved a few boxes of cleaning supplies out of the way to make an open space for them to work in. He then stood in front of Faucet with his hands on his hips. His own hips. Not Faucet's hips. That would've been weird.

'Right then, let's see what you can do,' he said.

With that, Faucet started dancing like Michael Jackson if he'd been covered in itching powder, waving his arms around and thrusting his hips.

'Stop, stop! What are you doing?' the captain asked.

'You said you wanted to see what I can do,' Faucet explained.

'I mean with your water,' the captain groaned. 'Show me what you can do with your water powers.'

'Oh! I see,' Faucet said, chuckling and rolling his eyes at his own stupidity. 'Sorry, Mr Cane. Well, I think I've got the hang of turning it on and off now.'

He demonstrated by closing his left hand into a fist and tensing. As he did so, a squirt of water sprayed out and hit the captain in the face.

'Very good,' the captain grumbled as he wiped his face with his cape. 'I think we need to work on your aim first though.'

He walked over to the edge of the roof where there was a low wall along the perimeter, dragging a recycling tub full of cans with him. He started lining up a row of cans on the wall.

'We're lucky Flush drinks so much pop; the recycling people love us,' the captain said as he positioned the last can. 'Okay, so we're going to start by working on your aim. It's all well and good having powers, but if you don't know how to use them, then it's pointless.'

'Roger that. I'm ready Mr Cane,' Faucet replied, holding up his arms and taking a fighting stance.

'Now imagine these cans are criminals. See if you can hit the first can. Just a-' the captain started, but he was interrupted as Faucet shot a small burst of water which hit the can and knocked it off the roof. 'Right, yes, that's good. What I was going to say is just give it a quick tense up and thrust your arm forward as you release, so you only produce a small shot of water, like a bullet.'

'That's what I did,' Faucet replied.

'Yes, I know. I'm just giving you the tips that HyJean's told me on how to control your powers. I'm meant to be training you. Now why don't you try-' again he was cut off as Faucet repeated his water bullet technique and shot the next can off the roof with perfect aim, smiling triumphantly. The captain let out a little huff and continued, 'Yes, exactly. But with this next one, try to-'

Once again, Faucet wasted no time and hit the next two cans off the wall. This pushed the captain to his limit, and he grabbed the one remaining can and threw it at Faucet. 'Will you wait until I've told you what to do!' he yelled.

'Sorry Mr Cane, just a little excited is all,' Faucet said sheepishly.

'It's alright,' the captain sighed as he set up a few more cans. 'So, what I was going to say is try shooting from both arms at the same time, see how well you can aim in multiple directions.'

Faucet nodded and took his stance again, holding his arms up. He stared at the cans intently and waited.

'What are you waiting for?' the captain asked.

'For you to tell me when to go,' Faucet replied.

'You don't have to wait for me to tell you, just don't do it when I'm in the middle of-' before he could finish, Faucet fired and knocked two cans off at the same time. The captain sighed, '... a sentence. Okay, I think you've got the hang of aiming. Let's try some longer streams.'

'Alright, I'm up for that,' Faucet said flexing his arms and readying himself.

'See that graffiti on the wall over there?' the captain asked, pointing to some writing on the building opposite them that said "The Sanitary Squad Sucks". 'Aim for that and let's see if we can clean it off. Just tighten your fists, tense your wrists and try to hold it. The more you tense, the more force it should produce.'

Faucet nodded and took up his stance, eyeing up the graffiti on the wall. He'd been practicing with small bursts of water, but wasn't quite so confident at producing larger quantities – at least not intentionally. He took a deep breath and then tensed his arms up, firing a jet of water from each hand. It was plentiful, but with little force behind it, so the water didn't reach the target and instead dropped down over the edge of the roof. He unclenched his fists and the water stopped.

'That's fine, it's okay,' the captain reassured him. 'It's only your first go and you're nervous, it's not surprising you're having trouble getting it up.'

'The words no man wants to hear,' Faucet groaned.

'This time aim a little higher,' said the captain, pointing to above the graffiti. 'The trajectory is going to dip as it gets further away, so you need to take that into account.'

Faucet took his stance again and focussed on the target. He clenched his fists and tightened his muscles as tightly as he could, firing out another jet of water from each wrist. This time, he pointed his arms higher, and the two streams were much closer to the target. The force was greater, so he had to adjust his stance to make up for it. He tweaked the angle of his trajectory a little, spraying all around the target, but the pressure on his arms became too much he couldn't hold it long enough to get a good aim. He relaxed and the streams died down, the water dropping to the floor.

'That was much better,' Captain Clean said, genuinely impressed by his new recruit's efforts.

'I can do this,' Faucet said, psyching himself up.

'I know you can, but don't push yourself too much,' the captain advised.

'Nope, I'm gonna do it. Here goes.'

He took a strong stance, squinted a little as he aimed and then fired his jets of water. The blasts were just as powerful as before, and as he got used to the force, he was able to control it more. He inched his arms upwards until finally he hit the graffiti. He held it for a few seconds and then relaxed. When the water disappeared, the graffiti was gone.

'Excellent!' Captain Clean cried. 'That was incredible, well done. And we finally got rid of that blasted graffiti.'

'Thanks Mr cane,' Faucet said, with a satisfied grin as he eyed up his work.

'You seem to be a natural. Which is good really, because I doubt we've got time for a longer training session' the captain said as he patted Faucet on the back like a schoolchild. 'Right, one more exercise and then we're done.'

Captain Clean left the ledge and moved back to the centre of the roof, gesturing for Faucet to join him. From his pocket, the captain took out a remote control. He pressed a button and a metal pole sprung up to their left with a metal disc on the top that had an angry face spray painted onto it. The surprise made Faucet jump on the spot and cower from the metal assailant. The captain pressed the other buttons and further metal targets with angry faces popped up around the roof in quick succession. There were hints of pink goo and other substances on the targets, which had clearly been used many times before by different members of the squad.

'These are your targets. They represent criminals attacking you,' he explained. 'Now, criminals may be violent, but they're also surprisingly polite. They'll usually stand around in a circle waiting to attack you one at a time.'

'What, why?' asked a confused Faucet.

'Nobody knows. It's like an unwritten rule of criminal combat,' the captain replied. 'But anyway, what you've got to do is be aware of everything around you and be ready for an attack to come from any direction. So, I'll set these up and when one pops up, you fire at it. Got it?'

'I think so, yeah,' Faucet nodded as he positioned himself and looked around, trying to memorise where all the targets he'd seen were situated.

Captain Clean stepped back out of the way, pressing a button to retract the targets, and watched Faucet closely. When his trainee was ready, the captain launched the first target. Faucet took a couple of seconds to find it, but when he did, he fired and just missed the target. Faucet shook himself to relax and focus. The captain set off the next target a few yards away, which Faucet was quicker to spot and managed to hit. Another target went up behind Faucet, which caught him off guard, but he span around and hit it. The targets continued to pop up, appearing quicker and quicker, which affected Faucet's aim. Just as the captain was about to launch another target, the roof door opened and Carol the receptionist stepped out onto the roof. Faucet only saw movement and assumed it was another target, spinning around and spraying her in the face with water.

'Captain Clean, we are- aaaaargh!' she garbled as she stumbled back in surprise.

The captain saw what happened and rushed forward to help the woman whose name he never bothered to remember, 'Madam!'

But again, Faucet mistook his movement for that of a target and quickly sprayed him with water before realising his mistake.

'Oh crap, I'm so sorry! I thought you were a target,' Faucet said as he saw the captain drying himself off with his cape. He then turned around and saw Carol and now he felt even more embarrassed. 'I'm so sorry, ma'am. I thought you were a target.'

Carol shrugged Faucet off and marched over to the captain furiously. She grabbed his cape and wiped her face.

'Captain Clean, we are trying to have our annual charity barbecue in the garden downstairs and you've drenched us all!' she shouted, holding up one of the recycling cans. 'And thrown cans at us! What an on Earth do you think you're playing at?'

The captain walked over to the edge of the roof and looked down at the garden. Faucet's streams of water had dropped down onto the crowd of people, extinguishing the barbecue and soaking the guests. His eyes widened and he blushed under his mask. He turned around and gulped. He quickly pointed at Faucet, 'He did it.'

'What?!' cried Faucet. 'You told me to!'

'I don't care whose fault it was,' Carol said, putting her hands on her hips to show some form of authority, despite being one of the lowest ranking employees in the community centre. The only reason she'd come up was because nobody else wanted to deal with the squad. 'You're going to come down and help us all dry off, and then you're going to order us all pizza to make up for the ruined barbecue.'

Captain Clean was about to protest, but he could see from Carol's eyes that she was not in the mood for an argument.

'Fine,' he sighed as he walked past her and led the way back downstairs to face his own army of angry-faced targets.

♦ ♦

Meanwhile, in the home of the Carbunkles, the couple was sat on the sofa, Blackhead attending to his wife's wounds.

'She chased you through the whole shopping centre?' Blackhead asked as he added another plaster to her arm, which was now almost completely covered in plasters.

'Yeah, we caused quite the scene, but I got away, and got the cream,' she said with a slight wince as he touched one of her scars.

'How did she even find you?' he asked.

'I… I may have posted that I was going shopping on Jargle,' she admitted.

'What?' he cried. 'How many times do I have to tell you to stop using that bloody app. We're supposed to be criminals keeping a low profile. How are we ever going to do that if you keep posting every damn thing you do on social media? Honestly, we've only got one more day to go and you could've blown the whole thing.'

Pimple didn't have a suitable answer, so she did the only thing that she could think of and started to cry. Her husband instantly fell for her sympathy attempt and put his arm around her.

'Aww, it's okay. I'm sorry, darling. I'm just a bit on edge because of this whole grease thing,' he said, stroking her hair and holding her close. 'Once it's over, we can have a nice break away and relax.'

'That'd be nice,' she nodded as she wiped away her crocodile tears.

'Right then. I'll go finish washing up while you try out that new cream,' he said, giving her a kiss on the top of her head and heading off to the kitchen.

Pimple got up and wandered into the bathroom, opening her new cream and staring at her reflection in the mirror – her spotty face making the mirror look like an obscene dot-to-dot book. Despite washing regularly, eating healthily and always keeping clean, the two had never found a cure for their skin complaints and left countless doctors baffled. Every time she looked into a mirror, she was reminded of her condition and the bullying she faced in school, through college and in any job she worked at. It only made her more determined to get some payback. She shuddered again at the sight of her spotty face and started smearing the cream all over.

'I'm so excited for tomorrow,' Blackhead called through from the kitchen. 'The last batch of grease, and then we can dump it all.'

'And then everyone will be spotty like us,' said Pimple dramatically, grinning maniacally at her white, cream-covered face.

Their plan was to collect all the grease from the four greasiest restaurants in the city, mix it with various chemicals to hide the smell and colour, then dump it into the city's water supply. They presumed that infecting people's water with grease would irritate people's skin and cause them to break out in spots. Their lack of scientific knowledge meant they had no idea whether their plan would actually work or not, but even if it didn't, they figured it would be a fun prank. Blackhead sauntered into the bathroom and wrapped his arms around his wife. He placed his head on her shoulder and smiled at her in the mirror.

'What's say we prepare ourselves properly with… an early night,' he said with a teasing smile.

'Good idea,' she replied as her face lit up with excitement. 'I'll go make the cocoa, you get the crossword book.'

♦ ♦

HyJean arrived back at the base to find a grouchy Captain Clean and an exhausted Faucet sat at the central table. It looked as though neither had spoken to the other in quite a while, with that awkward silence where you feel it should be broken, but as soon as it is it just irritates you even more.

'Where's Suds?' the captain asked.

'It's his night off,' HyJean said. 'It's their anniversary, so he's taken Mary to Greasy Pete's for a slap-up meal.'

'Aww, that's sweet,' said Faucet. 'How long have they been together?'

'13 years,' said HyJean.

'Wow. What's that? Is there like a gold or ruby thing for 13 years?'

'Yeah, it's lace.'

'Oh, that's a bit rubbish.'

'On the contrary, Mary showed me some new lacy lingerie she bought for tonight, so Mick's in for a treat,' HyJean said with a grin.

'What did you say?' asked Captain Clean.

'I said she's bought some new lingerie,' said HyJean.

'No, before that.'

'About the 13 years?'

'No, before that.'

'I said it's his night off.'

'No, the bit after… look, where did you say they've gone for food?'

'Greasy Pete's Steak House.'

The captain thought for a moment, wondering why the name sounded familiar, then a metaphorical lightbulb illuminated above his head. 'Didn't you say earlier that Pimple went there for lunch? On her Jungle website thing?'

'Oh, yes!,' HyJean nodded. 'On her Jargle profile.'

'Well then, I think we know where our dermatologically challenged duo will be heading next,' the captain grinned.

'Of course!' said HyJean, realising what the captain meant.

'Where?' asked Faucet, who was still waiting on the platform to join them on their train of thought.

'Greasy Pete's,' the captain explained. 'They must've been there yesterday to check the place out.'

'It'd make sense, it's the greasiest steak house in town, hence the name,' said HyJean. 'They've robbed the three fast food joints and now they're going for the big one. And going by the news reports, they've been robbing a place every 2 days, so all we have to do is go there tomorrow and wait for them.'

'Wait a minute,' said Faucet. 'You mean we're going to stake out a steak house?'

'Exactly,' said the captain.

Greasy Pete's Steak House was a restaurant with zero Michelin stars run by a man called Peter Lanolin. He'd wanted to name it Greasy Peter's, but friends and family members insisted it sounded like a seedy backstreet adult club, and that Greasy Pete's somehow sounded better and friendlier. He argued that nobody ever called him Pete, and, in fact, he hated being called Pete. Truthfully, he hated being called Peter, and always thought he'd be more suited to a name like Rick or Elvis, but he didn't have the confidence that usually went with those sort of names. And so it was, the restaurant opened as Greasy Pete's. The food was surprisingly good, while the décor was just surprising. Rather than having a rustic Americana or warm log cabin theme, it instead had large paintings of boats and seascapes on the walls, which his wife had painted. She'd suggested he could use them in his restaurant, and while he wasn't overly keen on the idea, he figured it would be better than having them around the house. To continue the uncharacteristically nautical theme, the toilets were all completely blue, with blue walls, blue cubicle doors and blue sinks. It was a design choice that Peter made purely so he could refer to them in his best Elvis voice as his "blue sprayed loos".

'Well Marigold, it's been really nice getting away from work for the night,' said Mick as he tucked into his steak.

'I thought we agreed not to talk about work,' said Mary, pointing at him with her fork.

'I'm not. I was just saying it's nice not to be at work.'

'There, you've done it again!'

'Fine, what do you want to talk about?'

Mary sat and thought for a moment. Their work consumed much of their lives and left them little free time for other hobbies or interests. She casually looked around the room as she thought, but her eyes suddenly stopped and her mouth dropped.

'Captain Clean!' she said in a surprised tone.

'Now who's talking about work,' said Mick with a slight frown.

'No, the Captain's just walked in,' she said, pointing across the room.

Mick span round and saw that Captain Clean was indeed walking into the restaurant, dressed in his full grime fighting attire.

'Oh jeez,' groaned Mick. 'Can he not leave us alone for one night!'

As if on cue, Captain Clean caught sight of his two colleagues sat amongst the crowd of tables. He gave them a little wave and Mick gestured back to go away. The captain realised he was interrupting and sheepishly mouthed an apology, holding up his cape to try and conceal himself as he slowly crept over to the front desk - little realising that most of the restaurant was now staring at him.

'Go sort him out will you,' Mary said to her husband as she stabbed her knife into her steak in quite an aggressive manner.

Mick obliged, leaving his own steak and quickly walking across the restaurant over to his boss, pulling the cape down swiftly.

'What are you doing here?' he hissed.

'I'm so sorry,' said the captain. 'We think Blackhead and Pimple are going to rob this place tomorrow, so I'm going to try and get the manager to set up these hidden cameras.'

The captain held up a bucket with a pile of small cameras inside.

'This is my night off with Mary,' Mick said. 'Why are you doing this to me?'

'I know, I'm sorry. I did try to be inconspicuous,' the captain replied sheepishly.

'How?' Suds asked frustratedly. 'How did you try?'

'I'm wearing the dark blue cape.'

He held up his cape, which was indeed a dark blue instead of his usual mustard yellow.

'You know what would've been more inconspicuous?' said Mick. 'Not wearing a cape!'

'But the cape completes the outfit,' the captain argued.

Mick was just about to grab his fellow grime fighter and throttle him when he was interrupted by a waiter.

'Excuse me sirs,' said the waiter in what was clearly a posh voice he was putting on, 'can I help you?'

'Yes, I'm Captain Clean from the Sanitary Squad,' said Captain Clean.

'Really, I never would have guessed,' the waiter replied in a deadpan tone.

'I need to speak to the manager immediately. The restaurant is under threat.'

'Very well, I will take you to the manager,' said the waiter before turning to Mick. 'Are you with this Captain Clean, sir?'

'Um, no… I just want a spoon,' Mick lied.

'Hm, yes. Don't we all,' said the waiter, flicking his long fringe as he turned his head and led the captain away to find the manager.

💧💧

The following night, Captain Clean, Suds, Faucet and Flush were all sat in the Driver's taxi, parked in the car park on the opposite side of the road to Greasy Pete's Steakhouse. Flush was in the front because he'd called shotgun, the others in the back, with the captain squished in the middle. Faucet had been allowed to accompany them, on the strict instruction that he not get involved in any of the action, he was there purely to observe. HyJean was back in the base at her computers, keeping an eye on the restaurant via the cameras the captain had installed.

As they waited, The Driver tapped his fingers on the steering wheel in time with the bhangra music playing on the radio. While his colleagues had requested different music several times, Flush was quite getting into it, performing his own little dance that he'd come up with and singing along with what he thought were the right lyrics but were mostly just the names of random footballers. They had been in the car for just over an hour and Captain Clean in particular was getting restless. He didn't enjoy music of any kind. Every genre seemed to taunt him. He didn't like rock because rocks were dirty. Folk reminded him of hippies camping out in fields, getting dirty. Jazz was popular in New Orleans, which had swamps that were very dirty. Classical was from the old days in which people had poor personal hygiene. And he didn't even want to think about grime or grunge. He was struggling to think of a reason not to like the bhangra music that was playing, so he returned his thoughts to the mission they were on.

'HyJean, is there...' he tried to reach for his communications headset, but his arms were jammed between the two men either side of him. He turned to Suds on his right and said, 'Can you?'

Suds shuffled around, reaching across with his free arm and pressing the button on the captain's headset.

'Thanks a lot,' he said.

'What for?' a confused HyJean on the other end asked.

'No, I was talking to Suds,' said Cap. 'Is there any action on the cameras?'

'Hold on, let me check.'

HyJean put down her magazine and looked up at the monitor to see a black and red polka dot van had appeared in the Steakhouse car park. Her eyes bulged out like a constipated toad and she bit her bottom lip to keep from cursing too loudly.

'Damnit,' she muttered. 'Uh, yes, they've just arrived.'

'Okay, let's go! Go! Go!' shouted the captain, with a notable sense of excitement in his voice.

The men piled out of the car, took a brief moment to stretch their legs and then dashed out of the car park and across the road. However, in all the excitement, they forgot to look both ways and Flush was the unlucky one to get hit by a car, which suddenly screeched to a halt as its driver saw the costumed men appeared from nowhere. Flush tumbled onto the car's bonnet and slid onto the floor, his friends stopping to help him up.

'I'm okay,' Flush said wearily.

'He's okay!' Suds called to the driver.

'Do you want to go back to the car?' the captain asked.

'No, no,' Flush insisted. 'You carry on, I'll limp over in a minute.'

'Oi, what are you doing?' called a voice from inside the car. 'Running across the road like that, you could've been killed.'

The captain walked around to the window to address the man, who was clearly on his way home from work, though his appearance made it hard to guess what his job was. Too casual for the corporate world, but not scruffy enough for a tradesperson. He didn't smell of fish and there was no spacesuit on the back seat. But the captain wasn't interested in his job, only his attitude.

'Sir, we are grime fighters on a very important mission where time is of the essence,' he explained.

'Grime fighters? What are you talking about?' the driver asked. 'Are you lot a stag do?'

As the captain argued with the driver and the others helped Flush up, Blackhead and Pimple were busy inside the restaurant. They'd been there for a while already, had hooked up their machine and were draining the Steakhouse's kitchen of its grease.

'You know love, I've really enjoyed doing this grease stealing operation with you,' said Blackhead with a smile.

'Me too,' Pimple smiled back. 'It's been so nice to do something together for a change.'

'And maybe if we have some grease left over, we could…' his voice trailed off and he gave her a cheeky wink and a playful grin.

'Ooh, you like a greasy woman, do you?' she asked, seductively wiping a bit of grease off the top of the fryer and licking her finger seductively. She immediately spat it out with a groan and wiped her tongue in disgust.

Suddenly, they heard the commotion outside and Pimple went to take a look out of a nearby window. Seeing the members of the Sanitary Squad fumbling around in the middle of the street, she ran to the van, switched the machine off and rushed back into the Steakhouse to warn her husband.

'Honey, I think it's broken,' Blackhead said as he fiddled with the fryer.

'It's not broken, I turned it off,' she explained. 'The clean freaks are outside; we need to go.'

'Holy crap,' said Blackhead as he detached the tube. 'God, why didn't we think about the possibility of this happening? We really should've planned for this eventuality.'

'Just come on,' called his wife.

They rushed back to the van and thankfully the mob of traffic had slowed the squad down just long enough for Blackhead to drag the pipe into the back of the van and Pimple to jump in the driver's seat and speed off with a loud screech. The acceleration caused Blackhead to stumble farther back into the van, tripping over the pipe. They were getting away, but in the rush, Blackhead didn't have time to close the van doors. Outside he could see the squad chasing after them on foot. They were obviously much slower than the van and quickly began to fade away. But Captain Clean persisted and spotted an opportunity as he saw a young man riding towards him on a skateboard. The captain quickly pushed him off and grabbed the skateboard, shouting a brief explanation at him.

'Need to borrow this! Bad guys getting away!'

He jumped onto the skateboard and kicked off. Though he wasn't at all experienced on the primitive mode of transport, he soon started to get the hang of it and, slowly but surely, began to catch up to the van whilst not enjoying himself at all.

'What's going on back there?' Pimple called out, looking round through the meshed window at her husband and the equipment sliding around the back of the van.

'Captain Clean is chasing us on a skateboard!' he shouted back.

'Well, there's something you don't see every day!' his wife replied.

Despite the van's speed, the captain soon caught up to them. Throwing caution to the wind, he leapt off the board and landed in the back of the van, clutching onto the floor of the vehicle as his legs dangled out the back. He tried to pull himself in, but the floor was wet with grease, making it difficult to get any kind of grip.

Thinking on his feet, Blackhead grabbed the pipe and flipped a few switches on the machine, turning it on and switching it from suck to blow. The grease shot down the pipe and burst out of the end. Blackhead aimed it at the captain, who bravely resisted the onslaught of grease.

'What are you doing?' Pimple shouted through. 'We need that for the plan!'

'If we don't stop him, there won't be a plan!' he reminded her.

There was a slight pause and then she replied, 'Good point!'

Blackhead kept the pipe aimed at Captain Clean, who was reliving one of his nightmares as the torrent of thick, slippery sludge rained down on his face. He held on for as long as he could, but in the end, it was too much. The grease covered his hands and made him lose his grip. The greasy current sent him flying back out of the van, throwing him down onto the hard tarmac road. Blackhead turned off the machine and closed the doors. As the captain lay in a puddle of grease, he looked up and saw the van speeding off into the night.

'Damnit,' he said with a heavy sigh as sat up and looked around. He pulled out a wet wipe and started the arduous process of cleaning himself.

💧💧

'You were so sexy back there,' Pimple said as she walked around the side of the van that was now safely parked in their garage. The sudden rush of adrenaline had her pumped up. She pushed her husband against the side of the van and gave him a passionate kiss on the lips. 'I wish we could go to bed right now.'

'So do I, love, but we've got to dump this grease. Now that they're onto us, we can't wait,' he said, patting his wife's arm.

She sighed and nodded, 'I guess you're right. Let's get these other barrels on the van.'

They headed over to the other side of the garage, where there stood three barrels filled with grease. One by one, they shuffled them across the garage floor and lifted them up into the van.

'We really should've got one of those vans with the lift at the back,' Blackhead groaned as he heaved the final barrel up.

'Yeah, but we're on a budget,' Pimple replied as she lifted it from other end and dragged it into the van.

'We wouldn't be if we stopped buying all those bloody creams,' he muttered to himself.

'What was that?' she asked with a raised eyebrow.

'Nothing, nothing,' he said, holding out his hand to help his wife down.

'Because if you were moaning about the skincare creams…' she started.

'No, I wasn't, I was just-' he said, but his wife was quick to interrupt.

'For years I suffered bullying at school,' Pimple said, putting her hands on her hips.

'Here we go again,' Blackhead sighed.

'People calling me all sorts of names. Spotty, dotty, dalmatian girl, polka-dot face, dot-to-dot girl, bubble-wrap head, the walking Liechtenstein painting… and all through life I've been held back by my looks. Boys refusing to go out with me, employers refusing to employ me, masseuses refusing to massage me. It's been hell. So, if I can find a cream that clears my skin up, even if I have to pay a million pounds, I'm going to do it. Until then, the world can bloody suffer with me and have greasy skin. Now let's go and dump this grease.'

'Yes dear,' Blackhead nodded.

The two closed the van doors and climbed in the front of the van. Blackhead started the engine and chuckled to himself.

'Walking Liechtenstein painting. Haven't heard that one before,' he said. 'That's a good one.'

'Just shut up and drive,' his wife barked.

And so, the two criminals set off in their van, which was now weighed down a little by the copious amounts of grease sloshing around in the back. The river was only few miles away, so it was a relatively short drive. As they got closer and closer, their excitement rose, and they shot each other the occasional giddy grin. Pimple was glad to be finally getting some revenge, but she was even more glad that she was doing it with her husband. Blackhead was just glad she hadn't hit him for laughing at the nickname.

♦ ♦

'What happened?' asked the familiar voice of Sergeant Suds from the window of the Driver's taxi as it slowed down to drive alongside the now less greasy Captain Clean.

'They got away,' the captain huffed as he walked defeatedly along the pavement back towards the restaurant. 'Fired a load of grease at me and I couldn't hold on.'

'You should've come and got me,' said the Driver. 'I would've caught up to 'em.'

The idea of following the van in the Driver's taxi hadn't occurred to the captain. Nor had it occurred to the other members of the squad. Caught up in the action, they'd forgotten that their associate was sat waiting across the road listening to music on the radio. Once the captain had disappeared dangling from the back of the van, the other members of the squad had returned to the taxi to drive around looking for him.

'Come on, let's go back to the base, we'll never find them now,' Suds suggested.

'And besides, you could do with a shower,' Flush added. 'You smell awful.'

The captain sniffed and realised that although he'd wiped the grease off, the smell still lingered on him. But the sniffing caused him to stop in his tracks as an idea came to him. He continued to sniff frantically, turning his head around and leaning forward purposefully as he did so.

'What's wrong with Mr Cane?' asked Faucet as the taxi stopped next to the sniffing captain. 'Has he gone mad?'

'No, that happened a long time ago,' Flush replied.

'I think he's trying to sniff them out,' said Suds. 'Trying to follow the smell of the grease.'

'What? Can he really do that?' asked Facuet.

'You'd be surprised,' Suds replied with a slight smirk as he watched the captain march confidently over to the taxi. 'He's got a well-trained nose, like a sniffer dog, but for unhygienic smells. Legend says he can smell a mouldy sandwich from over a mile away.'

'What legend?' asked Faucet curiously.

'Well, me. I said it once,' Suds admitted.

Captain Clean climbed onto the bonnet of the car, on all fours as if he were imitating a hood ornament. He took a big sniff and then pointed ahead, clinging onto the front of the car.

'That way!' he shouted, and the taxi once again set off at a slower speed into the night, following the captain's nose to find the two criminals.

💧💧

CLICK! SPLAT! FIZZZZZZ!

The noises came from the other side of the garage door as a circle of the metal door began to fizz and melt away, revealing Sergeant Suds on the other side aiming his powerful soap gun. He switched it back from the acid setting to the default soap stun setting while Captain Clean strode forward and peered through the hole.

'We've got you now!' he said, triumphantly.

Flush poked his head through the hole next to him and eyed up the dark, empty garage. 'Uh Cap, I don't think they're home.'

'That's what they want us to think,' the captain replied, stepping back away from the garage. 'Suds, another hole please.'

'I think he's right, Cap. Their van isn't there,' Suds pointed out.

'Suds, another hole please,' the captain repeated in the exact same tone as before.

Suds rolled his eyes. He knew better than to argue with Captain Clean. Even when the captain was clearly wrong, he never gave in. Suds changed the setting on his gun back and shot another two holes, making a gap big enough for a stubborn human being to fit through. The captain waited for the acid to die down and then stepped through into the garage. He looked around and saw no signs of life, but he wasn't about to give in just yet.

'They must be inside,' he said as he grabbed a paint can and threw it at the window on a nearby door, which smashed instantly. He then tried the handle and realised the door was already open. He disappeared into the house and was gone for a good minute or so. When he finally reappeared, he walked straight out of the garage and over to the taxi.

'They weren't in there, were they?' Suds said as he passed.

'No,' the captain grumbled.

The squad piled back into the taxi and Suds instructed The Driver to take them to the river, where he wished they'd gone straight to in the first place.

💧💧

As the taxi rapidly approached the river, one of the back doors flung open and Captain Clean leapt out, tumbling down onto the grass and inadvertently rolling himself up in his cape. He pulled himself up, a little dizzy from the fall, and tried to pose heroically. The car screeched to a halt a few metres away and the others got out.

'Cap, what on Earth are you doing? We were just about to stop,' Suds asked as he helped the captain up and unravelled his cape.

'I thought it'd look more dramatic,' the captain replied, dusting himself off.

'There they are!' Flush called as he spotted Blackhead and Pimple a short distance away.

'Quick! We've got to get to them before they contaminate the river,' said the captain.

'Not so fast!' came a voice from behind. The squad looked around to see three people wearing what looked like punch bags, like they were on their way to a gym-themed fancy-dress party. 'We're the Bag Boys and we're gonna beat you up, 'cause that's what we do.'

'Oh, for heaven's sake,' said the captain.

'Don't worry Mr Cane, you carry on, I've got this,' said Faucet, lifting his fists and taking a combative stance. 'I've prepared for this very moment.'

'Good man,' said the captain, as he, along with Suds and Flush, ran off to stop the two spotty criminals, calling back. 'And don't use my real name in public!'

Faucet ran at the Bag Boy, letting out a battle cry as he sprayed them. They were clearly surprised by his powers, as most of them promptly turned and ran. One stayed behind, but Faucet kicked him and he fell over, rolling down the grassy bank and landing in the river, crying out 'I'll get you for this!' as he slowly floated across the water. By the time the squad members got to Blackhead and Pimple, they were still unloading the third barrel of grease off the van.

'I wouldn't worry Cap,' said Suds. 'Looks like we got here with plenty of time to spare.'

'Really? That almost never happens,' said Flush. 'Usually we get here like seconds before.'

Blackhead and Pimple gasped as they saw the captain and his men standing a few yards away.

'Damnit, I told you we should've dumped each barrel of grease as we got them off,' Pimple groaned.

'Shh!' her husband said, ushering her aside. 'They might not know what we're doing here.'

'What? Of course they do,' Pimple cried. 'And even if they didn't, what would we say? Oh, hello, we're just taking our pet barrels out for a walk.'

'We do know what you're up to, and we're here to stop you,' Captain Clean said, stepping forward to confront them.

'Oh yeah, well… well… take this,' she ran behind one of the barrels and tried to tip it over onto Captain Clean, but it was too heavy for her to lift on her own. 'Don't just stand there, Gerry, come and help me.'

Blackhead stood frozen to the spot, not sure what to do now that he was surrounded by a bunch of men dressed as superheroes. Suds took the initiative and stepped in, trying to restrain the woman who started splashing him with grease and running around the barrels. While the squad were distracted with his hysterical wife, Blackhead seized the moment and darted off, running down the riverbank. Captain Clean turned to chase him.

'I'll get hi-iiiiiiieeee!' he cried as he slipped on a puddle of grease and fell flat on his back.

'Facuet, stop him!' Suds called over to Faucet, who had finished chasing off the Bag Boys and was now waiting by the taxi in the direction that Blackhead was running.

'But I was told not to get involved!' Faucet called back.

'Forget about that!' Suds shouted. 'Spray him!'

'Okay! I can do that!' Faucet replied, excited to have permission to try out his powers on his first mission.

'Stop!' he shouted, lifting his hand up and using his new bracelet to spray Blackhead in the face. The strong jet of lukewarm water sent Blackhead flying back and down onto the ground. Faucet gasped and quickly relaxed his hand to stop the water.

'Maybe use a lower setting next time,' Captain Clean said as he and the other grime fighters joined Faucet, with a restless Pimple in tow.

'Yeah, sorry Mr Cane,' said Facuet. 'I'm still getting used to these things.'

'Captain Clean,' the captain hissed.

'Oh, sorry captain.'

As Blackhead slowly got to his feet, Pimple let out a cry of shock. Although the water had not harmed her partner in crime and life, it was now dripping down his face, taking with it many of the spots, boils and pimples that had once prominently adorned his features, leaving his face, for the most part, clean and smooth.

'Gerry!' she cried, running over to her husband. 'Your spots are falling off!'

Blackhead's eyes nearly popped out at his wife's words. His face looked worried, and he quickly tried to think on his feet.

'Uh… oh wow,' he stuttered, 'That's incredible. It must be uh… it must be something in his water!'

Faucet looked down at his arm with a curious expression, wondering if his unique bodily water really did have some sort of magic healing power. There was still a lot he didn't know about his new biology, and it didn't seem beyond the realms of possibility given what he'd heard thus far. Pimple swiped some of the water off Blackhead's face and splashed it on her own, rubbing it into her spots vigorously.

'Is it working?' she asked excitedly.

'Um… no,' Blackhead replied, scratching the back of his neck awkwardly.

'Quick, spray me,' she said to Faucet.

Faucet looked unsure what to do and slowly raised his hand, looking around to Captain Clean as if asking for permission. The captain just shrugged and nodded.

'No, stop!' Blackhead warned Faucet. 'It… it's not going to work.'

'What do you mean? How do you know?' Pimple asked.

Blackhead sighed. 'The water didn't clear my spots.'

'What? Then what happened? Why has your skin cleared up?'

'You know that new cream you bought a couple of weeks ago, the one that didn't work? Well, I tried it, and it worked on my skin,' he explained. 'It cleared up some of my spots, but I didn't know how to tell you.'

'So, you lied to me for weeks?'

'I was going to tell you once we'd done this grease thing. See if there was something we could do for your spots.'

'You liar!' she said, hitting her dirty - although comparatively clean - stinking liar of a husband on the arm.

'Darling, please, just listen…' he begged.

'No, you listen! I've had enough of this! How could you do this to me?

All this time I thought we were the same, but now you... you go and do this!'

'But I didn't mean to, I-'

'Ahem,' coughed a voice from behind them.

They turned around and saw Captain Clean holding two pairs of handcuffs.

'Sorry to interrupt,' said the captain, 'but you two are-'

'You can wait a minute!' snapped Pimple, raising a finger to him.

The captain was stunned. Assessing the situation, he nodded and let her finish her argument. She continued to shout at her husband about how he never respected her, how he always had less spots than her and how he always took the toffee sweets when they had a tin of Quality Street. Blackhead tried to defend himself, but quickly gave up and just stood silent, letting her yell at him and completely embarrass him in front of the local heroes.

'You see, it's like I always say, it's not about the spots on your face, it's what's underneath that counts,' the captain said quietly to HyJean.

'Yeah,' she nodded. 'Hey, that's quite sweet for you.'

'What?' said the captain. 'I was talking about the sebaceous glands and the build-up of sebum that causes the spots.'

'Of course you were,' sighed HyJean.

Eventually Pimple seemed to run out of things to berate her husband for and finished her tirade. Suds gave the captain a little nudge and he stepped forward once again.

'Right, if you're finished,' he said with a disapproving look at Pimple, 'you two are coming with us.'

The captain took hold of Pimple, while Suds grabbed Blackhead. They led them over to their van and sat them down on the floor while Flush made himself useful and called the police. As they waited, the captain decided to learn a bit more about the villainous couple.

'So, the Scarlet Pimple has returned?' he asked, looking down at the familiar criminal.

'I'm just Pimple now,' said Pimple.

'And who's this guy you're with?'

'I'm The Blackhead,' said Blackhead.

'The Blackhead? Never heard of you,' said the captain.

'Really? I was involved in some pretty big robberies a couple of years back.'

'Nope,' confirmed HyJean, scrolling through her phone. 'We definitely haven't got a Blackhead in our database.'

'It's not Blackhead, it's The Blackhead,' he corrected her.

'Oh, sorry,' said HyJean. 'Well, The Blackhead, I still don't think-'

'No, it's not The Blackhead when you're talking to me. Then it's just Blackhead.'

'Huh?' said a confused HyJean, her fellow heroes sharing her confused look.

'It's simple, when you're referring to me, it's The Blackhead, and when you're talking to me directly it's Blackhead,' the villain explained.

'Man, why do you guys have to have such complicated names?' asked Flush. 'Can't we just call you…. I dunno, Blacky?'

'No, that sounds racist,' Suds pointed out.

'What about The Head?' Faucet suggested.

'That makes him sound like he works in a school,' said HyJean. 'Plus, it doesn't solve the "The" issue.'

'Look, my name is The Blackhead!' shouted the annoyed villain.

'The Filthy Liar, more like,' said Pimple with a sneering glance.

'Alright, alright. Calm down,' said Captain Clean. 'We don't want to set her off again.'

There was an awkward silence for a while, but fortunately the police soon arrived. The two criminals were stuffed into the back of a police car while the crime scene investigators took photos of the van and barrels of grease as evidence.

'I guess I ought to congratulate you Mr Clean,' said Chief Inspector Dovedale.

'All in a day's work Chief Inspector,' smiled the captain as he casually leaned on one of the barrels. However, as he did, it tipped over onto its side with a loud thud and the captain fell to the floor while the grease from the barrel started to spill out and run down towards the river.

'Noooo!' the captain cried as he quickly jumped down and crawled along the floor, getting ahead of the flow and trying desperately to stop it with his cape. Chief Inspector Dovedale just shook his head and called a couple of his men over to pick the barrel back up.

♦ ♦

A short while later, Gerry Carbuncle was being led down the corridors of Rotenhell Prison by a bald, muscly guard who looked so mean that a rumour was spreading around the prison that he lost his hair when he ripped it out in a fit of rage and forced someone to eat it. The prison was a modern, mixed-gender facility designed to be more of a rehabilitation centre, but the quality and service it could afford on the city's low budget meant it was really as bad as the worst prisons. The walls were dirty and the floors even dirtier, like they were competing to see which could be dirtier. The toilets were surprisingly clean, but this was mainly because nobody dared use them – they instead found alternative methods, which didn't help with the overall lack of hygiene. Still, the management tried. The rooms were fitted with outdated televisions (though channels were restricted), the food was decent, and they had arts and crafts sessions on a Wednesday where inmates were constantly told not to make shivs from the pipe cleaners and lollipop sticks.

'So, what's it like here?' Gerry asked the guard. 'Is the food any good?'

The guard just grunted and gave him a shove to carry on walking down the long, dank corridor.

'I'll take that as a no.'

The guard stopped outside a cell and opened the door. He looked at Gerry with a look that told him that they were never going to become good friends like in some movies where a prisoner befriends a guard. They were destined to share as few words as possible during his time there, and the first three that he decided to share were, 'In you go.'

Gerry entered his new home and was horrified to see a familiar face sitting on one of the two beds that furnished the dark, damp room.

'Oh no,' he sighed. 'Hello dear.'

A LOAD OF RUBBISH

The squad were in good spirits as they sat waiting for the captain to join them, watching MOP (their Mechanical Office Pet) trundling around showing off a new trick it had been programmed with. It moved around the base picking two things up at a time and holding them up proudly. Prior to this, MOP had only been able to compute instructions for one thing at a time, but HyJean had since programmed it to be able to understand more than one instruction at once, thus making it more efficient than the staff at Homebase. As the squad watched and applauded at MOP's successes – as parents do when children complete the easiest of tasks in three times the amount of time it'd take an adult to do it – Captain Clean entered the room and cleared his throat. MOP held up a piece of paper and a glove and the captain just shook his head.

'No, thank you,' he said, brushing the robot away. It returned the items to the table it had got them from and waited for further instructions.

'Today we're going to look at what to do if someone attacks you with a knife,' he began. 'So, let's get right into it. Flush, can I borrow you?'

Always one to enjoy a bit of action, especially in front of a crowd, Flush nodded and dutifully rose, walking over to stand in front of the captain and puffing his chest out a little with pride at being picked.

'Right, I'm going to come at you with a knife,' the captain said, taking a combative stance.

'Wait, a minute,' said Flush. 'What sort of knife are we talking about?'

'Does it matter?' asked the captain.

'Of course it matters. I need to know how far away I need to stand. If it's a pen knife, I'll be closer, but if it's a machete I'll stand way back.'

'Okay, it's a pen knife,' said the captain.

'Pfft, that's no problem.'

'Oh really? Okay, we'll see about that. MOP, fetch me the pen knife.'

The robot stayed motionless where it was. The captain looked at it disapprovingly, waiting for it to do something.

'You have to say please,' HyJean pointed out.

The captain let out a heavy sigh, and repeated the instruction through gritted teeth, 'MOP, fetch me the pen knife, please.'

The robot sprung to life and trundled over to a table where numerous tools, weapons and other assorted objects were spread out. Meanwhile, HyJean smiled, pleased with herself that she'd managed to make the robot respond to good manners. MOP then slowly trundled back over to the Captain Clean, holding a plastic knife in one mechanical arm and a ballpoint pen in the other.

'No, I said pen knife, you stupid robot, not a pen and a knife. That's wrong!' Captain Clean held up his arms, crossed in an X shape as if this would help the robot understand. MOP showed absolutely no emotion in return, other than the painted on smiley ace below the screen that teased the captain even more. He snatched the pen and knife off the robot and instructed it again. 'Go and fetch me a pen knife. A PEN KNIFE. All one word. Go! Please!'

The robot once again went over to the table and returned again with yet another combination of plastic knife and ballpoint pen.

'Oh for God's sake, I'll do it myself,' muttered the captain as he went and picked up a pen knife from the table, muttering under his breath, 'I don't even know how he got that second knife, there was only one on here.'

He returned and took his place in front of Flush. 'Right, are you ready?'

'Yup,' nodded Flush.

Cap whipped out the pen knife and swung it at Flush with a mighty 'Aha!'

Flush just stood where he was and smirked. Whilst the captain's handling of the pen knife looked impressive, he'd mistakenly flipped out the bottle opener attachment instead of the knife.

'Cheers cocker,' said Flush as he picked up a bottle off the table and opened it with the bottle opener.

'Alright, you're obviously not taking this seriously,' the captain sighed. 'Sit down. Faucet, get up here.'

While Flush returned to his seat and sipped on his drink, Faucet got up and, just as Flush had, stood in front of Captain Clean to await an attack.

'Okay, so this time it's a real knife. Something bigger, like... a katana!' said the captain, pretending to hold up his imaginary katana.

'Ooh, now we're talking,' said Faucet with a smile.

Before he could carry on, Captain Clean was interrupted by MOP as he drove slowly towards him holding out a banana, much to the amusement of everyone except the captain.

'No! Wrong!' he shouted, crossing his arms again. 'Go away! Please!'

MOP left to head back to its home in HyJean's office, still holding the banana like it was about to go and eat it. Captain Clean turned back to Faucet.

'So, if I came at you with a katana, what would you do?' he asked.

'I'd spray you with a jet of water to blind you and then attack you,' replied

Faucet.

'Okay... that's good,' the captain nodded. It wasn't the answer he had hoped for, but he was pleased that Faucet was at least thinking tactically. 'But what about the others? They don't have water jets, so what would they do?'

'They'd call me,' Faucet replied with a slight smirk.

'But what if you weren't around. How would you stop the attacker?'

'I wouldn't need to, I'm not there,' he shrugged.

'That's not... you know what, fine, go sit down,' the captain said with a groan. 'Mick, help me out here, come on.'

Faucet returned to his seat with a self-satisfied grin, receiving a high five from Flush as he sat down. Suds got up and took Faucet's place.

'Okay, I'm coming at you with a katana, what would—'

Before he could finish, Suds whipped out his soap gun, which he routinely kept at the lowest setting by default, and shot the captain in the face, covering his head in a sticky, pink goo.

Suds turned to the others and said, 'Drink?'

The guys all agreed and got up from the table, high fiving Suds and patting him on the shoulder.

'I think we've earned it,' said Faucet.

'Yeah, three of us just survived getting attacked with a bottle opener,' chuckled Flush as they headed out of the base, leaving HyJean to deal with a frustrated captain.

'I don't think they're taking these lessons very seriously,' said Captain Clean as he wiped some of the goo off his face.

'No,' said HyJean, handing him a towel. 'I don't think they are.'

'I don't know why you insist on keeping that thing, he's useless,' said the captain as he took the towel and began wiping his face with it. 'He can't even follow basic instructions.'

'Come on, Faucet isn't that bad.'

'Not Faucet, the robot!'

'Oh! Well, he's still learning,' HyJean shrugged with a little sympathy for her robot. 'The more we use him, the quicker he'll learn.'

'He'd better,' said the captain, scrunching up the towel in frustration and handing it to her.

'He is trying y'know,' she said as she took the towel from him.

'Yes, you're right,' said the captain. 'He is very trying.'

Later that morning, the captain was in his office, while HyJean and Mary were enjoying a nice cup of tea at the main table. The two of them often enjoyed a cup of tea together; a brief break from the chaos that seemed to plague the squad. Their choice of accompanying biscuit would depend on how stressful the day was. If it was a relatively calm day, they would enjoy a Malted Milk, but if the toils of being a grime fighter were really getting to them, they'd break out the chocolate digestives. They kept a pack of Hob Nobs in a Tupperware box for emergencies. The morning had been very quiet, so they were taking turns to see who could dunk a Malted milk for the longest. Their competition was interrupted when the doorbell went, causing Mary to jump a little and drop her biscuit in the tea.

'I'll get it!' the captain cried, almost breaking his office door off its hinges as he flung it open and bolted across the room. HyJean and Mary were equally surprised by the captain's speed, which they'd never seen the like of in the base before. Even in an emergency, he would walk calmly as he had a bad habit of tripping on his cape or getting it caught and being pulled to the ground. The captain skidded to a halt and opened the main door. He was surprised to find a cheery looking woman on the other side holding a parcel. She had short grey hair and was dressed like someone considerably younger than she looked. She didn't seem at all surprised to be greeted by a man a man wearing a mustard yellow cape, but the captain looked at her with a furrowed brow.

'Who are you?' the captain asked.

'It's me, Carol,' said Carol.

'How did you find our secret base?' he said with a whisper, leaning in and looking around the corridor.

'I work downstairs on reception, and I do the knit and natter sessions on Fridays,' she said, following his sideward glances to see what he was looking for.

'I don't like nits, they're unclean,' he said dryly.

'Yes, well anyway, this parcel came for you, I had to sign for it. And there's a few other bits too,' she said, holding out a bundle of mail.

The captain held up his hand to stop her, before reaching over and picking up a bottle of anti-bacterial spray and spraying the mail. He wanted to spray Carol too, as she looked like she could do with a clean, but he resisted.

'Thought I'd bring them up, save you having to come down and get them,' she said with a smile.

'Thank you, Carol from downstairs,' he said, taking the mail and nodding to her. 'Tell nobody of our location.'

'Okie dokie, love. See you later,' Carol said with a smile as she left to return to her desk in the reception area of the community centre. Captain Clean shut the door and brought the mail over to the main table, walking with a slight spring in his step.

'One for you Mary,' said the captain, handing her what was probably another invoice or complaint about the squad's activities. He flipped through the rest and tossed a copy of Foot & Ball Magazine onto the table. 'I keep telling Will to stop having his magazines delivered here.'

Finally, he opened up his parcel with a childlike excitement. After tearing into the paper like a homeless person at a buffet, his face suddenly dropped as held up a small piece of yellow cloth, about the size of a small hand towel.

'What is it?' asked HyJean.

'It's too bloody small is what it is,' the captain groaned in frustration.

'Is that the cape you ordered?' asked Mary.

'Yes! I had it made especially, and I specifically put 180 centimetres,' he said, eyeing up the small piece of cloth that definitely wasn't anywhere near two metres in either direction.

'Are you sure you typed 180 and not 18?' asked Mary.

'Of course I did… I think,' he replied indignantly. 'Anyway, they should know that an 18-centimetre cape is too small.'

'I think you should keep it,' said HyJean as she tried to stifle a laugh. 'It looks cute.'

'I'm not keeping this,' said the captain. 'Mary, can you send it back to the tailors please?'

'Yes Captain,' she nodded as she took another biscuit. 'If you leave it there, I'll take it this afternoon and get one the right size. I've got to go that way anyway, to pick up Nelson's mask and your new brush.'

'Who's that one addressed to?' asked HyJean, gesturing to a small envelope that lay on the table. The captain picked it up and opened it, taking out a letter.

'Nobody,' he said. 'It just says The Sanitary Squad.'

'How strange,' said HyJean. 'What does it say?'

'Dear Sanitary Squad,' the captain read out. 'I am writing to you on behalf of the Filtham neighbourhood watch group to see if you can help. Three people have gone missing from our cul-de-sac in the past month and have returned two days later beaten and bruised. My husband was the latest victim. We've spoken to the police, and they say they are looking into it, but whenever we chase it up, they say they're busy with other things. Nothing connects these incidents, and we can't think who would have any motives to do such a thing, but there is one detail that made us think of reaching out to you. All the attacks happen on a Wednesday night when they're taking their rubbish out, and as well as the people going missing, their wheelie bins are vanishing too. We're all scared to put our bins out now. Could you please help? Mrs Tara Herman. And there's an address at the bottom.'

The three squad members all looked at each other, sizing up everyone's reactions, which were all a similar look of bewilderment and intrigue. The sort of look you might have if you saw a rabbit playing a saxophone. Captain Clean was the first to break the silence.

'How did she get our address?' he asked. 'This place is top secret.'

'The police must have given it to her,' said HyJean, taking the letter to investigate it further.

'So, somebody's kidnapping people and their wheelie bins, beating them up and then dumping them back a couple of days later?' Mary surmised.

'That's what it sounds like' said HyJean as she read through the letter.

'Just a theory,' said Mary, using her biscuit to point like a detective making a deduction. 'But could we be dealing with living wheelie bins?'

The captain and HyJean looked at her silently with the same jazz rabbit look and she shrugged, 'What? Mick and I were watching an episode Doctor Who the other night and it had living plastic wheelie bins.'

'I think it's more likely that people are using the wheelie bins to transport the bodies,' suggested HyJean.

'But they're putting the bins out on bin collection night, they'd be full, wouldn't they?' said Mary. 'Not much room for a body.'

'Good point,' the captain said, stroking his chin. It was at times like this that he wished he had a beard, but he would never grow one as it was far too unsanitary. 'It's bin night tomorrow, so we'd better not waste any time on this.'

He folded the letter neatly and put it in his pocket, before walking over to the table and taking a seat, staring blankly at the wall in front of him.

'What are you doing?' asked HyJean.

'I'm waiting for the others to come back so we can fill them in and go investigate,' he replied. 'There's no time to lose.'

'Evidently,' said HyJean as she picked up the copy of Foot & Ball Magazine and started flicking through it to check out the handsome football players whilst trying to convince herself she really was interested in Filham City's latest transfers.

About twenty minutes passed – for the duration of which, Captain Clean stayed staring at the wall expressionless, as if in some sort of trance – before Sergeant Suds, Faucet and Flush returned. As soon as the door opened, the captain snapped back to life as if someone had unpaused him with a remote control, quickly showing them the note and filling them in.

'Suds, we'll go speak to them, see what we can find out. HyJean, have a look at their profiles online, see if there's any clues. Flush and Faucet, you can come too, check out the area, ask around to see what people know.'

'Ah, I can't Cap, I've got work,' said Flush sheepishly.

'Fine,' the captain said with a sigh. 'HyJean, can you go with Faucet?'

'I am a grown up, y'know,' said Faucet. 'I'm allowed to talk to strangers now.'

'You haven't completed your training, and yesterday you almost blinded a woman trying to wave at her yesterday. You need supervision,' the captain pointed out.

'Fine,' Faucet sighed. 'I'll go with HyJean.'

'You know I'm really trying not to take offence here,' said HyJean as she clipped on her utility belt. She gave him a nudge and headed over to the door. 'Come on, we'll be like Mulder and Scully.'

'Make sure you hold his hand when he crosses the road!' Flush called out with a snigger as they left.

💧💧

Whitehouse Way was a cul-de-sac not far from the community centre, but in the nice bit of the city. It was a usually quiet place to live where everyone tended to keep themselves to themselves – rather than keeping themselves to other people, which would be both exhausting and legally questionable. In a small house on the left side of the cul-de-sac lived the Hermans – sadly no relation to anyone from the 60s pop group Herman's Hermits.

There was a knock on the door and Tara Herman made her way to the door. She was a short, rotund woman, with messy hair that seemingly repelled hairbrushes. Whenever she went out walking, she would notice birds looking at it with admiration, getting tips from it for their nests. One bird even tried to nest in it once. She was out sunbathing and woke up to find a starling nestled in her locks, trying to feed a worm to her ear. But today, Tara Herman hesitated at the door, before cautiously opening it just a few inches.

'Mrs Herman?' Sergeant Suds asked.

'Y-yes,' she replied, timidly, wondering if the army were doing house visits now.

'I'm Sergeant Suds from the Sanitary Squad, we're here about the disappearances and beatings,' Suds said with a sympathetic smile.

She opened the door a little more to let him in, but gave a curious look as she looked past him, 'What's he doing back there?'

'Oh, that's Captain Clean,' said Suds, turning around to see the captain sweeping up the leaves with a broom he'd taken from the neighbouring garden. Suds coughed loudly to get his attention. The captain placed the broom to one side and quickly hurried over to greet the woman.

'Mrs Herman, I'm Captain Clean from the Sanitary Squad, we're here about the disappearances and beatings,' he repeated.

'Yes, I know, he just said all that. Come on in,' she said, gesturing for them to enter and glancing around the cul-de-sac before she closed the door and joined them, ushering the two grime fighters down the tight corridor to the room at the end.

'You say your husband was taken and returned beaten up?' asked Captain Clean.

'That's right,' she nodded. 'Went missing last Wednesday night, turned up again Friday. He couldn't remember much. Just in here.'

They entered the small kitchen and found Mr Herman sitting at the kitchen table. His face was covered in cuts bruises – from the deep purple bulges around his eyes to the red cuts along his mouth – so that his battered face looked like the leftover paint on an artist's palette after they'd finished painting a rather nice sunset. His body fared little better, with a neck brace, an arm in a sling and a leg in a cast. Captain Clean and Sergeant Suds recoiled a little when they saw the unfortunate man, who barely moved when they entered – mainly because it was too painful.

'Mr Herman, I'm Captain Clean and this is my colleague, Sergeant Suds,' said as he sat down opposite, inadvertently pushing the table into Mr Heman, who let out a little yelp of pain.

'Please, call me Herman,' he said with a wince.

'I thought I did,' said the captain, looking at Suds in confusion.

'Herman, we're investigating this strange case,' Suds explained. 'Could you tell us what happened to you?'

'I'll try,' Herman replied. 'Last Wednesday, I was putting the bin out, when something hit me from behind and it all went dark. I woke up with my hands tied to a pole above my head and I was blindfolded. There was a man in the room. Every now and then he'd come and beat me, and I'd hear him laughing. He gave me bread and water to keep me going, but it was rough. A few days later, he knocked me out and I woke up outside my house.'

'Interesting,' said the captain. 'Did he say anything? Give you any kind of clues why they did this?'

'No, that was the strangest thing,' Herman explained. 'I don't understand what he got out of kidnapping me and beating me up.'

'Did you recognise the voice?' asked Suds.

'Sergeant Suds, please, I've got this,' said the captain, holding up a hand to silence Suds. 'Mr Herman, did you voice the um… did you recognise what voice the uh… whatever he said."

'Uh… no… I don't think so,' he replied, sounding a little unsure of himself. 'I thought he sounded a bit familiar at one point, but I couldn't quite place it.'

'Was it your neighbour?' the captain asked.

'No, I don't know who it was,' Herman sighed.

'Was it your boss?'

'No, it wasn't my boss,' Herman replied. 'I don't know who it was.'

'Your postman? Your dentist? Your butcher?' the captain persisted.

'No, no! Look, I told you, I don't know who it was,' Herman snapped.

'Alright, I was just trying to help you remember,' the captain said, throwing his arms up. 'I thought maybe if I listed some names you might… your old school teacher?'

'Will you stop it,' said Mrs Herman, smacking Captain Clean across the back of his head. 'He's in no fit state for your silly games.'

'Okay, I'm sorry. I think we've got a good picture of what happened now. I just have one more question,' said the captain.

'Alright, what is it?' asked an exasperated Mr Herman.

The captain paused for a moment and then leaned in with a serious look on his face. 'Was it your barber?'

♦ ♦

Meanwhile, Faucet and HyJean were busy across the road, individually speaking to the neighbours to see if they had seen or heard anything. HyJean hadn't learned much, but her gentle, friendly approach was working out better than Faucet's, who had discovered that he now leaked a little water when he was nervous, and people were put off by a man who looked like he was melting on their doorstep. He had just had another door closed in his face when a little old lady ran over to meet him at the front gate. Her hair wasn't messy; it was curly and grey, like most old ladies' hair. And she was wearing a cardigan that she'd knitted herself, evident from the knitting needles still dangling from the bottom.

'Excuse me, dear,' she said in a voice that sounded as frail as she looked. 'Are you with the Sanitary Squad?'

'Uh, yeah, I am,' said Faucet, a little unsure how much he was supposed to divulge about the squad and his role within it. But the woman seemed to already know of the squad, so he figured it wasn't that much of a secret.

'My name's Mrs Begonia. I wonder if you could help me, I live just around the corner,' she explained.

'I'm not sure how I can help with that,' Faucet replied. 'I can't see any houses for sale.'

'No, that's not the problem, silly boy' said the old woman with a slight frown. 'It's littering. Follow me.'

'Littering?' repeated a surprised Faucet as he watched her walk off. He looked around to see if HyJean was nearby, but couldn't see her, so he followed the woman, who was already halfway down the road. She led him out of the cul-de-sac, onto the main road.

'There's a young boy, you see, keeps throwing his rubbish in my garden,' she explained as they walked. 'The first time he did it, I told him off and now he seems to be making a point of chucking his wrappers and cans into my garden every morning and every evening on his way to and from school.'

She stopped outside a house and pointed down to a small pile of rubbish on the other side of a small hedge. Faucet peered over the hedge and, unsurprisingly, saw a large pile of crisp packets, chocolate wrappers, soda cans, receipts and even a jacket potato skin.

'Yep, that's littering alright, no doubt about it,' he said, confidently, nodding as if he were making some clever deduction.

'I can't keep coming out and picking it up, it's doing my back in,' she sighed. 'I've asked Mr Grudgely next door - he used to be a bin man you see, so he doesn't mind picking rubbish up, used to it - but he's not always in and it's becoming a nightmare. It's every flipping day – if you'll excuse my language. Can't you do something? You and your lot deal with this kind of thing, don't you?'

'Well, yes, uh… we do. I think. I'm not sure if littering counts as sanitation… or a crime,' Faucet said scratching the back of his neck as he tried to think what the captain would say for him to do. He looked down at the little old lady and saw the desperation in her eyes. 'Okay. I'll take your details and see what I can do.'

'Oooh, thank you!' she said, giving him a hug and then instantly regretting it as she pulled away and wiped the damp patch on her chest. She gave him her name and address, and he borrowed a pen to make a note of the details on the back of a receipt from the rubbish pile.

💧💧

'You accepted a case without consulting us?' Captain Clean asked in a tone that was angrier than Faucet had expected. 'What were you thinking?'

'I was thinking that I was doing a good deed helping a nice old lady,' Faucet replied.

'You should really have come and asked me,' HyJean pointed out, her tone a little friendlier, but still disapproving. Like the nice teacher in school who begrudgingly has to tell you off.

'It's okay, I'll handle with this one on my own, you won't have to do anything,' said Faucet, desperately trying to plead his case.

'No, that is not happening,' said the captain, holding up his arms, crossed in an X shape to further emphasise his point.

'Aww, c'mon Cap, you didn't see that old lady, she needs our help,' Faucet pleaded. 'I thought that's what we did, helped people in need?'

'No, I'm sorry but you're just not ready and it's not an issue that we need to concern ourselves with,' said the captain resolutely.

HyJean could see how much Faucet wanted to do this, and she thought it would be good for him, so she paused for a moment in thought. An idea came to her, and she gave Faucet a subtle wink.

'You're right, Captain,' she said. 'It's only a bit of littering, it's not that bad.'

'Not that bad?' the captain repeated, his voice going a little squeaky in disbelief. 'I'll have you know littering is a very serious offence. It can lead to flies and foxes, contaminating the area with their germs, not to mention all manner of odour issues spreading around… People and animals can cut themselves on discarded sharp items… And have you heard how many car accidents occur due to cars trying to avoid litter that's blown into the road?'

'Hm, sounds like someone should really deal with it then?' she said nodding her head slightly to gesture towards Faucet.

The captain was about to protest, and opened his mouth to do so, but after a couple of silent seconds, he merely let out a defeated sigh. 'Fine, but he's not doing it alone. And he's not doing anything without me approving it first,' he said sternly.

'I agree,' said HyJean. 'Faucet, why don't you and Flush come up with some ideas how to resolve the littering and we'll go from there.'

'Great! Will do. Thanks guys, I really appreciate it,' said Faucet, beaming at the idea of taking the lead in his first case. As he turned to leave, though, he suddenly remembered something. 'Oh, have you had any luck finding out anything more about me or who experimented on me?'

'We're working on it,' the captain nodded.

'Awesome,' Faucet replied.

He shook HyJean's hand and turned to the captain, his hand hovering as he hesitated and decided to just give him a thumbs up instead, before rushing off, with a joyful bounce in his step, to find Flush to tell him the news and get started on their plans.

'Are you really working on it?' HyJean asked quietly as she watched Faucet running away like a monkey on a sugar-rush.

'To be honest, I'd forgotten all about it. But I'll get around to it at some point,' the captain replied. He too was watching Faucet and shook his head a little. 'I don't like this, Jean. He's only been here a week and he's already gone rogue.'

'I know, but give him a chance. He's just trying to make a good impression,' HyJean replied. 'Besides, someone going against the rules and authority to try and make things cleaner. Doesn't that remind you of anyone?'

'Does it? Yes, it does. Of course it does. It's just like uh…' the captain said, pausing to think of an answer to prove to HyJean he knew who shew as talking about. 'Gandhi?'

'Yes, he's the next Gandhi,' HyJean said, rolling her eyes.

♦ ♦

Mary left the tailors after returning the captain's tiny cape and dropped a sample of a new micro-fibre material she'd picked up into her tartan shopping bag, which also contained a new waterproof rubber mask for Faucet and a replacement toilet brush mace for the captain that she'd picked up from a man who was an actually an artists that worked nearby making all sorts of weird things out of metal, like saxophone lamps and hubcap hats. She walked down the street, heading back towards the community centre. However, as she passed an alleyway, she heard cries of help coming from inside the alley. She looked closer and saw that somebody inside was being mugged. Mary looked around for any sign of police or someone who could help, but the street was quiet. Then she looked down at her bag. There was a weapon inside. And a mask to conceal her identity. And a piece of fabric that was enough for a small cape. She looked around the street again. It was still deserted. She quickly opened her bag an took the mask out. She tried it on tied it behind her grey, curly hair. She took the fabric out and tied it around her neck, then took out toilet brush mace and threw the bag down behind a bin at the entrance to the alley.

'Oi, you!' she shouted, running into the alley and lifting the toilet brush up. As she got closer, she saw that it was a man in a balaclava tugging at a young woman's handbag and brandishing a knife. Had she seen the knife earlier, she might not have been so keen to step in, but she was already running now. Mary swung the toilet brush mace down at an angle and hit the man square on the back. He cried out in pain, dropping the bag. He turned to face Mary, but before he could use his knife, she'd swung the toilet brush back up again and knocked it out of his hand, breaking several fingers in the process. The woman whom he had been trying to mug just stood and watched in disbelief, still shaking and wincing with every hit that the man took. Mary gave him one last uppercut to the jaw with the toilet brush mace that seemed to knock him unconscious, sending him falling down into a puddle. Mary picked up the bag and handed it to the trembling woman.

'There you go dear,' she said with a smile. 'Now you run along and avoid coming down this way in future.'

The woman took the bag and clutched Mary's arms, 'Thank you. Thank you so much.'

She quickly left the alley and Mary looked down at the unconscious mugger on the floor. She was unsure what to do next, as she'd never done anything like this before. She felt a rush of adrenaline that she hadn't felt in many years. Better even than finishing a cryptic crossword in the newspaper without having to Google anything. All she could think was that it felt good helping someone and giving a criminal what he deserved. After a brief pause, she removed the mask and returned to her bag. Putting the mask, cape and brush back inside, she took one more look back at the unconscious man on the floor and giggled to herself.

'I can see why Mick likes this job,' she said quietly, before continuing her journey.

💧 💧

Later on, back in the Sanitary Squad's base of operations, Captain Clean and HyJean were sat around the central table, ready to hear Faucet's plan for dealing with the serial litterer.

'Okay, we've done some brainstorming and we've got a few ideas to present to you,' said Faucet as he and Flush stood before them. The captain shuffled uncomfortably in his seat, while HyJean sat upright looking as keen as she could.

'We're all ears,' said HyJean.

Faucet looked down at his handful of cue cards, which shook a little nervously in his hands. 'Okay, so the first idea is to talk to him and try to reason with him, tell him what he's doing is wrong and convince him to stop.'

He looked up half-expectantly and was disappointed to see that HyJean was biting her bottom lip and shaking her head slightly, whilst the captain had his head in his hand, sighing frustratedly.

'That doesn't usually seem to work, strangely enough,' said HyJean. 'Let's move on. What about your other ideas?'

'Ah, well this next idea is much more exciting,' said Flush, stepping forward. 'Okay, picture this. We get one of those German helmets with the spikes on the top, strap it to his head, and then pick up him and use him as a human litter picker.'

Flush demonstrated his suggestion with a mime, waving his hands about quite enthusiastically and hoping it helped them visualise it. Again, both grime fighters looked despondent, with the captain trying not to lose his temper and HyJean desperately trying to find something positive to say.

'It… it's an interesting idea,' she said, 'but I think we could get into trouble for doing that. Sorry boys. Have you got anything else?'

'Yes,' Faucet said with the slightest hint of a smile. 'We thought you might not like those ideas, that's why we pitched them first. But we've got one more that – and I might be biased here – but I think it's pretty awesome. Flush, hit the music please.'

'Music? Oh no,' groaned the captain.

Flush tapped his phone and music started playing. HyJean immediately recognised it as Wake Me Up Before You Go-Go by Wham!, but the boys had their own lyrics.

'Litterbug… litterbug, woooh!' they sang in unison, swinging their arms and clicking their fingers in time to the music. 'Pick me up, before you go-go. Don't just throw me on the floor, no-no. Pick me up, before you go-go. Don't you litter again.'

The music ended and they both struck a pose with jazz hands and broad grins on their faces.

'I don't get it, what's the idea?' asked the confused captain. 'Are you going to sing to them?'

'What? No, the litterbug,' Flush replied.

'The plan is to get lots of litter and make it into a costume, like a litter monster,' Faucet explained.

'Or a litterbug, if you will,' Flush added.

'Then we track the guy down and jump out on him wearing the costume,' Faucet continued. 'Scare him straight sort of thing, y'know?'

'Well… it's not the worst idea I've ever heard,' said HyJean with a little shrug.

'I don't even know what to say,' said the captain. He sat there for a moment in silence, a stunned look on his face. Then suddenly he punched the palm of his hand with his fist and beamed with delight. 'I love it!'

'You do?' asked HyJean, taking the emotional baton and adopting the stunned look that the captain had just disposed of.

'Of course,' said the captain. 'The kid gets the message, nobody gets hurt, and as far as I can work out it's not illegal.'

'Oh… right… well, I guess that's a yes then,' HyJean said with a bemused thumbs up.

'Bostin!' said Flush.

'Awesome!' said Faucet, bouncing on the spot happily like a rabbit that had just won gold in the hurdles event at the pet Olympics. 'We'll get to work on it right away. I'll ask Carol downstairs if we can raid the bins.'

The two gave each other a high five and made for the door, eager to get started on their big project.

'Make it outside! I don't want any rubbish in here!' the captain called after them, before turning back to HyJean. 'And in the meantime, I think we should pay a visit to the council's waste department, see if they know anything about these wheelie bin attacks.'

Mary returned to Filtham Community Centre later that afternoon, a spring in her step as she put the bag down on the large central table in the main room of the base. She was still pumped from her recent experience, and it was quite visible to the others.

'What's got you so excited, Marigold?' asked Suds as he walked over and gave his wife a peck on the cheek.

'Oh Mick, it was so thrilling,' she said, barely able to contain her excitement as she took his hands and wiggled them about a bit in that way that people do when they're excited. 'There was a woman being mugged… he had a knife… nobody was around… I had the mask… and the cape… and the mace brush… so I put them on and… and I… I stopped him!'

You stopped him?' Suds asked, a little concerned. 'The mugger? What do you mean?

'I used the brush to beat him up and rescue the woman's handbag,' she said with a proud grin.

'What? Mary, you could've been hurt!' Suds replied, his voice almost angry. 'And you can't just go round beating people up, you could get arrested.'

'I know, I know, but I just couldn't help myself,' Mary replied, her excitement fading a little as she didn't get the reaction she'd been hoping for.

Suds noticed her disappointment and pulled her in for a hug. He kissed the top of her head and sighed as he held her tightly.

'I'm sorry. You did a good thing and I'm proud of you for helping that woman,' he said in a gentler tone. 'It just worries me you could've been hurt.'

'I know, and that's how I feel about you doing this every day,' Mary replied quietly. 'But now I can see why you do it, the thrill of the fight and helping someone.'

'The difference is I've had training and I can handle myself,' Suds pointed out. He paused for a moment, thinking, and Mary knew what was going through his mind. Finally, he pulled away and looked at her face for a while, then gave her a loving smile. 'Maybe I could speak to Cap about getting you some training, learn to defend yourself if anything ever does happen. You'll probably need it the way this city's going.'

'Oh Mick, that would be lovely! Thank you!' she cried, pulling him back in for a hug, this time squeezing him and shaking slightly from side to side like he was a metronome, swinging in time to the joyous song in her heart.

'But this isn't so you can start going out fighting people,' he said sternly. 'It's purely defensive, understand?'

'Yes, yes! Whatever!' she said as she danced back to her office cheerily.

Meanwhile, Captain Clean had taken out his new brush, which he swung in the air to test, whilst making the wooshing and smashing sound effects with his voice – because at heart he was still a kid who dreamed of being a superhero one day. He then took out the waterproof mask and took it over to Faucet, who was sitting at the computers and definitely not playing an online game no he was just checking his emails and clicked on that by accident honest.

'Here you go, Faucet,' said the captain, holding out the blue rubber mask.

'This mine?' asked Faucet excitedly as he took the mask.

'Your name's Faucet, isn't it?' said the captain in a slightly irritated tone.

'Yeah, but… it's so cool,' Faucet replied, taking the mask and trying it on. It fit perfectly, with the material stretching to allow him to wrap it around his head and tie it at the back.

'This is so cool! I love it, captain. Thank you so much,' said Faucet excitedly. 'I'm gonna wear this all the time.'

'No you're not,' said the captain, holding up his hands in an X shape. 'It's only for missions, to conceal your identity. Plus we don't want to wear it out too much; it costs more than ours and we can't afford to keep replacing it.'

💧💧

Flush and Faucet were hiding across the road from Mrs Begonia's house, trying to be as inconspicuous as two people in home-made superhero costumes could be. As Faucet peered over the hedge, Flush felt a tap on his shoulder. He turned round to see a grumpy-looking bald man wearing a purple cardigan that matched the hue of his face.

'Excuse me, what on Earth do you think you are doing, apart from trampling on my roses?' he growled.

'I'll have you know, we're here on a very important mission investigating a dangerous criminal,' Flush explained, bending the truth a little in the hopes that the neighbour would be more obliging. '

'What… but… who are you?' he asked, still struggling to understand what two strangers were doing lurking in his front garden.

'We're from the Sanitary Squad,' Flush explained. 'Look, we're just looking for a guy, we'll be out of your hair in a few minutes,' adding with a mutter, 'what's left of it anyway.'

'Mrs Begonia said he usually walks by this time every day,' said Faucet.

'And what does this person look like?' the neighbour asked.

'Young, black guy, usually wears a tracksuit and a black cap, often seen littering,' Faucet replied.

'You mean like him,' the neighbour said, pointing across the road to someone who matched Faucet's description exactly walking down the road.

'Yes! That's him!' said Faucet, as he realised he'd been looking at the wrong house.

He clambered over the hedge, followed by Flush, who called back, 'Sorry we hurt your roses, mister!'

They ran across the road and hid behind a tree, watching as the boy unwrapped a chocolate bar and tossed the wrapper into Mrs Begonia's garden. Right on cue, the old woman came out and started shouting at him, waving her knitting needles around. The boy just scoffed and pushed her away, sending her toppling over into the hedge. Faucet went to run out, but Flush held him back. The boy snorted and carried on down the road. Once he was far enough away, Flush and Faucet ran over to the woman and helped her up.

'I told you not to interact with him, Mrs Begonia,' said Faucet. 'Leave it to the professionals.'

'Sod, damn, blast and bleeding sodding damn it,' the woman grumbled as she brushed herself down. 'I hate that arrogant little toerag.'

They encouraged her to go back inside and continue her knitting, then quietly and carefully followed the young man all the way down the road and farther, until eventually he arrived home. They watched from behind another tree as he entered the house and then turned to each other to plan their next move.

'Okay, so we knock on the door, speak to his parents and try and get inside so we can work out which room is his bedroom,' Flush explained.

'Got it,' Faucet nodded. 'But what's our story going to be?'

'Hm, I don't know. If only there were some group we could pretend to be from that investigated things like toilets and sinks,' Flush replied sarcastically.

'Oh yeah, right,' Faucet replied. 'Good point.'

They waited a few awkward minutes so as to not look too suspicious, then walked up to the door confidently and rang the bell. A middle-aged woman with a lifetime of exasperation on her face answered it, frowning as most people did when they saw members of the squad for the first time.

'Yes?' she asked in a slightly disgruntled tone.

'Hello ma'am, we're from the Sanitary Squad,' Faucet began.

'Are you from the council to do with the water? They said they were going to send someone out, is that you?' the woman asked in the sort of tone that someone might use if they'd been arguing with their local council for weeks about issues with the water supply.

Faucet was about to correct her, but Flush stepped in. 'Yep, that's us. Council water people. Can we come in?'

'Well, you're not going to be able to check the water from out here, so I think that'd be a good start,' the woman said with a roll of her eyes. 'I must say though, you came quicker than I expected. Usually have to wait weeks for a response. Do you always wear these ridiculous outfits.'

'Yes ma'am, standard issue these days,' said Flush. 'Focus groups found it made people feel more reassured.'

'Not the word I would've used,' she replied as she led them inside the house and down the hallway, past the living room where the young boy they'd just been stalking was watching television, and into a small kitchen.

'Nice house you've got here, Miss um…' Faucet said, hoping to catch her name.

'Throwett, Mrs,' she replied. 'Isn't that on your file?'

'Oh, we don't have a file on you,' said Faucet without thinking.

'Uh, what he means is we don't have the file on us, it's out in the van,' said Flush quickly after seeing the Mrs Throwett's suspicious reaction.

'Maybe you should read it before you come in next time,' she muttered.

'Are they here about my glasses?' came a screechy, ancient voice from behind that made Flush jump.

He'd not noticed a little old lady sitting in the corner eating a bowl of soup. She looked like Mrs Throwett, but with considerably more wrinkles and whiter hair that was thinning on top.

'No mom, they're from the water company,' said Mrs Throwett.

'I don't care who they are, as long as they fix my glasses,' the old woman replied. 'Can't see a thing without my glasses.'

Her point was evidenced as she dipped a knife into her soup and tried to use it to drink the contents.

'Ignore her, she's staying with us for a few days,' said Mrs Throwett. 'The toilet's through here. It flushes, but the water doesn't go down.'

'Okay, Mrs Throwett, we'll take a look,' Flush said, giving Faucet a wink to signify he knew what he was doing. 'In the meantime, my colleague needs a tour of your house.'

'A tour? Why?' she asked, her frown reappearing even deeper, like the microbes on her face had been digging a cave on her forehead to mine for treasure.

'It's uh… so we have a layout of the house. It can affect the water, depending on what's in each room,' Faucet said, thinking on his feet.

'Fine, whatever. If it gets the job done,' she said with another roll of her eyes. 'Come on then, this way.'

Faucet followed Mrs Throwett around their small, semi-detached council house. As they passed the living room, she poked her head inside and said in a frustrated tone, 'Kiefer, I told you to sort that sofa bed out.'

The boy just sucked his teeth and ignored her, so she shut the door with a huff and continued the tour, pointing out each room as they went: the dining room, bathroom, hallway – the last one seemed redundant to point out, but she figured this pair of strangely dressed council workers weren't the brightest tools in the toolbox that they'd left in the van. The made their way upstairs, where the bedrooms would be and where Faucet was most keen to go - but not for the reason most young men are keen to follow women to bedrooms for. When she started pointing out the bedrooms, Faucet pressed her for more information.

'And who sleeps in here?' he asked, walking into the first bedroom.

'Um, is that important?' she asked.

'Could be,' Faucet nodded, now getting used to the character. 'Younger generations tend to use more electricity, which could affect the polarity of the neutron flow in the house.'

'I... see,' said Mrs Throwett, giving in and deciding it was easier and quicker just to answer. 'That's my son's bedroom.'

'And these other rooms? Who sleeps in those?' asked Faucet, so it didn't sound suspicious that he was only interested in the one room.

'That's the spare room,' she said pointing to the next room. 'And that's my room at the end of the hall.'

'Right, got it, thank you,' Faucet said as he drew a little diagram and scribbled down a note of each room on the back of the receipt with Mrs Begonia's details on.

'Can't afford notebooks, hm?' asked Mrs Throwett.

'Council budget,' he shrugged.

♦ ♦

Captain Clean and HyJean sat on uncomfortable plastic seats in the reception of the council building. HyJean often theorised that they purposely used these chairs to make visitors feel uncomfortable and inferior, leaving them waiting as long as possible to baste them in a layer of desperation that only they, the council, could remove. She now sat and wondered if it would make more sense to make their visitors comfortable in nice, soft armchairs so that they were happier and less irritable going into the meeting. But that seemed unlikely to ever happen. They'd both come dressed in their grime fighting outfits, hoping it would give them more authority, but the dull brown chairs seemed to have the power to strip anyone of any authority, as they were sat awkwardly squeezed together and slightly too low down.

When the head of waste management, a Mr Derek Tritus, appeared, they wasted no time in getting to their feet. Derek was a rotund man – and that was putting it politely. He spent all day at his desk and all evening on his couch, happy to roll through life with the minimum of effort, which made him a model employee for the council, but gave him a figure that meant he would never become a model, unless it was for a duvet cover that doubled as a t-shirt. He had a thin layer of greasy ginger hair on his head and a bushy moustache that twitched as he moved. The captain instantly recognised the mouth movements as someone trying to dislodge a bit of food from between their teeth. As Derek walked towards them (although "waddled" might be more appropriate) he proudly adjusted his name badge, which had gotten lost in the folds of his skin.

'He should go to the gym and try a different kind of waist management,' HyJean muttered to Captain Clean.

Despite being a generally kind person, HyJean had very little time for the council. Although they funded the squad's operations, they often proved themselves to be more of a hindrance, refusing them permissions to do things or taking forever to get back to them whenever they needed something. Most of the employees knowingly mocked the squad too, though, believing they shouldn't be getting paid to run around in silly costumes pretending to clean up the city.

'Ah, Captain, HyJean. Good to see you both,' Derek said as he put out a hand that could've been easily mistaken for a packet of sausages. The captain flatly refused the gesture, as he always did, so Derek turned his attention to HyJean. She reluctantly shook the porky protuberance, discretely wiping the greasy sweat off her hand after.

'Mr Tritus, thank you for arranging this so quickly,' said the captain.

'Well, here at the council, we pride ourselves on working quickly and efficiently,' he said as gestured them to follow him down a corridor.

'He means it. He actually means it!' HyJean whispered in amazement to the captain from behind as they walked down the dimly lit, drably painted corridor.

After a long, slow walk – with Captain Clean and HyJean having to walk at speeds that a snail could have beaten – they finally reached the waste management department, walking past a few rows of desks and into Derek's office. It was a small room, with rows of folders all lined up on high up shelves, while cardboard boxes stuffed full of papers, workwear and other equipment were strewn along the floor. Derek slumped down into a chair behind his desk, which was had a slightly curved indentation to accommodate his large belly. HyJean wasn't sure if this was how the desk was made or if it had just been warped over time. Meanwhile, the captain looked around at the thick layers of dust on the shelves and thought about what a field day he'd have if he were let loose in this office with a vacuum and feather duster. Their thoughts were interrupted as they were swiftly joined by three men, all of whom were well built, with their impressive muscles showing through their shorts and fluorescent jackets. Once they were all in and the door was shut, there was barely room to move. One of the muscly men had to perch himself on the desk to avoid being squashed.

The other two – one with a stubbly beard, which the captain was trying hard to ignore, and another who was very tall and had to bend a little to avoid hitting his head on the low ceiling – stood behind the captain, pressed up against the wall.

'Captain, HyJean, these are my three top senior waste operatives,' Derek said, gesturing to the three men in fluorescent jackets with a raise of his hand that seemed like it required a great deal of effort. 'If anything's going on, they'll know about it.'

'Shouldn't you know about it, being their boss?' asked HyJean, who couldn't help but take a jibe.

'I'm a very busy man,' Derek replied sternly. 'I can't be everywhere at once.'

'You're having a good go at it,' HyJean muttered under her breath as she looked down at the edge of the desk disappearing into his stomach.

'Gentlemen, thank you for coming,' said the captain, addressing the three waste operatives. He filled them in on the letter from Mrs Herman, the testimony from Mr Herman and they listened with some surprise. 'So, have you heard or seen anything that might shed some light on this?'

'I've not noticed anything,' said the waste operative who was perched on the desk.

'Are you sure this is true,' said the operative with a stubbly beard. 'I mean those lot on Whitehouse Way are always complaining about something, they're a right pain.'

Derek cleared his throat loudly and gave a piercing stare at the operative. The kind that a boss usually gives someone as a discreet warning, despite the fact that anyone within a few yards will have heard it. If anything, it only serves to draw attention to the fact that whatever was just said was something that shouldn't have been said.

'Sorry, I mean they liaise with us regularly and provide useful feedback to help us improve our service,' the operative said, correcting himself.

'Yes, it's true,' the captain nodded. 'We've spoken with them ourselves and seen the damage.'

'Have any of the other bin men reported anything?' asked HyJean. The seated waste operative visibly winced at the term "bin men" and the tallest of the three puffed his chest out a little.

'Waste operatives,' he corrected her from above.

'Of course, I'm so sorry,' HyJean said with a slight hint of sarcasm in her voice. 'Have any of the waste operatives reported anything?'

'Nothing,' said the stubbly waste operative. 'Although… my guy Brian did mention about seeing a wheelie bin moving down the road on its own last Wednesday. Could that be anything to do with this?'

HyJean struggled to contain her frustration at this revelation, now speaking with unreserved sarcasm. 'Ooh, I don't know. Let me think. Could a wheelie bin moving on its own on the night of the kidnapping be relevant? Gosh, I just don't know. What do you think captain?'

The captain frowned behind his mask and gave a disapproving grunt, before turning back to the stubbly waste operative.

'Yes, that definitely sounds suspicious,' he said. 'Do you know where abouts it was?'

'I think he said… um… where was it now?' the operative muttered, tapping his head as if trying to press a refresh button on his brain. 'Ah! Walker Street, that was it.'

The captain made a note of the name in a little notepad. He then turned to the tall waste operative who loomed over him like a faulty streetlamp. He was busy looking down at the desk, so the captain gave a little cough to get his attention.

'Ahem. You… you have you seen anything, have you?' he asked a little timidly.

'I don't know nothing,' the operative replied, giving the captain a hard stare as if he were trying to read his mind. The captain just smiled awkwardly.

'Right, well, you've been most helpful, thank you,' he said, turning to leave. 'Please keep in touch if you hear anything else.'

'Happy to be of service, captain,' Derek called out, with his moustache masking some of the sarcasm in his tone. 'Always willing to support your worthy cause.'

It was a tight squeeze to turn around and leave, and when Captain Clean tried the handle, the door wouldn't open. He grunted as he pushed and pulled on the door.

'That blinking handle,' said Derek. It gets a bit stuck sometimes. You have to twist and push… no, twist and push. Barry, give him a hand will you.'

The stubbly waste operative leaned over the shoulders of Captain Clean and reached down to the handle. The captain winced and cowered away from the beard that was inches from him. The door eventually opened and they tumbled out into the main office. The grime fighters brushed themselves down and promptly left.

♦ ♦

Flush and Faucet had put together their litter monster costume on the roof, which took longer than expected since it was a windy day and the lighter wrappers and packets kept being blown away. Eventually they'd finished and Flush tried on the suit, leaving the head off for now so he could see. On the way down they bumped into Carol, the receptionist, who nearly had a heart attack and screamed so loudly that the even the windows were worried about smashing. She berated them about wandering around scaring people and sent them on their way. They managed to sneak into the base and into the shower room, where they could assemble the suit for the big reveal.

'We'll be out in a minute, just putting the last few finishing touches on,' Flush called out to Captain Clean, HyJean and Sergeant Suds, who were sat at the main table, unsure whether to be excited or worried about what was going to be presented to them. Suds had been told only that the boys were working on something to stop a serial litterer, so that his reaction would be even more genuine. He sat reading through the captain's notes on their earlier investigation at the cul-de-sac and whilst HyJean got him up to speed about the meeting with the waste department.

'It took some convincing, but I assured the other residents that we'd keep them safe and a couple of them have agreed to put their bins out as normal,' HyJean explained. 'One at 7pm, the other at 7:30pm. So, we'll go there and keep an eye on them.'

'It's definitely the tall one,' said the captain, staring blankly into the distance.

'The tall one what?' Suds asked, looking up.

'The waste operative, he knows something,' the captain explained. 'You heard him, he practically confessed.'

'Did he?' asked HyJean. 'He hardly said anything.'

'He clearly said "I don't know nothing",' Cap reminded her. 'That's a double negative, so that means he does know something.'

'I don't think so,' said Suds. 'It's just the way some people speak. People use double negatives all the time, doesn't mean it's some kind of code.'

'But these are smart men,' the Captain said, folding his arms and resting his chin in his hand in thought.

'Cap, they're bin men working for Filtham council,' HyJean said with a roll of her eyes. 'They're hardly the Sopranos.'

'They are waste operatives, Jean,' the captain corrected her. 'And you underestimate them. I think I'll go check them out later.'

'We're supposed to be keeping an eye on the bin tonight. It's Wednesday, remember?' Suds pointed out.

'You two can do that,' said the captain, brushing it away. 'This requires some serious investigative skills.'

'You're getting someone else in then?' said HyJean with a smirk.

The question went unanswered, as Faucet poked his head around the corner with an excited grin on his face.

'Okay, we're ready,' he said, before disappearing back around the corner.

The lights were dimmed, with only a single light in the middle of the room acting like a spotlight. Captain Clean, HyJean and Sergeant Suds sat up, drawn in by the theatrics and eager to see what they'd made.

'Gathered grime fighters, welcome,' said Faucet in a deep, commanding voice. 'We are proud to present to you… the litterbug!'

From out of the shadows stepped a large, bulky figure, completely covered in crisp packets, sweet wrappers, crumpled paper, bits of fabric, banana peels and all manner of rubbish. Captain Clean gave a little shriek and fell off his chair as he jumped back in fear of this collection of filthy rubbish. He crouched down behind the table, peering over the top to look at the monster before him. For someone who had dedicated their life to being clean, this was a nightmare for him. HyJean, meanwhile, sat with her jaw dropped, shaking her head and laughing in disbelief, while Suds was frowning with complete bemusement.

'I am the litterbug!' Flush boomed in his unmistakable Brummie accent. 'The remnants of all you have littered! You shall pay for your crime against cleanliness!'

'Is this for real?' asked Suds, turning to his fellow grime fighters. 'Can you two see this as well, or is it just me?'

'Oh, I can see it alright,' HyJean muttered as she watched Flush's litter monster stomping around on the spot. 'But I don't believe it.'

'And remind me, why is he covered in litter again?' asked Suds.

'They're going to try and scare the kid straight by… uh… being the ghost of their litter? I'm not too sure.' HyJean said, pausing to down at Captain Clean, who was still cowering behind the table. 'But as crazy as it sounds, I think it might actually work.'

'G-get it out!' whimpered Captain Clean, who was still cowering behind the table. 'And get me a sponge!'

'Yep, that's a definite thumbs up from him,' Suds told Faucet, who was standing to the side watching.

'I can't quite believe I'm saying this, but nice work lads,' added HyJean.

'You might want to work on the voice a bit though,' said Suds. 'The accent kind of spoils the effect.'

'You shall be thrown away into the bin of doom, you selfish miscreant!' continued Flush, pointing at Suds with a glove made out of Happy Happy Burger wrappers and cigarette butts stuck to a bin bag.

'Alright, enough trash talk,' HyJean chuckled. 'Go get ready to scare your kid. We've got to get ready.'

♦ ♦

HyJean and Suds sat on tree stumps behind a large bush on Whitehouse Way that almost covered them. The Driver had dropped them off, but was unable to wait around with them, as he was going out on the town with his mates, where he would get very drunk and go home with a woman he barely knew. HyJean was sat looking through a pair of binoculars, scanning the street for any signs of movement. There had been very little movement all evening, save for a drunk couple returning from a party and a suspicious looking cat – Suds had argued that all cats looked suspicious in general, so they let it off the hook this time.

'That's it, it's been over an hour, I need to stretch my legs,' Sergeant Suds grumbled as he turned to stand up.

'No you don't,' said HyJean, grabbing his vest and pulling him back down behind the bush. 'If we're seen, it might compromise the whole mission.'

Suds sat down with a huff and looked in the bag for something to do. HyJean, being a mother, had naturally packed some snacks, but they had foolishly gorged early on and were now left with just an oat bar that neither of them really wanted to eat. Finally, HyJean's phone beeped, signalling it was 7pm and time for the first bin to be put out.

'Look, there he is,' HyJean said as she spotted a nervous-looking woman leave the house with two bin bags and tentatively put them in the wheelie bin.

They leant forward, watching, waiting for something to happen. The woman dragged out two black bin bags, lifted the lid on the wheelie bin, put the bags in and closed the lid once again. She gave a little shrug and went back inside. It was a distinctly disappointing turn of events and made for quite boring viewing.

'It's not often I find myself disappointed when a woman doesn't get attacked by a wheelie bin,' said Suds with a sigh. 'But I do feel a bit short changed.'

'Don't worry, there's still one more to go yet,' said HyJean as she sat back on her stump.

They were in for another long wait, as the two grime fighters took it in turns to keep watch for the next half an hour.

💧💧

While Sergeant Suds and HyJean were keeping an eye out for any strange wheelie bin activity, Captain Clean wanted to confirm his suspicions. Carrying a large ladder with him, he made his way to the council offices, which were now closed for the night. The outside looked just a drab and uninviting as it did during the day, with its brutalist architecture and windows that were almost opaque with dust and dirt. It took all of the captain's strength to resist cleaning them, though even if he had it would've taken all night. He made his way quietly around the back of the building, knowing the layout by heart after he'd memorised it years ago for something to do. He found the window where Derek Tritus's offer should be and propped the ladder up against the wall. He climbed up and peered through the window, which was hard to see through, as it had a layer of grime on that was thicker than any PE teacher. But he could just make out the rows of folders and the slightly curved desk. Taking a little tool out of his utility belt, the captain picked the lock and edged the window open. As he swung his leg over to climb in, his weight shifted and pulled the ladder across, which slowly tilted and then collapsed onto the ground. Captain Clean was left dangling from the windowsill holding on for dear life.

'Bugger,' he grumbled, before scraping his feet against the brickwork and pulling himself up and through the window. He turned and looked down at the ladder on the ground and muttered, 'It's never as easy as it looks in films.'

Nevertheless, he was here now, and he had work to do. He held up a flashlight and started to run his finger along the labels on the row of files to look for the employee records, but he winced at how much dust collected on his tip and resorted to just using his. He found the right file and took it out, placing it down on the desk and opening it up. Inside the ring binder, there were several plastic wallets with sheets of paper in. He flipped through them until he found the records for the tall waste operative. He took the papers out and started to read through them.

'Perry Soal… thirty four… started four years ago…' he muttered as he read the file. He flicked through the pages to find the notes on any sickness, incidents or customer complaints. But just as he was reading about a time when Soal had mistaken a garden ornament for a bin bag, he heard a noise coming from behind him. He turned his head quickly, listening hard to make certain he had heard something. Then he heard it again. Footsteps. Gradually getting louder. He panicked and stuffed the papers into the ring binder, without putting them back in the plastic wallet. He looked at the shelves on the wall to see where he'd taken the file from, but the neighbouring file had fallen over and now he couldn't remember where he'd got it from. They all looked the same, he thought. In a panic, he threw the file in the bin and ran to the window. He started to climb out of it, but when his feet hit nothing solid, he remembered about the ladder. He clung to the window frame, his legs dangling in mid-air as he watched the door slowly open. A figure walked in, ducking slightly to fit through the doorway.

'You!' the captain gasped. 'I knew it. Come to destroy the evidence, have we?'

'Evening, Captain. I thought you might come back here,' said Perry Soal, the tall waste operative, as he walked over and helped the captain back into the room. 'I am here to destroy evidence, you're right. But not for the crime you were on about earlier.'

'What?' said the captain, a little surprised at the man's honesty and his lack of surprise at his being there.

Perry merely crossed to the desk and picked up a letter from the inbox tray. He showed it to the captain before stuffing it in his pocket.

'An old man claimed I was stealing his plants the other day,' he explained. 'A right nutter, but you can't be too careful these days. Another complaint and I'll be out on my ear. I saw this had arrived earlier and recognised the handwriting. Luckily you turned up, so Mr Tritus didn't have chance to open it.'

'I see,' said Captain Clean, though he didn't really see. 'So, that was why you were acting all shifty? You really didn't know anything about the wheelie bin case?'

'Nope, sorry,' he said with a little shrug.

'But… you said you don't know nothing… the double negative… it doesn't mean anything?' said the captain, stumbling over his words as he tried to come to terms with the reality of the situation.

'What? Of course not,' said Perry, frowning slightly. 'Why would you think that?'

'I don't know, look it doesn't matter,' said the captain, waving his hand to brush the topic away. 'Look, I need your help to get back out of here. Can you run down and put my ladder back up, please?'

'Yeah, sure. Or you could just come down with me?' Soal suggested.

Captain Clean chuckled and patted Soal's arm, 'See, I told HyJean you were clever.'

♦ ♦

'Eighty-four. Eighty-five. Eighty-six.'

Sergeant Suds had resigned himself to counting the leaves on the bush in order to pass the time away. It was a poor choice of things to count, because all of the dark green leaves that made up the bush looked almost identical. He'd already had to restart twice, but when he was interrupted this time, he was glad.

'There he is,' said HyJaen in an excited whisper, nudging Suds' arm. Sergeant Suds sat up and spotted the man that HyJean had pointed out. He was quite a short, stocky man, barely taller than the wheelie bin that he was approaching. Whilst HyJean kept a close eye on the man through the binoculars, Suds scanned the cul-de-sac for any other signs of movement. There had to be someone sneaking around waiting to pounce. But there was nothing. No suspicious movement, no eerie noises. They thought they were in for another false alarm, but as the man lifted the lid of the wheelie bin and peered inside, HyJean was surprised to see a puff of gas shoot out, causing the man to drop the bags. She was then horrified to see something from inside pull the man down into the bin.

'Suds, look! There's something in the bin,' she said, slapping his arm as she stood up and dived out from behind the bush. As they ran out and over to the road, something very strange happened. The bin suddenly started to roll away, slowly at first, but picking up in speed as it made its way out of the cul-de-sac, the man's feet poking out from under the lid.

'How's it doing that?' asked Suds as they stood, stunned.

'I don't know, but we need to follow it,' said HyJean.

They set off in a hurry, running after the rogue wheelie bin. It was surprisingly fast, considering its size and contents, and of course, it had the advantage of knowing in which direction it was going. As the bin escaped the confines of the cul-de-sac, it veered violently left, turning onto another road and whizzing down at the same speed. HyJean and Suds ran along after it, neither being particularly fast runners.

'That bloody Driver!' Suds cursed as he thought of their taxi driver, who could've easily caught up with the bin and blocked its path.

'It's times like this I regret wearing heeled boots!' cried HyJean, as her feet grew uncomfortable with every stride.

'At least you're not wearing big, heavy army boots!' Suds grumbled.

Their bickering quickly died out, as they struggled to speak through heavy panting and needed to conserve their energy. The bin careered down the road, turning this way and that as it weaved through side streets and passageways. They almost lost it at one point as it turned a couple of corners before they could, but to their relief, when HyJean and Suds span around the corner, they saw a wheelie bin stood in the middle of the road. They didn't question why it had stopped, they were just glad to have caught up with it.

'There it is,' said HyJean, clutching her chest as she caught her breath. 'This must be where they pick it up.'

'Let's get it,' said Suds, wiping the sweat from his forehead.

They ran towards the bin, half-expecting it to launch into another chase at any moment, but oddly it stayed still. When they reached it, they flung the lid open and were surprised it was empty.

'What?' gasped HyJean.

'How is that possible?' asked Suds. 'We were right behind it.'

'It's clearly not the same bin. It's a decoy,' said HyJean slumping down onto the bin. 'We'll never catch it now.'

'We should've put a tracker on it,' said Suds.

'Yeah, well, if Cap hadn't accidentally stuck it on that pigeon last month, we'd still have one left,' HyJean replied grumpily. 'Come on, we'd better head back to the house. Let's see if we can get some food on the way.'

◆ ◆

Later that night, Flush and Faucet were preparing to enact their plan and bring the litterbug to life. As the ladder from the base had been taken, they had to rely on their ingenuity to get up to the second floor of the house. The wheelie bins were out for collection, but fortunately Faucet spotted a large storage box, which, with some effort, he was able to drag underneath their target's window. Still not quite reaching, they topped it with a garden chair. Faucet climbed up first to open the window, which was already open a little to let in some air. He heaved it up as quietly as he could and then surveyed the room inside. It was almost pitch black, so it was hard to make anything out, but he could see the outline of a person sleeping in the bed. He turned back and gave Flush a thumbs up, before climbing back down.

'Okay, he's in there,' he said. 'Let's do this.'

Faucet gave Flush a boost to help him up onto the storage box. He found it was tricky to move in the costume and almost fell off more than once.

'Dude, be careful,' hissed Faucet. 'We've gotta keep quiet.'

'Sorry, this thing ain't exactly made for stealth y'know,' Flush replied, brushing away a crisp packet on his face so he could see a little better.

He climbed up onto the garden chair and finally through the window, which was the most difficult task as it was quite a narrow gap to fit through and the costume rustled loudly with each movement. Fortunately, the bedroom's occupant must have been quite a heavy sleeper, as they barely stirred. Flush crept over to position himself beside the bed on the side nearest the window, while Faucet went to the other side, holding the torch ready. They silently counted to three, and then Faucet switched on the torch. It emitted a blindingly bright light that illuminated the litterbug and woke the startled sleeper.

'I am the litterbug!' boomed Flush. 'You shall pay for your littering!'

The plan had the desired effect, and there was a loud, terrified scream coming from the bed. However, Faucet couldn't help but notice it sounded higher in pitch than he'd expected. And a little croakier. He lowered the torch slightly and was horrified to find that instead of a young man cowering in the bed, there was a little old lady. Not Kiefer, but his grandmother! The pensioner continued to scream, letting out shrill, piercing wails as she cowered under the sheets.

'Crap, it's the nan!' said Flush, suddenly making the litterbug look much less intimidating as he stood quivering in a panic.

Faucet heard movement from the other rooms and made to dart across the room, but the stress of the situation had caused him to leak – as he often did when experiencing heightened emotions – and he slipped on the water and fell flat on his back.

'What are you doing? Come on, let's get out of here,' Flush cried in a hush whisper as he helped him up, which wasn't easy to do with the floor being wet and his body being covered in litter. They reached the window and climbed through, Flush going first to avoid a potentially wet ladder. The two grime fighters just about managed to get out and hide before the bedroom door burst open. The family rushed in to see what the matter was, and while they comforted and questioned the old woman, Faucet and Flush rearranged the garden furniture into place.

'Mom, what is it?' asked Mrs Throwett as she pulled the sheets down.

'A m-m-monster!' the woman cried, pointing to where Flush had been standing.

They looked around, but the room was in darkness again and there was no sign of any monsters. Kiefer crossed to the window and looked outside, but saw nothing out of the ordinary.

'It sh-shouted… at me… about l-l-littering,' the old woman continued.

'Littering?' said a stunned Mrs Throwett. The mother and son exchanged baffled looks and Kiefer shook his head. Mrs Throwett turned back to her shaking mother. 'I think you just had a nightmare mom. Probably because you're staying in Kiefer's room. It's strange being in someone else's bed.'

'I don't like this room. The bed's too small and he's got all those creepy posters,' the grandmother muttered, pointing to posters of rappers and R&B artists on the wall.

They took the old woman downstairs and made her a mug of hot chocolate, sitting with her until she'd calmed herself down. Eventually, she agreed it must have been a dream and they all went back to bed. By this point, Flush and Faucet were long gone, having had to walk back to the base since The Driver refused to pick them up again after the mess they'd left his car in on the way there.

💧💧

It was early the next morning when the members of the Sanitary Squad gathered around the central table to discuss their night's adventures. Captain Clean was repeatedly spraying Flush with disinfectant, despite the fact he'd taken the litterbug costume off the night before and stored it at his own home.

'Will you stop it!' Flush said finally, swatting away the spray bottle. 'I told you; I had a shower before I came and a shower when I got here, there's nothing on me.'

HyJean snatched the spray bottle of out of the captain's hands and put it to one side.

'So, who wants to go first?' asked Suds, hoping if he asked the question then it wouldn't be him.

'Well, ours was a total disaster,' Faucet sighed. 'We broke into the wrong room and scared the kid's nan by mistake.'

'Oh, the poor thing,' said HyJean sympathetically. 'Was she okay?'

'I dunno, we scarpered as quickly as we could,' admitted Flush.

'But don't worry, we reckon we know which room it is now, so we'll go back again tonight,' said Faucet confidently.

'You will not,' said Captain Clean sternly. 'I think you should leave that family alone for a while or you'll end up arrested.'

'Can you be arrested for scaring people?' asked Faucet.

'You can if you give them a heart attack,' Suds pointed out.

'Well, I guess we'll have to tell that poor old woman we've let her down and just let the kid litter every day,' said Flush in a tone of mock defeat, knowing the effect his words would have.

'Now hold on,' said the captain, and everyone knew what was coming. Flush had hit a nerve and, as just as he'd planned, changed the captain's mind. 'If you're sure which room it is this time, then I think we could still let the plan go ahead.'

'Bostin!' Flush grinned. 'Thanks Cap.'

'So how did you get on with your investigation?' asked HyJean, trying to change the subject before he could change his mind back.

'Ah, well it didn't quite go as planned either,' said the captain, scratching the back of his neck awkwardly. 'It turns out I was right to be suspicious about that waste operative, but for the wrong reason. He'd had some trouble with a mad citizen and was trying to cover it up. He really does know nothing about the wheelie bin case.'

'I could've told you that,' HyJean muttered quietly.

'Well, at least that's one thing cleared up I guess,' said Suds. 'We didn't fare much better. Nothing happened with Mrs Mallard at half seven, but then at eight, Mr Nobble was um… kidnapped by a bin.'

'Kidnapped by a bin?' asked Flush as the squad all looked at each other with a look of confusion.

'Something pulled him into the bin,' explained Suds. 'And then it uh… it drove off.'

'Drove off? On its own?' asked the captain.

'Well presumably someone was driving it, either from inside or via remote control. I'd say remote control seems more likely, as there's not much room in those things,' HyJean surmised. 'We pursued it on foot the best we could, but it got away.'

'And what about the bin bags? Where did they go?' asked Faucet.

'Well, that's the strangest thing,' said Suds, choosing that moment to take a sip of water and prolong the suspense. 'When we got back, they were inside a wheelie bin outside their house.'

'Mrs Nobble said it just appeared there when she wasn't looking,' said HyJean.

'So, we're back to square one then,' the captain sighed.

'Not really, we know how they're being taken away now and that someone's probably piloting it remotely,' said Suds.

'Okay, square three then,' said the captain. 'And it'll be a week before they strike again. Any ideas where we go from here?'

The squad sat in silent thought for a moment, taking sips of water and scratching their heads, until finally Faucet broke the silence.

'What about Mrs Begonia's neighbour?' he suggested. 'She said he used to be a bin man, maybe he could have some insider knowledge?'

'Don't be ridiculous,' said the captain. 'If he's retired then he won't know anything.'

Faucet looked a little disappointed, but HyJean wasn't quite so quick to dismiss his suggestion.

'Actually, I think that's quite a good lead,' she said with a smile towards Faucet. 'It'd definitely be worth talking to him. Like Nelson said, he knows the area and he knows bins.'

'Well, you go and speak to him if you think he's that great,' said the captain like a schoolboy who'd just lost an argument.

'Do you want your disinfectant back?' HyJean replied with a raised eyebrow.

'Fine, I'll go,' the captain replied with a groan, like the schoolboy was now being forced to do extra chores.

'I'll come with you,' said Faucet keenly.

'Oh no, you've still got training to complete,' said the captain. 'You've been falling behind while you've been doing these jobs. I want to see the vacuum cleaner re-assembled and a thousand-word essay on the importance of toilet flushing on my desk before you leave tonight.'

Now it was Faucet's turn to groan like a disciplined teenager, letting out a groan that made Captain Clean feel a little better about his own situation.

💧💧

Captain Clean looked at the note with the scribbled address that Faucet had given him and then looked up to check the number on the door. He rang the doorbell and waited, staring at the smudge on the little pane of glass on the door and trying to ignore it. As the seconds passed, a desire burned inside him and eventually he gave in. He leaned in to discreetly breathe on the glass, but as he did, the door open and he found himself breathing into the face of an old lady.

'Can I help you?' she said as she moved her face in disgust and brushed him away.

'Oh, yes, sorry,' stuttered the captain, 'I'm from the Sanitary Squad.'

'Oh! Well, it's alright, I've got one of your team looking into it, thank you,' she said and began to close the door.

The captain stepped forward, pressing a hand against the door to hold it open, 'No, no, it's not about that. I'm looking for your neighbour.'

'Try the house next door, dear, that's where neighbours usually live,' said the old woman.

'No, I know that, but my colleague hasn't said which house he lives in, he's just given me your address' the captain explained. 'It's the former waste operative I'm looking for.'

'Waste operative? What are you talking about?' asked Mrs Begonia.

'Bin man,' the captain clarified. 'The former bin man.'

'Oh! You mean Mr Grudgely. He lives at 91, just on the left there,' she replied, pointing out the house.

'Brilliant, thank you,' said the captain. 'And uh, sorry again about the… y'know… breathing on you.'

'It's quite alright dear, lots of people struggle with introductions. Maybe just a hello next time though, hm?' she said with a sympathetic smile before closing the door.

Captain Clean took the opportunity to quickly clean the smudge off the glass, but was dismayed to find the smudge was on the other side of the glass. He cursed under his breath and contemplated ringing the bell again but resigned himself to leave it for now. He made his way around to the Mr Grudgely's house and rang the bell. He waited for a while, controlling himself and standing still, but there was no answer. He knocked on the door and even tried knocking the window. After a few minutes, he gave up and went back to Mrs Begonia's house. When she answered, she seemed a little surprised to see him back.

'He's not in,' said the captain.

'I know,' she said. 'He's never in on a Thursday morning.'

'Then why didn't you tell me that?' the captain asked in a frustrated tone.

'You never asked if he was in, you just asked where he lived,' she retorted in a similarly frustrated voice.

'Well, can you tell me anything about him?' the captain asked. 'You said he used to be a bin man; do you know why he left?'

'Ooh, I'm not sure,' said the old woman. 'It might've had something to do with all the complaints made about him.'

'Complaints? About him directly?' asked the captain.

'Yes, well he was always a bit standoffish with people, you see,' she explained. 'Didn't suffer fools and wasn't afraid to have a go back. I think that's why they got rid of him. But he's always been very pleasant with me.'

'I see, that's very interesting,' said the captain. 'One last thing, could I come inside for a moment?'

'What for?' asked Mrs Begonia, a little suspicious.

'Well… I'd just like to clean that smudge off your window,' he said, pointing out the mark on the glass.

'You cheeky sod, there's nothing wrong with my windows. Get out of it, go on,' she said, pushing him back and closing the door. As Captain Clean turned to leave, the letterbox flapped open and Mrs Begonia's voice shouted out, 'And pick some of that litter up on your way out!'

The captain picked up the sweet wrappers and put them in the bin a few yards away. As he deposited them, he looked at Mr Grudgely's house, then looked around to see if anyone was watching. There was something off about this neighbour, he could feel it. But he needed more evidence. He made his way over to the Herman household and knocked on their door. When they answered, he wasted no time in questioning them.

'Did you or your husband ever make a formal complaint about Mr Grudgely' he asked.

'Oh, Captain Clean, I wasn't expecting you. Would you like to come in?' Mrs Herman asked.

'Did you or your husband ever make a formal complaint about Mr Grudgely' the captain repeated in exactly the same tone.

'Um, I think we did, yes,' she nodded. 'Why? Has he said something?'

Captain Clean said nothing. He simply turned on his heels and walked away. Mrs Herman called after him, but he ignored her. He was onto something now. He asked did the same thing at another of the houses who had reported a kidnapping. They too had complained. The final victim too admitted that they had complained about Mr Grudgely in the past. It was all adding up now, the captain thought. He made his way back to Mr Grudgely's house and down the alley between the two houses. At the back, he was met with wooden gates and fences either side. Wishing he'd brought his ladder with him, he clumsily climbed up the gate and over the fence, landing with a thud on the other side. When he landed and turned around, he was only half surprised to see no less than four wheelie bins in the small back yard.

'Either he really gets through rubbish, or I'm on to something,' the captain muttered to himself. He opened the lids of one of the wheelie bins and looked inside. It was dark inside, but he could make out some wires and machinery at the bottom, including what looked like a hose pipe and a metal claw.

'Gotcha,' he said with a satisfied grin.

'I was thinking the same thing,' came a voice from behind. But before Captain Clean could turn to see who it was, he felt a blow to the back of his head, and everything went black as he slumped unconscious onto the bin.

💧💧

The next evening, Faucet was helping Flush into the Litterbug costume once again in the shower room when there was a knock at the door. HyJean stood in the doorway, looking a little worried.

'Hi boys, um… have either of you heard from Cap?' she asked. 'I've not seen him since he went off to speak to Mrs Begonia's neighbour, and I can't seem to get hold of him.'

'Not a sausage, sorry,' said Flush, the newspaper on his shoulders rustling as he shrugged.

'Does he usually go off the grid like this?' asked Faucet.

'Not really, he's too egotistical to stay quiet for too long,' HyJean replied, sound more than a little concerned.

'Tell you what, it's on our way, so we can drop you off in our taxi and you can find out what's going on,' said Flush.

'Thanks. I just need to do one thing first though,' said HyJean. She left the room and returned seconds later with a can of air freshener, which sprayed all over a surprised Flush. 'I'm not sharing a car with you smelling like that.'

'Aww man, that's part of the effect!' Flush groaned.

'I'll go let Suds know. Give us a shout when you're ready,' said HyJean as she left the room.

A short while later, the Litterbug was ready and the four grime fighters gathered outside the Filtham community centre waiting for a regular taxi, since The Driver refused to pick them up. This time they had the benefit of the ladder, which Faucet was carrying, to make the climb up to the window easier.

'You know what we need?' said Flush as they waited.

'A shower?' Suds suggested.

'No, a car,' said Flush. 'Then we wouldn't have to rely on The Driver or public transport all the time.'

'You mean like the Batmobile?' said Faucet excitedly.

'Exactly, all the best superheroes have their own vehicles,' Flush nodded. 'The Batmobile, Wonder Woman's invisible jet, the Teenage Mutant Ninja Turtles van.'

'So, we're on the same level as mutant turtles now?' chuckled Suds. 'Nice.'

'Forget it, there's not enough in the budget for a bicycle, let alone a van,' HyJean pointed out.

'And if there was, Cap would probably point out how bad for the environment they are,' added Suds.

'We could get an electric car,' suggested Faucet.

'Oh yeah, that'd be great,' said HyJean sarcastically. 'Halfway through chasing a criminal we have to pull over to recharge. And who's going to drive this car anyway? Can either of you drive?'

'Not legally,' Flush replied.

Faucet thought for a moment, 'You know, I can't remember.'

'Don't worry, we'll get a driverless car,' said Flush. 'They're all the rage now.'

'No, I don't trust them,' said Suds, shaking his head.

'Do you trust it more than Cap driving?' asked HyJean

'Good point,' said Suds.

The conversation continued in much the same fashion until the taxi arrived, and by the time it pulled up, they were all discussing the pitfalls of having a company helicopter. The taxi driver wound down his window to get a closer look at Flush. The others had gotten used to the sight of his litter-covered outfit, but the taxi driver, seeing it for the first time, was simultaneously astonished and baffled by it.

'Is this some kind of Lady Gaga fancy dress thing?' he asked.

'No, we're going to scare a kid to stop him littering,' Flush explained as he climbed into the passenger seat of the taxi.

'Oh… okay,' said the driver as he gave Flush another look of disbelief. 'Just make sure you take away anything that drops off.'

They set off on to their destination, with HyJean, Suds and Faucet squeezed into the back and the ladder across their laps and hanging out of the window. The driver constantly glanced across at Flush, taking in every piece of litter on the incredible costume.

'Excuse me, can you keep your eyes on the road please,' said HyJean, leaning forward and tapping the driver. 'If you want to look at litter, I can direct you to a particularly popular bin on Gilbreth Street.'

The driver apologised and stayed focused on the road for the rest of the journey. They dropped HyJean and Suds off on the main road just outside the cul-de-sac, and then continued down to the Throwett household. They paid the driver, giving him a generous tip to keep quiet about what he'd seen, and then they found themselves once again climbing into the back garden of their victim's house.

'I was so sure it was that room,' whispered Faucet, looking up at the window they'd climbed through the night before. 'I must've drawn it wrong. It was that one he sleeps in.'

He pointed to the window to the right of the one he'd thought was Keifer's bedroom, and they propped the ladder up against the wall.

'Okay, you go up first and open the window, I'll follow when you're in position,' said Flush.

Faucet climbed the ladder and was disappointed to find that this one was shut. It made sense, he thought. Given what had happened the night before, they probably wanted extra security. He had no tools to open it, but he had an idea. He pressed his fingers against the seam between the window and the and tensed his wrists. Water shot out against the slight gap and he felt it hit against something. He wiggled his fingers up and down and the pressure of the water managed to catch the locking mechanism. The handle moved with a little click and he was able to pull the window open, before looking down at Flush and giving a thumbs up.

'When did you learn to do that?' asked Flush in an excited whisper.

'About ten seconds ago,' Faucet whispered back.

He climbed inside the room and made his way carefully across the room, the moonlight highlighting the furniture and objects in the room. Flush then made his way up the ladder and awkwardly through the window, while Faucet took out his torch. They looked at each other and nodded. Faucet mouthed counting up to three and then shone the torch on the Litterbug.

'I am the litterbug!' boomed Flush once again. 'You shall pay for your littering!'

There was a loud scream from the bed that sounded worryingly familiar. Flush's eyes widened and Faucet shone the light on the bed to reveal Keifer's grandmother looking terrified. Fortunately, the torchlight blinded her and she covered her eyes as she continued to scream.

'Run!' cried Flush and they both darted across the room, out of the window and down the ladder, pushing the window shut as they left. They had just made it to the bottom of the ladder when they saw the bedroom light come on and heard the sounds of people rushing to the old woman's aid. Wasting no more time, they ran from the garden, carrying the ladder and jumping over the fence to hide in the trees behind the house.

'How does this keep happening?' asked an exasperated Faucet.

'I dunno,' said Flush, through heavy panting. 'Let's just get out of here.'

💧💧

Meanwhile, HyJean and Sergeant Suds were busy investigating their boss's disappearance. They surveyed the neighbour's house from behind the hedge in the front garden. The lights were off and there were no signs of movement.

'Looks like they're asleep, or out,' said HyJean.

'Reckon you could pick the lock on the front door?' asked Suds.

'Easily,' HyJean nodded. 'But I'm not going to.'

'What?' Suds replied in some surprise. 'Oh, come on. It's not like we're robbing the place. We just want to have a look around. And besides, Cap might be in trouble in there.'

'Yes, I know all that,' said HyJean with a roll of her eyes. 'I mean I'm not going to because we don't need to. The living room window is open.'

She pointed to the bay window on the house, and sure enough, one of the windows was still open just enough to fit a small rat if it had recently been on a diet. They crept up to the window and HyJean pulled it open, before giving Suds a smug look. He gave her a boost up and she climbed in through the window and into the living room, her feet landing on a side table, which acted as a step down into the room. The lights were off, so the room was lit only by the streetlamps outside. It was a typical living room, with a sofa, television and large fireplace. Even in the dark light it looked cosy and inviting. HyJean began to look around, but she suddenly winced with shock as she heard a crash behind her. She looked around and saw Suds, halfway through the window, with his leg stuck in a hole that he'd just made in the top of the side table.

'Sorry,' he mouthed.

HyJean let out a little groan and helped him into the room without damaging anything else. They quietly and carefully looked around the room, not really sure what they were looking for – perhaps some clues as to Captain Clean having been here? Some note on a scrap of paper about a kidnapping plot? A torch that they could use to see better? Sadly, they found none of these things, and as they moved into the kitchen, that room fared no better either. Everything looked frustratingly normal. But then, just as they were about to exit to the back garden, a light came on. They gasped and span around to see a large, shadowy figure behind them. The face was shrouded in the darkness of the hood of a long, black robe. One hand was hidden under the sleeve, but the other was clearly visible. It was pale white and bony, holding onto a scythe, with a long, wooden shaft and a rusted metal blade at the top, glistening slightly in the light. The two grime fighters let out a scream and HyJean quickly burst into a barrage of excuses and pleas.

'I'm sorry! We're not burglars! Please don't kill us! We were just lost and wandered in!' HyJean babbled.

Sergeant Suds, however, was more proactive, and ran towards the reaper, shouting at him wildly, 'You creep, you kidnapped our boss!'

He swung a punch at the man, who didn't seem to block it. Instead, he took the hit and stumbled back, dropping his scythe. As the man stumbled back against the wall, the hood of his robe fell down, revealing a young man with a bleeding nose.

'Wait… stop… who are you?' he asked frantically.

Suds grabbed him by the robe and pushed him back against the wall, lifting him up off his feet.

'We're from the Sanitary Squad,' growled Suds. 'And we're here to find our boss, Captain Clean.

'He came to talk to you yesterday and he's been missing since,' added HyJean from behind, dancing around on the spot trying to be seen behind Suds, unsure whether to help her fellow grime fighter or the man in the grim reaper costume.

'What are you talking about? Came to talk to me? Nobody's been to talk to me,' stuttered the man, who seemed genuinely confused and more than a little frightened.

'He said he was coming to talk to you about the recent kidnappings,' said Suds, still holding him firmly.

The man let out a little cry of pain and HyJean finally acted, rushing forward, trying to pull Suds off the whimpering reaper. 'Okay, Suds, I think we should let him go now.'

'I agree with her! Let me go!' cried the man.

'He said you used to a bin man, so you might know something,' Suds continued, ignoring HyJean tugging at his arms.

'A bin man? I never used to be a bin man,' the young man replied. 'I'm an accountant!'

'But… Mrs Begonia said… she said her neighbour…' HyJean said, momentarily letting go of Suds.

'That's Mr Grudgely, he lives two doors down,' the man explained.

There was a brief silence in which HyJean and Suds looked at each other awkwardly, then back to the terrified young man.

'Ah,' said Suds, slowly loosening his grip and letting the man slide back down so his feet were on the floor. 'I think we may have broken into the wrong house.'

Suds brushed the man down, as if trying to wipe off the pain and upset he had caused.

'I think you have,' said the man, pulling himself up.

'Then what are you dressed like this for?' asked Suds.

'I'm going out to a fancy dress party tonight,' the man explained. 'Or at least I was.'

'Well, not to worry. No harm done, eh?' said HyJean with an awkward chuckle as she tugged Suds arm as a signal to leave. Suds patted the man's chest and gave an apologetic smile, then they both swiftly left through the front door without another word.

'That was so embarrassing. That poor man,' said HyJean as they walked quickly down the garden path. 'Why did you hit him?'

'Did you not see his dirty great scythe?' asked Suds as they passed Mrs Begonia's house.

'Oh come on, I doubt he would've used it,' said HyJean as they made their way into the right neighbour's front garden.

They walked up the path and rang the doorbell. They waited for a minute or so, but there was no answer. HyJean peered through the window, but could not see any signs of light or movement. Meanwhile, Suds had spotted the alleyway at the side of the house. He walked down it and peered through a gap in the fence, through which he was just able to make out the row of wheelie bins. He eyed up the fence and gate to see if he could climb it and noticed a few scuff marks on the wooden fence. Inspecting it closer, he noticed a bit of yellow fibre that had stuck to the wood. It was the same shade of yellow as Captain Clean's microfibre cloth cape. He whistled to get HyJean's attention, but got no reply. He tried again, but still nothing. With a huff, he walked back down the alley to the garden, poking his head around the wall. He whistled again loudly.

'Oh, that's you,' said HyJean, looking up from the gnome she was holding. 'I thought there was an excited bird around here.'

'Whatever, just come on. I think I found out where Cap went,' he said, gesturing for her to follow him down the alley. He pointed out the marks on the fence and the small thread of fabric.

'Let's have a look inside, shall we?' said HyJean. She lifted her leg to get another boost from Suds, but her fellow grime fighter merely shoulder-barged the gate and smashed it open. She sighed as he continued through into the garden. 'That works too, I guess'

Their first course of action was to inspect the contents of the wheelie bins, inside which they saw the mechanics that had grabbed the victims. She leaned in close and took photos of the devices on her phone as evidence.

'So, this arm piece grabs them and pulls them in, but what's this box with the light on for?' she mused. 'There's a flashing light on it. Aha! This must be the signal for the remote control. So, he is controlling them remotely, but not from here. So where is he? Maybe we should try and get inside and look for-'

She was cut off by the sound of glass smashing behind her. She looked around and saw that Suds had knocked out a pane of glass from the window with his soap gun.

'Way ahead of you,' he said with a grin as he unlocked the back door and opened it.

'Mary's going to love you with all these repair bills,' HyJean said as she rolled her eyes and followed him inside.

They moved around the house, looking for anything that might give them more answers. The kitchen looked normal, as did the living room, but down a small corridor there was a door that was slightly ajar. HyJean opened it and saw a small study that could have been mistaken for a broom closet. The tiny room housed only a chair, desk and an old-looking laptop.

'Suds,' she called out in a loud whisper. 'Come see this.'

She sat down at the laptop and opened it up. She was surprised to find that it wasn't password protected, and she could access the files with great ease. As Suds joined her and looked over her shoulder at the screen, she pulled up a page that showed a map with several flashing red dots on it.

'It's the cul-de-sac, look,' she said, pointing out the circular road near three flashing red dots. 'These must be the three bins out back.'

'There's two more, look,' Suds said, pointing to a red dot higher up on the map. 'It's less than a mile away.'

'Maybe that's where he's keeping his latest victim,' said HyJean.

'And I bet you anything the other dot is Cap,' added Suds.

HyJean picked up the laptop and stood up. 'Let's go save our boss.'

The two grime fighters quickly made their way down the road, checking the map on the screen every now and then to make sure both that they were going in the right direction and that there were still two dots flashing. The night was dark and the streets were empty - it was a mugger's paradise. There was a certain eeriness to it, as the wind whistled softly and an owl hooted in the distance, which was odd because owls weren't usually found in suburban streets like these. It may well have been a different bird, imitating the cry of the owl, or a human with a very unusual choice of ringtone. Sergeant Suds contemplated all of this as he directed HyJean over a patch of well-trodden grass that led to a set of storage facilities.

'Oh great, now we've got to figure out which of these boxes he's in. It's like Deal or No Deal,' groaned Suds.

'And you're no Noel Edmonds,' muttered HyJean as she walked along bent over, scanning the rows of metal shutters for any signs of light or movement.

'Have you tried calling his phone?' Suds asked.

'Noel Edmonds? I don't have his number,' said HyJean. 'Besides, what's he going to do?'

'No, I mean Cap's phone,' Suds clarified.

'No point, he never has his phone on him,' said HyJean, but a sudden thought made her stop dead in her tracks. 'But we could call Mr Grudgely'

'How? We don't know his number,' Suds replied, looking confused.

'Hm, if only he had a computer to store that kind of information on,' said HyJean, walking back to Suds and handing him the laptop to hold, using his hands like a makeshift desk. She tapped away and soon enough she'd found the number they needed. She took her phone out of a pouch on her utility belt and dialled.

'What are you going to say?' asked Suds. 'We're here to foil your plan but could you give us some directions?'

'Shh,' HyJean said, holding up a finger.

'Hello,' came the voice of Mr Grudgely, although since they'd never met, HyJean had to assume it was the right voice.

'Hello, is that Mr Grudgely,' she whispered quietly. Suds frowned, wondering why she was being so secretive.

'Hello, who's this?' Mr Grudgely said. As soon as he started speaking, HyJean put the phone to her chest and looked around, hoping to hear his voice coming from one of the storage units, but she heard nothing.

'Hello, is that Mr Grudgely' she repeated in the same muted voice.

Mr Grudgely said something down the phone, which she didn't hear as she listened.

'I'm calling about your pension,' she said, still quietly muttering.

'What? Speak up! I can't hear you!' Mr Grudgely said loudly. This time HyJean was able to pick up roughly where the voice was coming from. She pointed down a row and led Suds down there.

'I'm sorry mister csshkrsshk I can't quite pssshkrsh you, there seems to be csshkrsshk connection,' she said, this time louder so he could hear her. This confused Suds even further, but Mr Grudgely's reply made things very apparent.

'Ugh, I can't hear you, there's a bad connection,' he replied in a very frustrated tone. 'Hang on, I'll come outside.'

Seconds later they saw one of the shutters in the distance rising up and a shadowy figure stepping out.

'There! Go get him,' HyJean said triumphantly.

Suds ran and was close enough that Mr Grudgely had very little time to react when he noticed Suds running towards him and aiming his soap gun. He turned to run back inside his unit, but Suds fired and a large blob of pink gloop landed just in front of his feet, causing him to slip as his foot landed. He fell down face first and Suds was quick to jump on him and pin him to the ground. HyJean meanwhile ran inside the unit and saw two men sat on chairs with bags over their head. Both looked weak and beaten, but only one was wearing a long yellow cape and marigold gloves.

'Captain!' HyJean exclaimed as she rushed over and took the bag off his head.

'HyJean!' he cried weakly. His face was covered in several cuts and bruises, making his smile of relief somewhat painful. 'I knew you'd find me.'

'I'm here too y'know!' came a sudden voice from the other chair. HyJean had forgotten all about the other man.

'Oops, sorry,' she said as she reached over and took the bag off his head.

'Thank you, now somebody call the police!' the other victim snapped.

'There's no need for that, I'm already here!' came a confident voice from behind that the grime fighters recognised immediately. They all turned and saw the shutter on one of the storage units opposite slowly and dramatically rise up, revealing a pair of shiny black shoes, then a pair of smart black trousers, and then… it stopped. The door had jammed with a worrying clunk, stopping at waist height.

'Bloody thing,' came the echoing voice from behind. 'Keeps on licking… uh, sticking.'

They watched as Officer Sidney Down wrestled with the shutter, but to no avail. In the end, he resorted to leaning back and trying to squeeze his portly body underneath the door limbo style. When that didn't work, he retreated and tried again, this time bending forwards. There was a clang as he hit his head off the shutter, at which the grime fighters winced. Finally, the familiar ginger-bearded police officer appeared, standing up straight and brushing himself down.

'Not quite the entrance I was hoping for, but still. Here I am,' he said, patting the metal shutter, which clicked and then rolled back down shut with a rapid drop, making the police officer jump a little. Although Officer Down would have been none of their first choices for an authority figure to be conveniently present, they were still somewhat grateful to have him there. HyJean, the most affable of the group, stepped forward.

'Officer Down, this man is the one who has been kidnapping people in wheelie bins and abusing them,' she explained, pointing to Mr Grudgely.

'The what?' Officer Down asked, looking a little confused.

'He's the one… the kidnappings on Whitehouse Way, with the wheelie bins… it's been all over the local news,' she said, trying to jog his memory.

'Nope, sorry,' the officer shrugged. 'I've been on holiday for a few weeks, you see. I've just got back and came here to pick up my scooter. It was a nice break though. I went to heaven… uh, Devon. Lovely place, lots of nice peaches-'

'Okay, okay,' HyJean said, interrupting him before he could tell them any more about his holiday, which he was clearly about to do. 'Well anyway, we just need you to arrest him. You'll find all the evidence in that lockup and on his computer.'

'Evidence for what?' asked Officer Down.

'For the kidnappings, you moron!' shouted Suds, who had become increasingly irritated by Officer Down's lack of understanding.

'Oh, sorry,' Officer down chuckled. 'I thought you were on about Devon. I was going to say, there was no trouble there. I mean I paid £6 for an ice cream, but I don't think we can arrest anyone for-'

'Just come and cuff him up before I shove you in a wheelie bin,' Suds grunted.

'I've got one spare in there,' said Mr Grudgely, gesturing to his storage unit.

'Don't tempt me,' Suds muttered.

'Right yes, I'll just get my… oh, where are they,' said Officer Down, patting his jacket and fumbling around in his pockets, looking for his handcuffs. 'Oh bother, I think I left them in there.'

He turned back towards his storage unit and crouched down, trying to lift the shutter back up. The door had clearly become just as fed up with its owner as the people around, as it put up quite the fight to be opened.

'Come and give me a hand will you,' the officer asked with a clear hint of desperation in his voice.

HyJean rolled her eyes and walked over to the storage unit, turning the key that the absent-minded officer had left in the lock on the wall next to the shutter and pressing a button that made the shutter slowly rise all the way up.

'Oh, would you look at that,' Officer Down chuckled. 'It's alternated… uh, automated.'

They retrieved the handcuffs, and the grime fighters were quite relieved when Mr Grudgely was finally apprehended. Mr Grudgely himself was obviously not as relieved, but criminals are rarely pleased when they are being arrested. Although some are, of course, as they commit crimes with the intention of being caught and becoming infamous, but that's more for things like murder or robbery, not kidnapping people in wheelie bins. The police were called (once Officer Down remembered the number) and soon Mr Grudgely was being driven away to a nice warm cell. Well, a nice cell. Well, a cell. Despite Captain Clean's many protests, the living conditions in Rotenhell Prison were not the most hospitable. If they were, maybe more criminals would be relieved to be arrested.

♦ ♦

The following day, the squad arrived at Whitehouse Way to inform the residents who the culprit was behind the kidnappings and to let them know that he had been arrested. In a police interview, Mr Grudgely had revealed that he had suffered years of complaints from the cul-de-sac while he had been working as a waste operative and had spent his retirement planning a scheme to get revenge on those who had been so petty and unforgiving.

'I guess we do complain a lot,' said Mrs Herman, looking slightly ashamed as she stood amongst the small crowd of locals that had been gathered to hear the news in the middle of the cul-de-sac.

'But they still don't take all my rubbish,' an old lady in the crowd grumbled.

'It's probably because you pile all the bags up in your back garden instead of putting it in the wheelie bin out front,' an unseen voice called out.

'I can't be carting that big heavy thing back and forth every week,' the lady protested. 'I've got arthritis in my legs and my hands.'

'Then maybe you should ask someone to help you,' HyJean suggested.

'I'll help you, Mrs Pottage,' said a younger woman in the crowd.

'Oh no, I don't want her helping me,' Mrs Pottage grumbled, 'She'll be rifling through my bins trying to find my pension cheques.'

'How dare you!' the woman shouted. 'Cheeky old hag, no wonder nobody wants to help you.'

'Who are you calling an old hag, you nosey mare?' Mrs Pottage retorted.

While the neighbours argued and Captain Clean tried in vain to defuse the tension, Mrs Begonia came tottering down the driveway and over to the squad. Flush noticed her and gave Faucet a nudge. When she got to them, Faucet was quick to react.

'Don't worry Mrs Begonia, we're still working on your case,' he said in a hurried voice. 'There's just been a few complications that we-'

'No, no, it's okay,' Mrs Begonia interrupted. 'It's all sorted now.'

'It is?' asked Faucet and Flush in a surprised unison.

'Yes, the boy's mother came around this morning and told me that her mother, who had been staying in her grandson's bed, had been scared half to death by something in the night. They moved her to a sofa bed in the spare room and, would you believe it, the same thing happened again!' she explained. 'And when she found out the boy had been littering, the grandmother swore she'd beat him to a pulp if he ever littered again. He's been round and apologised and everything,'

'Oh,' said Faucet. 'Well, I guess that's good then.'

'I don't know what you boys did, but I'm very grateful,' Mrs Begonia said with a warm smile. 'Thank you, both.'

She patted them both on the arm and gave them both £5 each for their trouble, before returning to her home with a noticeable spring in her step. Flush and Faucet smiled at each other, satisfied with their work, but also stunned at how it had resolved itself.

'Nice work, you two,' said HyJean, who had overheard the conversation.

'Never doubted you for a moment,' added Captain Clean.

HyJean gave him a look of resentment, but then her eyes grew wide and a look of slight panic covered her face as she spotted someone over the captain's shoulder.

'Oi, you! I want a word with you!' shouted Mrs Begonia's other neighbour, who still had a bandaged nose from where Suds had punched him.

'Oh crap,' HyJean muttered, tugging Sergeant Suds' arm and pointing out the angry neighbour.

'Quick, leg it!' Suds whispered in a panic, and the two grime fighters ran off down the road and out of the cul-de-sac.

A PENNY WELL SPENT

Inside Filtham community centre, in a little office tucked away on the second floor, Mary Goldman was busy putting through a purchase order for some new gloves for Captain Clean, who had burnt his last pair by using them to take a pizza out of the oven. His gloves weren't insulated or anything like that, he just believed that they imbued him with powers and abilities far beyond those of mortal men. As he repeatedly found out the hard way: they did not.

Mary's work was interrupted as the phone suddenly rang in the disruptive way that phones always do when you're in the middle of something that you're trying really hard to concentrate on. Mary answered it before the phone had chance to reach three rings and, in her usual polite tone, said, 'Hello, Sanitary Squad, Mary speaking. How can I help?'

'Hello, my name is Tanya' said a foreign sounding woman on the other end of the phone whose name clearly wasn't Tanya. 'I'm calling from Injury Advice Helpline about an accident you or your partner were involved in at work.'

'Okay, you may have to be a little more specific,' Mary said, not realising the type of call this was.

'Was it you or your husband who was involved in the accident?' the woman on the phone asked, feeling a slight tingle of delight that her caller had not immediately dismissed her.

'It was probably my husband, Mick. He's got quite a dangerous job,' Mary explained.

'What job does he do madam?' asked Tanya.

'He's a grime fighter.'

'Crime writer?'

'No, GRIME. With a G. He's a grime… FIGHTER. He fights grime, you see,' Mary explained.

'He fights grime?' Tanya repeated slowly.

'Yes.'

'Oh, um… okay,' said the woman on the phone. She'd heard many different job titles in her time, but grime fighter was a new one on her, and it threw her slightly. Still, sticking to the script, she continued. 'Do you remember when the accident took place?'

'Ooh, I'm not sure. He gets into accidents all the time. I'll go and ask him. Hold on a minute.'

Mary pressed a button on the phone and a low-quality recording of When I'm Cleaning Windows played over the phone while she went and asked her husband, Sergeant Suds, if he'd been in an accident recently. When she returned, she picked the phone up and her voice changed to a deeper, more serious tone. The room around her seemed to darken, as if the lights had picked up on the change of atmosphere. Even the flies outside the window stopped buzzing to hear what was about to go down.

'Right, listen dear. I don't know who you are. I don't know what you want. If you are looking for money, I can tell you we're funded by the council, so we're skint. But what we do have is a very particular set of cleaning solutions that we've acquired over a very long purchase order. Cleaning solutions that make us a nightmare for stains like you. If you hang up and never call back again, that'll be the end of it. We will not look for you, we will not pursue you. But if you call back again, we will look for you, we will find you, and we will make you drink bleach.'

'Y-yes… yes, I understand… I'm sorry!' the woman cried, before quickly hanging up. Mary put the phone down and looked up at the lights, two bulbs of which had gone out.

She tutted. 'We really need to get them sorted out.'

💧💧

'Today's lesson is puns,' said Captain Clean to his gang of grime fighters, who were all sat around the table in the centre of the base. 'A good pun can be as effective as any weapon. Puns are our bread and butter; without them we'd be toast. Today we're going to look at attack puns. When you hit someone, you should be able to deliver a witty remark along with your attack to increase the impact. For example, just before you punch a postman, you might say "Special delivery." This also gives them a bit of a laugh just before they're hit, maintaining our friendly image. So, to start off, I'm going to give you each a profession and you think of a witty phrase you could use when attacking them. Let's start with Flush. A waiter, go!'

'Order up!' Flush replied quickly. As the joker of the squad, he was always ready with a quippy response.

'Very good. Faucet, a pirate, go!'

'Um… Polly want a cracker?' he said without a trace of confidence.

'Needs work. HyJean, a paramedic, go!'

'Why am I hitting a paramedic?' she asked.

'No questions,' the captain replied, holding his hands up in an X shape to emphasise his point. 'A paramedic, go!'

'Oh, I don't know, uh... clear.'

'Clear?' asked a confused captain.

'Yeah, you know... the defibrillators,' she explained, miming using a pair of defibrillators.

'I haven't got time for pop music,' the captain said with a roll of his eyes, 'let's just move on.'

HyJean turned to the others with a frustrated look, and they gave her sympathetic smiles.

'Okay, so now you've got your puns, you need to think about delivery,' continued Captain Clean. 'It is important to remember that you must never laugh at your own pun. They may be hilarious – except for HyJean's, which was just confusing – but for maximum impact, you must deliver them with a straight face. The easiest way to do this is to imagine something sad. Faucet and Suds, can I borrow you?'

Faucet and Sergeant Suds got up and the captain positioned the two of them facing each other. He handed Suds a pad to hold up and then explained the exercise.

'Okay, so Faucet, you're going to throw punches at Mick, and to get you to keep a straight face, I will call out some sad affirmations. Right, both ready? Okay, Faucet, let's see your punch. Go!'

Faucet wasted no time and threw a punch at Suds's face, hitting him square in the jaw. Suds was tough and merely recoiled a little, but then reacted instinctively and threw a punch back at Faucet, knocking him to the floor.

'Stop! Stop!' the captain cried as he stood between them. 'I meant hit the pad, Faucet! What did you think he was holding the pad was for?'

'Oh crap, sorry Mr Goldman,' said Faucet, realising what he'd done as he pulled himself up. 'I don't know, I... I thought it was some kind of fashion accessory.'

'Never mind, sit down,' the captain said, waving him away. 'Flush, get up here.'

As Flush got up to face Suds, HyJean helped Faucet back to his seat and checked he was okay.

Upon Captain Clean's command, Flush started throwing punches at the pad. He wasn't the best built of the group, but he was agile and had a pretty strong punch that stood him in good stead. After a few hits, the captain started his heckling.

'Your phone battery has died!' he shouted.

Flush tutted and continued punching.

'Your favourite TV show has just been cancelled!' the captain continued.

'Aww man,' Flush groaned, now punching with a disappointed look on his face.

'Good, now imagine your cat is dying!'

'I don't have a cat,' replied Flush as he almost clipped Suds himself with an impressive right hook.

'Imagine you do have a cat!' the captain growled.

'Okay… Oh no, the cat's dead! Oh my god! Oh fluffy!'

'Okay, that's good. Tone it down a bit though,' said the captain, holding up a hand

'Oh poor fluffy! You were such a kind cat! Why has this terrible fate befallen you? WHY! Take me instead!'

'Alright stop,' said the captain, stopping Flush who by this point was now clutching the air with his fists, giving a dramatic performance that was almost Oscar worthy. 'That was a bit over the top.'

'Sorry,' said Flush. 'I just got into it and now I can't stop thinking about the poor cat.'

'It's fine, just go and sit down,' the captain replied, dismissing him.

Flush returned to his seat, sobbing a little. HyJean put a comforting arm around him and tried to remind him that the cat wasn't real and had never even existed.

'It never existed? Oh god it gets worse!' Flush bawled. 'He was never born and now somehow he's dying!'

💧💧

As Captain Clean and Suds were packing away the table of props that had been used during the lesson to demonstrate how objects could inspire puns, one of the computer screens on HyJean's desk started flashing. Flush was the first to notice it.

'Hey guys, it's a video call from Dumbdale,' he pointed out.

Captain Clean and HyJean went over to the desk and accepted the call. Chief Inspector Dovedale's haggard face appeared on the screen, jittery at first as the connection was unstable.

'Hello inspector,' said the captain.

Chief Inspector Dovedale mouthed something, but they couldn't hear him.

'Hold on inspector,' said the captain, 'we can't hear you.'

'Probably for the best,' muttered Suds in the background, giving a little smirk to Flush who stifled a laugh.

HyJean fiddled with the computer and pressed a few random keys, hoping that she'd accidentally stumble upon the right key to fix it, as most people do when trying to solve a technical issue.

'We need to get this fixed,' whispered the captain. 'We can't keep having this happen.'

After the traditional back and forth routine of asking if they could hear each other and trying the same troubleshooting steps several times, HyJean eventually got it sorted.

'What's the problem inspector?' asked the captain.

'I think my microphone was muted,' he replied.

'No, I mean why are you calling?' asked captain, trying his best to not sound like somebody trying to get information out of a senile elderly relative.

'Oh right, yes.' He cleared his throat. 'What do you know about the council's toilets?'

'I avoid them at all costs, they're filthy,' the captain admitted.

'Not quite what I meant,' groaned the inspector. 'Every year the council puts out a tender for a company to manage their sanitation. The company that's been the provider for the past two years, what was their name… Trev's Toilets, has mysteriously gone out of business overnight. The only other two companies left are Bathrooms R Us 4 U and Crapp Toilets, but Crapp is refusing to bid for the tender. Probably because of what happened last time.'

'What happened last time?' Faucet asked Suds.

'He installed loads of new toilets that turned out to be faulty,' Suds explained. 'Big controversy, his business almost went bankrupt.'

'This all seems very fishy,' continued the inspector. 'The council have asked me to look into it, just to make sure nothing dodgy is going on, but honestly, I think this is more your department. Can you do a bit of digging, see what you can find?'

'Of course, I'll look into it right away,' nodded HyJean as she made a note of the names he'd mentioned.

'This Trev's Toilets, have you contacted them?' she asked as she wrote.

'We've tried,' the inspector replied with a sigh. 'Can't get hold of them. Their website's down and you can't find their toilets anywhere, so we've got nothing to go on.'

HyJean quickly muted the call and the squad all looked away from the camera as they let out a laugh in unison. Once they'd settled themselves, she unmuted and resumed the call.

'Sorry about that, the connection went,' she lied.

'Never mind,' said the chief inspector.

Meanwhile, just off screen, someone handed the inspector a note scribbled on a piece of paper. The inspector read it and looked back up to the camera.

'Also, I've just been informed that there's an old man in a silly costume, calling himself the Commode Dragon, riding around on a commode throwing bedpans at people and spraying them with what we can only hope is yellow coloured water. I don't suppose you could look into that as well, could you?'

'Of course, Inspector,' Captain Clean nodded. 'Leave it to us.'

'Thank you, Mr Clean.'

They ended the video call and before the captain could correct him. As he turned around to address the team, Flush shouted 'Bagsy the old guy!'

He gave Faucet a nudge and he too volunteered to deal with the old man.

'Fine,' said Captain Clean with a slight sigh. 'You go deal with him. But if Faucet's going out as part of the squad, he'll need to start wearing a mask.'

The captain opened a nearby drawer and took out a generic-looking blue domino superhero mask that he'd bought as a job lot from a fancy dress shop when it was closing down. He handed it to Faucet as though it were some grand prize he'd just won. 'We'll get you a proper one made, but you can use this for now.'

'A mask?' Faucet asked took the mask and inspected it. 'Why do I need a mask?'

'To conceal your identity,' the captain explained.

'Okay, but… I have no identity. Even I don't know where I'm from or who I really am,' Faucet replied.

'Well, that's true, but what if you develop friendships or relationships outside of work, you won't want them being targeted, will you?' the captain argued. 'And we don't want people knowing you're associated with us, because then that puts our family and friends at risk. You've got to think about more than just yourself, Faucet.'

'Yeah, I guess you're right,' said Faucet. 'But how is this meant to hide my identity?'

'Trust me, put this on and nobody will recognise you,' the captain explained.

'Really? With just my eyes covered?' asked an incredulous Faucet. 'Won't they recognise my voice?'

'Nope. The mask gives you total anonymity,' the captain nodded. 'It's a very strange phemon… phemomom… it's a very strange thing that happens.'

'Alright, works for me,' Faucet shrugged as he put the mask on and admired himself in a mirror before leaving.

'Now, let's if we can track down this Trev's Toilets guy,' said Captain Clean, turning back to HyJean. 'Interesting name, that, Trev. I wonder what it means. Could be some foreign word that might give us a clue. I'm thinking maybe Russian… or possibly Swedish.'

'It's short for Trevor,' HyJean said dryly as she got to work locating the eponymous toilet retailer.

💧💧

Filtham City Retirement Home was home to many of the city's older generation. Their children were the type of people to chuck their parents in a home out of convenience, so they had more time to do important things like go to football matches and watch reality television. The old folk were secretly quite happy with this arrangement though, as they were fed up with their children's inane chatter about cancelled celebrities and air fryers, neither of which they really cared about nor understood. And besides, the retirement home was a nice enough place. The staff were friendly and the meals were hot, and on a Saturday night they'd play bingo, which was a popular favourite. Everyone enjoyed hearing ex-bingo caller Mr Riley – they always called him that because he was very formal and never responded to his forename because he'd forgotten it was his – do his bingo calls. He'd always mix it up, so one call might be "3 and 4, 34" but occasionally he'd throw in "5 and 6, 11" which always kept them on their toes. The 80s were a particularly fun set, as he would always describe them as "One fat lady and one thin lady, 81" or "One fat lady and her pet duck, 82". And if he ever pulled out the number 90, he'd say, "Top of the house?" and they'd all shout back, "The chimney!" Nobody ever tired of the same old jokes, except a woman called Maude who had once tried to steal the 90 ball in a daring Mission Impossible style heist, but her plan was scuppered when Frank, who was wheeling her through on a hoist that she dangled from, hurt his back and had to go sit down, which lead to him falling asleep and leaving her dangling there in a black jumpsuit and balaclava overnight. Despite all the fun of the home, some longed for more adventure, including one old man who had asked his son for a dragon costume for his birthday and decided to cause a bit of mischief.

'See, you've got to know which cases to pick,' Flush told Faucet as they made their way to Subplot Street, where the Commode Dragon had last been spotted. 'This old guy will be a piece of cake. Whereas the toilet bloke will be a lot of faffing about, going undercover, creating an alias, interrogating him… it's just too much work.'

'True. But surely the big jobs are more rewarding afterwards?' Faucet asked.

'I guess,' Flush replied with a half-hearted shrug.

'I don't know if I'm ready for this, y'know,' said Faucet. 'I still haven't had much training. Mr Cane has had me cleaning toilets and spraying things, and I've just started karate lessons, but that's about it.'

'Hm, yeah, you might need a bit more than that. I know, why don't you run up those steps over there?' Flush suggested, pointing to a large set of steps leading up to an important-looking building.

'Why?' asked Faucet as he eyed up the steps.

'We can get HyJean to edit it and put the Rocky music over the top and when you watch it back it'll feel like you've had loads of training.'

'I mean, that does sound fun. And there's no sign of the dragon guy,' Faucet said, eyeing up the steps. 'Okay, let's do it.'

They headed over to the concrete staircase and Faucet looked up, counting about thirty steps at least. He psyched himself up and then ran up to the top, turning on the spot and running back down again. By the time he reached Flush, he was panting breathlessly.

'Jeez, you really are out of shape,' said Flush. 'Did Cap not do a physical before you joined?'

'Nope. He kinda… skipped a lot of… things,' Faucet replied through heavy breaths.

'Typical,' Flush said with a roll of his eyes. 'C'mon, let's go find this old man. Maybe you can race him instead. You never know, you might win if he's on foot.'

They walked a little farther down the road and suddenly spotted the old man they were there to find, careering down the road on his pimped-out commode. He was dressed in a red jumpsuit that was a size or two too big for him and a dragon mask that enveloped his wrinkly face behind a set of foam teeth. His commode was a little more impressive. He had created a steering mechanism, added some sort of engine on the back that propelled him forward and stuck some cardboard flames and dragon-scales onto the sides. Despite the mischief it had been created for, the two grime fighters had to admit it was pretty cool.

'There he is,' said Flush. 'Right, you slow him down with your hose pipe hands and I'll lasso him.'

Faucet nodded and got into place. He was still relatively new to using his powers, but he'd been practicing and was a little more confident. As the old man sped towards them, Faucet jumped out in front of it and sprayed a jet of water from each hand at the commode, soaking the man and causing him to fall back into the seat and let go of the controls, bringing the commode to a halt. Meanwhile, Flush tied his toilet chain whip into a lasso, swung it around above his head like a modern-day cowboy and flung it over the dragon-themed man, pulling him off his vehicle and onto the ground. The old man stumbled to his feet in a dizzy confusion and from seemingly out of nowhere he pulled out a bedpan and threw it at Faucet. It bounced off his head with a clunk and he let out a whine of pain that made him sound less like a grime fighter and more like a young child that had been poked by his bratty younger sister.

'I am… the Commode… Dragon!' he shouted in a frail, croaky voice, pausing between words to catch his breathe. 'Prepare… to meet… your doom.'

'The game's up old Dragon,' said Flush, humouring the man's senile delusions, 'we're here to put a stop to your reign of terror.'

'Huh? Speak up boy,' said the old man, whose dragon powers clearly didn't include good hearing.

'He said we're here to stop you!' shouted Faucet moodily, still rubbing his head.

The old man looked at them, still none the wiser what either of them had said. Faucet turned to Flush and, remembering what they'd learnt that morning, suggested he try a pun. Flush was excited by the idea and, as loudly as he could, he yelled at the man, 'We'll be dragon you off to jail now!'

The old man definitely heard this, and upon hearing the pun – if you could call it that - he promptly clutched his chest in shock and keeled over, collapsing on the floor in front of them like a sack of gone-off potatoes.

'I did it!' cried Flush. 'It worked! My pun actually disabled him!'

'Dude, I think he's having a heart attack,' Faucet replied, looking down at the man writhing slightly on the floor.

'No, it was my pun,' Flush insisted. 'They're more effective than we realised.'

'No seriously, it looks like he's dying,' Faucet said, giving the man a little nudge with his foot.

Faucet was right. The old man's afternoon of tyranny and the sudden barrage of attacks from the two grime fighters had apparently taken its toll, and Flush's outburst had seemingly finished him off.

💧💧

After a morning of research and phone calls, Captain Clean and HyJean had been able to find someone who knew where Trevor of Trev's Toilets was. He'd abandoned his house and was currently staying with his wife and kids at his sister's house on the outskirts of the city. It had taken some convincing, but he'd finally agreed to speak to them. He sat nervously in an armchair, a number of bruises on his face and more on his body that nobody could see but everyone knew were there from the way he winced every time he moved.

'Thank you for speaking to us, Trevor,' HyJean said as she sat down on the sofa. Captain Clean preferred to stand, as he'd spotted a tiny ketchup stain on one of the cushions and could not be sure that it was the only one.

'Trevor, we'd like to know why you closed down your business so quickly,' asked the captain as he discreetly wiped a gloved finger across a side cabinet to check for dust.

Trevor bit his lip, a little unsure whether he could trust these people with the truth. They weren't exactly dressed like people he would naturally trust. People he could trust usually wore a suit and tie, or a nice floral dress - though never at the same time. Well, except once. But he later found out she wasn't a lawyer at all.

'Don't worry, you can trust us,' HyJean reassured him, as if she had read his mind. She did not possess mind-reading powers, but women often have a way of reading emotions that comes across like a mystical intuition in situations like these. 'We're here to help.'

'And if you don't tell us, we'll have you arrested and you can tell the police,' the captain added.

This made Trevor even more nervous, but HyJean gave her colleague a furious glare and calmed Trevor down.

'I… I had to,' he said, letting out a deep sigh, as if he'd been dying to tell someone his story for days. 'He forced me to.'

'Who forced you?' asked HyJean, leaning in and looking sympathetic.

'Bog,' Trevor replied quite dramatically, and sat still waiting for a response that didn't come. Captain Clean and HyJean just looked nonplussed. Sensing they didn't know who he was referring to, Trevor quickly added, 'I mean Walter Crapp.'

'Walter Crapp?' Captain Clean repeated in the shocked tone that Trevor had expected the first time around. 'But why?'

'I don't know,' admitted Trevor. 'He came round in this weird porcelain suit of armour, threatening me. He tried to buy me out, but I refused because his offer wasn't even half of what the company was worth. He trashed the place and beat me up. Said if I didn't take the offer and dissolve the company, he'd come after my family. I had to do it.'

'Why didn't you go to the police?' asked HyJean.

'He said if I told anyone or went to the cops then he'd have me killed.'

'But why would Crapp want you gone? And why now?' the captain asked the room as he paced its floor.

'To try and win the council tender?' suggested HyJean.

'But Dovedale said he's not bidding,' the captain reminded her. 'So what would be the point?'

'Did he say anything to you? Like why he wanted you gone or what he's planning?' HyJean asked.

'Not a sausage. Not even a chipolata,' Trevor replied sadly. 'I figured he just wanted to get rid of the competition.'

'And does he know where you are now?' the captain asked.

'I sure hope not,' Trevor said, with a slightly worried expression.

'Well don't worry,' said HyJean, standing to her feet. 'We'll make sure he doesn't find you and we'll investigate to find out what he's up to and get him put away so you can start your business back up again.'

'Oh, I'm not bothered about that,' said Trevor, smiling for the first time since they'd arrived. 'It's given me an opportunity to pursue my real passion – knitting jumpers for mice.'

He held up an example of one of his tiny jumpers, and HyJean and Captain Clean shared a bemused look, before moving a little quicker towards the door.

'Uh… right. Well, that's good then. One more thing,' Captain Clean said, pausing at the door. 'You called him Bog earlier. Is that a nickname or something?'

'Yeah, that's what we used to call him, because his toilets were cheap and nasty,' Trevor explained. 'Bog standard bogs, we called them. The name just stuck.'

'Interesting,' the captain mused.

As they left the house and reached the end of the driveway, HyJean turned to the captain. 'I think we should pay a visit to the bog.'

'Why didn't you go before we left?' he asked, before suddenly realising what he meant. 'Oh, I see. Yes, I think that's a good idea.'

'But we can't go like this,' said HyJean, gesturing to their outfits. 'He'll know we're onto him. We've got to be a bit more discreet with this one, he sounds quite dangerous.'

'You're right,' said the captain. 'Luckily for us, I've got something in mind that I think will work.'

The Commode Dragon still lay on the floor on Subplot Street. He'd stopped writhing about now, which the grime fighters were equal parts relieved and concerned about, but he still looked to be breathing, so he wasn't dead.

'What are we going to do?' asked Faucet nervously.

'Uh... I don't know,' said Flush. 'Haven't you done the medical training at the hospital?'

'No. So far I've only done how to fight bad guys, not save them.'

'Ah, okay.'

'What about you? Didn't you go on the course?'

'I did, but... well, I fell asleep.'

'You fell asleep during medical training?'

'Hey, I'd been out drinking the night before and it was so boring! Except for the part where I got to do mouth-to-mouth on the bird sat next to me. Boy, that was fun. Until the teacher told me I was supposed to be doing it on the dummy.'

'So now what do we do? Should we call an ambulance?'

'Nah, that'll take too long. I'll call The Driver.'

'Why, do you think he'll know how to save him?'

'No, so he can drive us to the hospital,' Flush said as he took out his phone.

'Oh yeah, duh. Sorry, I'm kinda panicking right now,' Faucet said, looking down at the old man lying on the floor. 'Jeez, my first proper mission and we've already screwed it up by nearly killing a guy.'

'Hey, what's this "we" business?' asked Flush.

'Yeah, you're right,' said Faucet. 'You screwed it up. I was just being polite.'

Flush called the Driver, who said he'd be there as soon as he could. The two grime fighters stood looking over the decrepit dragon. They watched in silence for a while, tensing up every time he exhaled, wondering if it was his last breath, and relaxing when he breathed in again.

'I'm not sure about taking him to the hospital,' Faucet said. 'What if they refuse to treat him?'

'Why would they do that?' asked Flush.

'He's dressed as a super villain and he's been causing trouble all day.'

'That's a point. What do you think we should do?'

'Well, I was thinking we should take his suit off. It's not good for someone his age to be in wet clothes either.'

They knelt down beside the old man and stripped him of his costume. They were surprised to find under the overall that the man was wearing pink frilly knickers.

'What the... is he wearing women's underwear?' asked Faucet.

'Yeah,' said Flush. 'How bizarre.'

'But why?'

'Well, it's more comfortable isn't it.'

Faucet gave Flush a curious look. His colleague often said things that made Faucet question his sanity, and he never really knew whether to take Flush seriously or not.

'I mean I assume it is... I wouldn't know,' he added quickly.

'Anyway, what are we going to do? We can't take him to the hospital naked in women's knickers. That'd be embarrassing if he woke up.'

They thought for a while, both of them trying not to stare at the pink underwear. Not because they were embarrassed by it, but because both of them were starting to think if an old man like this could feel free enough to wear them, then maybe it was okay and they could too. And if he was wearing them, there had to be a reason. Were they more comfortable? Did they make him feel sexy? Maybe they should try it out themselves to find out. Just for fun. As an experiment. Maybe. After a brief silence, Flush had an idea.

'I know, we'll get him some clothes,' he said as he stood up.

'Where from?' asked Faucet. 'There's no shops around here.'

'I saw one of those clothes recycling bins down the road, I'll go see if I can fish some clothes out of that.'

'Okay,' said Faucet. 'You do that, and I'll stay here and wait for The Driver.'

Flush ran down the road and found the clothes recycling bin on the corner of the road. It was quite fortunate that it was there, as there's not many of them about these days. Meanwhile, Faucet draped the old man's soggy dragon costume over him. Not knowing what to do with himself, he gently patted the old man on the arm and quietly reassured him that it was okay and they knew what they were doing, which, of course, they didn't.

Flush opened the flap on the front of the large, green recycling bin and peered inside. It was dark and he couldn't see much, but he could just make out a small pile of clothes at the bottom. He reached down but couldn't quite get them. Climbing up the grooves on the outside of the bin, he shuffled further in through the flap, which was just big enough for him to fit through. Flush stretched down to try and reach the clothes, and after a few swings he eventually grabbed hold of a jumper. He tugged on it, but it didn't budge. Instead, it pulled him down and he fell headfirst into the bin. As his feet slipped through the flap, it snapped shut and he lay on top of the pile of old clothes, imprisoned inside the dark, smelly metal prison.

'Bugger,' he muttered.

💧 💧

'My name is Bob Holness and you are my wife of 20 years, Janet. We're originally from Leicester but we moved here a few months ago to open up a patisserie, which we're looking to furnish with some of their toilets.'

'That's good,' said HyJean, 'except we're opening up a hotel, not a patisserie.'

'Ah, I was wondering why a patisserie would need so many toilets,' said the captain.

HyJean's idea was to visit Walter Crapp in disguise - posing as local businesspeople looking to purchase toilets - to try and find out information. They were now running through their back story one last time before they left, with Suds posing as the receptionist. They picked up their false IDs and Suds took off the blonde curly wig he'd been wearing. He was quite the method actor.

They had gone undercover the year before to spy on a company that was selling knock off wet wipes. Whilst working in the factory making them, they had discovered that the company had just been using regular cloths, dipped in water and sprayed with air freshener. The grime fighters were caught out though, when the captain was found cleaning the boss's office during his lunch break. Cleanliness had often been both Captain Clean's greatest strength and biggest weakness.

'I'm still not sure about Bob Holness,' said Suds. 'What if they used to watch Blockbusters?'

'Trust me, it's a pretty outdated reference; nobody will remember that show,' the captain argued. 'And besides, how often do you get to go around pretending to be your favourite television presenter?'

'Fair enough,' said Suds, placing his wig on a desk lamp in an unintended case of anthropomorphism.

The captain called their reliable chauffeur, The Driver, but he was busy driving to Flush and Faucet, so instead they had to take the to the Crapp Toilets manufacturing plant in the heart of the city. Fortunately, they weren't in costume, so it saved them the usual embarrassment. However, the captain had insisted on wearing wildly outdated glasses as part of his disguise and HyJean was almost as embarrassed to be seen with him wearing them as she was in her grime fighting attire.

♦ ♦

'What do you mean you're stuck in a clothes recycling bin?' asked Faucet.

'Well, I was looking inside a clothes recycling bin,' explained Flush, 'and now I'm sat inside it.'

'Why did you climb inside it?' asked Faucet, still struggling to understand his colleague's actions.

'I didn't climb inside it! I was looking in through the flap and I fell in. Now come get me out.'

'Okay. I'll be round in a minute.'

Faucet turned to the old man, still lying unconscious on the floor. He didn't want to move him, as he'd heard that moving someone when they're injured can make it worse. Although, given that he'd been lying on the floor unconscious for at least 15 minutes, there wasn't much worse it could get. Still, Faucet decided to leave him where he was. He scribbled a note on a scrap of paper saying "Do not touch this man" and left it on his chest. 'Stay there, I'll be right back,' he said, patting him on the arm.

He then ran down the road in the direction that Flush had gone and spotted a recycling bin on the corner of the road. He stopped to watch as a few young school kids walked past the bin. As they grew closer, there was a deep metal thud and a booming, echoey noise from inside bellowed out to them, 'I am the bin monster, and I am hungry! Give me your clothes!'

The kids all ran off screaming and the bin chuckled a deep, echoey chuckle. Faucet crossed the road and knocked on the bin.

'Hello hello hello, what's all this then?' he said in the poshest British voice he could muster. 'Have you been swallowing humans, bin monster?'

'Um… no officer,' came a more nervous booming voice.

'It's me, you idiot,' Faucet said in his normal voice. 'Come on, let's get you out.'

'Hang on, I think I'm gonna be…'

There was the sound of retching and then a number of articles of clothing shot out the flap in the bin, with a loud, 'Bleeeeuuurgh!'

'Very funny,' said Faucet, pulling a pair of trousers off his head. 'Now grab my hands.'

He reached in and with a great deal of struggling he managed to pull Flush out. Flush thanked him and as he stretched his aching limbs and dusted himself off, Faucet picked a shirt from the pile.

'They're a bit old fashioned, these clothes,' Faucet remarked.

'Well, I'm sorry to disappoint you Gok Wan,' said Flush sarcastically, 'but they'd just collected the last of the Ralph Lauren shirts.'

They gathered the clothes and headed back up the road to the old man. However, when they arrived, they were surprised to find that he was not where Faucet had left him.

'Where's he gone?' asked Flush.

'I don't know, I told him to stay right here!' cried Faucet.

They looked around, but there was no sign of the old man. His commode was still there, so he hadn't driven off, and his costume was in a crumpled pile on the floor, so he hadn't returned to his villainous ways just yet. As if on cue, a familiar looking taxi pulled up next to them.

'Alright mate,' said The Driver.

'Hey, have you seen a naked old man around here?' asked Faucet.

'Listen, what you two get up in your private life is up to you,' said The Driver. 'I prefer the more conventional dating sites.'

'No, he's the bad guy we're tracking,' said Flush, holding up the dragon outfit and pointing to the commode.

'Oh, that's a relief. Yeah, there's one just up the road there,' The Driver said, pointing behind in the direction he'd just come from.

Flush and Faucet ran down the road, where they found the old man crawling along the pavement. He still looked just as weak as he had done when they left him, although he was now conscious and moving, so that made a nice change.

'There you are! What are you doing?' Flush asked him.

'I'm late for dominoes,' he said in a frail, weary voice as he shuffled away slowly, crawling on the ground like a wounded soldier trying to subtly escape a battle he had not wished to join.

'Never mind dominoes,' said Flush, following along with tiny, slow steps. 'You need to come with us to the hospital.'

'Why, are you ill?' asked the old man, glancing back at them.

'What? No!' cried Flush. 'You're the one who's ill.'

'I'm not ill,' he said in a very ill-sounding voice.

'You are sir,' said Faucet, who by now had walked around to the front of the old man. 'You've just had a heart attack or a stroke or something.'

'I'm fine. It was probably just indigestion,' said the old man as he batted Faucet's leg and tried to carry on crawling down the road.

'You're not fine, look at you!' said Flush, now getting quite angry at the old man's lack of concern at nearly dying.

'Quick, grab his legs,' said Faucet.

'No, not my legs! I need them for walking,' cried the old man.

'You can barely crawl, mate,' grumbled Flush.

Together they lifted him up and carried him back, with quite a struggle, to the taxi. They sat him in the back and asked The Driver to take them to the hospital. With a curious glance at the semi-naked man in the back of his car, he obliged and set off for the hospital.

Captain Clean and HyJean – or Clifford and Jean, since they were dressed in everyday clothes to conceal their true identities – entered the reception of Crapp Toilets. It smelled faintly of disinfectant; a smell that Clifford loved. Jean not so much. They walked confidently (but not too confidently, because Clifford believed Bob Holness was quite shy in real life) over to the reception desk. Clifford instinctively pulled his sleeve down to wipe the bell before pressing it, but Jean nudged him and gave him a disapproving look. He stood for a few seconds, nervously trying to pluck up the courage to press the potentially germ-ridden bell. Eventually, Jean tutted and pressed it herself. A blonde-haired woman appeared, looking remarkably similar to how Suds had looked during rehearsals, only with more make up. Clifford contorted his mouth to hide his amusement.

'Hello,' said the woman behind the desk, with a half-hearted smile that looked so unnatural it could have been borrowed from someone else. 'May I help you?'

'Hello,' said Clifford, pushing the glasses that he'd worn as a disguise back up the bridge of his nose. 'My name is Bob Holness and this is my wife of 20 years, Janet. We're originally from Leicester but we moved here a few months ago to open up a patisserie or hotel, which we're looking to furnish with some of your toilets.'

Jean's face sunk and she let out a little whimper at her pretend husband's unconvincing acting.

'Forgive my husband,' she said. 'He's very excited. And he always acts like a total idiot when he's excited.'

'Of course,' said the woman sympathetically. 'Men do love their toilets.'

'Don't they just,' Jean replied with a fake chuckle. 'We have an appointment at 1pm to see Mr Crapp, we're a little early.'

Clifford had called up straight after the videocall with the inspector and managed to book an appointment under the false name. The woman tapped away at her keyboard – her long fingernails click clacking on each key – and read what was on the screen.

'You're very early,' she said. 'The appointment's not until tomorrow.'

'Oh, husband dearest, you really are the world's biggest moron,' Jean said as she slapped Clifford on the back of his head.

'Ow,' he said, flinching from the stinging slap and rubbing his head.

'As it happens, Mr Crapp has no appointments this afternoon,' the woman behind the desk said. 'I'm sure he'll be happy to see you. Let me just give him a ring.'

The woman turned away to her phone and called her boss. Neither Clifford nor Jean listened to the woman talking, but had they have listened, they would've heard her say 'Hello. Yes, I've got a Mr Bob Holness in reception… yeah, I think so… well he looks a lot younger than he does on the television.'

Instead, Clifford turned to Jean and said, 'That hurt y'know.'

'Sorry, I was getting into character,' she replied. 'See, I imagine Bob Holness is married to a strong woman who gets very annoyed when he messes up a perfectly simple plan.'

'Duly noted.'

The woman turned back and informed them that Mr Crapp would indeed see them, and that they should head to his office on the third floor. The only-fictionally-married couple thanked her and left to meet Mr Walter Crapp. As they did, the receptionist returned to her computer, humming the Blockbusters theme as she tapped away on the keyboard. Little did she know that she'd one day go on to not only appear on the show, but to win it. Sadly this would happen in a dream though, so nobody else would see it.

♦ ♦

Filtham General Hospital had a reputation for being quite good. They had once boasted the best-looking doctors and nurses in the county, topping the polls in some questionable magazines and putting out a saucy calendar at the end of every year. However, this led to many people feigning injuries just so that they could see one of these hospital hotties, which wasted a lot of important time and resources that could've been used to help treat patients who were actually ill. So, one summer, there was a major reshuffle, and many staff were transferred to neighbouring hospitals (though sparingly to avoid the same mistake) and the hospital advertised for less appealing staff. To nobody's surprise, the job advert's headline "Wanted: Ugly old trouts to work in Filtham General Hospital" garnered very little response and a media backlash, so the message was toned down and the management were more discreet in their choosing of less attractive staff. One of these nurses of average appearance was currently patrolling the ward, tending to the various patients and attending to the patient whims that required the least effort. In one of the beds lay an old man who'd once been dressed up as a dragon but was now wearing a hospital robe.

'Where am I?' asked the old man in a panic as he woke up and looked around at his surroundings.

'Calm down,' said Faucet, reaching out to settle him back down into bed. 'You're in a hospital. You had a stroke, so my friend and I brought you here.'

'Yes, that's right,' the old man nodded, looking around the ward. 'There was another young man, he hit me with his sex whip. Where is he?'

'It's not…' Faucet stuttered, glancing around awkwardly and lowering his tone, 'It's not a sex whip. That was Flush, he had to go to work, so I said I'd stay with you.'

'Oh, I see. Well, thank you, young man,' said the old man, lying back down on his bed. 'Did you bring me any grapes?'

'Um… no, sorry. We were kinda focusing on getting you hear. We didn't have time to stop for fruit.'

'Pity, I like grapes.'

'I can go get you some if you like?'

'No, don't bother,' he said, waving the offer away with his hand. 'You'll probably get the wrong ones anyway.'

'So, what's your name, mister?' Faucet asked as they both settled down in their respective bed and chair.

'George,' said the old man, as if he were reluctant to give the information away.

'Nice to meet you, George,' Faucet replied. 'I'm Faucet.'

'That's a ridiculous name,' said George with a slight laugh. 'Your parents must've been loopy.'

'It's not my real name. It's my grime fighter name. I'm not allowed to tell you my real name,' Faucet explained. 'Anyway, why have you been driving around in a pimped-out commode causing trouble?'

'Something to do,' the old man shrugged. 'Have you any idea how boring it is being an old man stuck in that retirement home? The most excitement we get in there is when someone loses their dentures. I needed more, so when my grandson came round with his new dragon toy and water pistol, it gave me the idea to become the commode dragon.'

'That's fair, I guess,' said Faucet with a shrug, finding the man's story to be pretty compelling.

The hero and the old man sat in silence for a while. Faucet watched the nurses walking up and down the room, attending to their patients and chatting amongst themselves. At one point he left the old man to sleep while he went and got a sandwich for himself. As he returned to the ward, a patient bumped into a young nurse, causing her to drop the jug of water she was carrying and fall over. The patient apologised profusely, but the nurse assured him she was alright and that it was an accident. Faucet rushed over and helped the nurse up, while one of the patient's family members took him back to his bed.

'Are you okay?' Faucet asked the nurse.

'Yes, I'm fine, thank you,' she said with a friendly smile.

She looked at the big pile of water on the floor and began to panic a little, glancing round to see if any other staff were watching. She'd only recently started working at the hospital and was worried about making a bad impression so early on.

'Oh no, I need to go find a mop,' she said, looking around a bit flustered.

'Don't worry,' said Faucet, 'I've got it.'

He bent down and put his hand on the small puddle of water. Slowly but surely, the puddle began to shrink as Faucet absorbed the water.

'There you go,' he said with a proud smile.

The stunned nurse stared at him for a few seconds, then said 'Eww, get away you freak.'

She rushed away from him, and Faucet let out a deep sigh. He returned to the old man's bedside and slumped down into the chair. For the first time since becoming a grime fighter, he suddenly realised that his new biology and abilities had their downsides. Whilst it was useful in grime fighting, it was hardly an attractive quality to need to wear bracelets on his wrists and ankles to prevent himself leaking all over people. He couldn't really remember if he'd been successful with the ladies before he was experimented on, but he definitely thought it would hinder his chances now. He sat and contemplated this aspect of his life for a while and was grateful when George woke up and provided him with a distraction.

'Want to see something cool?' Faucet asked, hoping he could entertain the man with some of his powers and feel a little better about them.

George nodded, and Faucet turned to face the bed on the opposite side of the room. He shot a droplet of water from his hand that flew across the room and landed perfectly in a plastic cup on the patient's bedside table. The noise of the water hitting the cup caused the woman in the bed to suddenly jump.

Faucet grinned at George, who just groaned, 'Bloody millennials.'

💧💧

Walter Crapp was a big man; almost 7ft tall with a big beefy body and the kind of face only a mother could love – and it wouldn't be his own mother. He looked like someone you wouldn't want to meet in a supermarket, let alone a dark alley. He walked with a slow stomp, resembling an elephant marching through the African wasteland. And with his huge figure, rippling muscles and aggressive demeanour, Crapp could probably beat an elephant in a fight.

'This is where the toilets are assembled,' said Walter Crapp as he led Clifford and Jean down a production line.

They'd managed to convince Mr Crapp to give them a tour of the factory floor, hoping that they might spot something that could give them a clue as to what he was up to. So far it had all been pretty standard stuff, interesting only to Clifford, who had always had a unique fascination with anything to do with toilets. Jean lagged behind, looking around for signs of anything usual. After a while she found something.

'What's behind that door?' she asked, pointing to a door with several locks and warning signs plastered all over it.

'Nothing,' grumbled Crapp in his rough East London accent.

'Awful lot of security for a door leading to nothing,' Clifford said, verbally poking their tour guide to reveal more.

'Awful lot of questions for a hotelier,' he said gruffly as he turned away and continued to walk.

Clifford and Jean followed. As they walked Clifford gestured towards the mysterious door with his eyes. Jean nodded. She knew what to do. Having worked together for years, they were now at the point where they could communicate silently, through eyebrow raises and other facial gestures. Though, like most forms of communication, there were the occasional misinterpretations, such as the time Clifford had something in his eye and HyJean thought his rapid series of winks were instructing her to open a trap door that subsequently led to hear being drenched in syrup.

The rest of the tour of the Crapp Toilet factory was just as uninteresting, culminating in a return to the owner's office. It was a large room that he probably looked quite nice once. Like its owner, it was bigger than it needed to be, with very little in the way of furnishings, save for a desk, a few chairs, a bookcase with only one book (a toilet catalogue from several years ago) and a water cooler that appeared to have been filled with beer. Clifford and Jean sat in two old chairs facing a desk that had a little plaque on it reading "Walter 'Bog' Crapp". Presumably, he had accepted his nickname and decided to own it. The boss was clearly not in the habit of entertaining visitors, as the chairs were the kind of cheap, plastic seats you keep in the shed in case you have an unexpectedly large party of guests over at Christmas. Walter Crapp sat on the other side of the desk. Clifford couldn't decide if the businessman was in a bad mood or if his face always had the same unpleasant expression.

'I must say, it's a fine place you've got here, Bog,' said Clifford, gesturing towards the sign on his desk.

'Only my friends call me that,' Crapp grunted.

'Oh, I'm sorry,' Clifford apologised, feeling a little embarrassed and more than a little intimidated.

Crapp's face turned very serious, as he leant forward ever so slightly and added, 'And my enemies.'

'That must be very confusing for you,' Clifford pointed out.

'So, what do you want?' Crapp said, ignoring the remark and changing the subject without a shred of politeness to his words.

'Well, we're opening up a new hotel in the city and we need a number of toilets installed,' explained Jean. 'We've heard excellent reviews about your products, so we thought we'd come to you direct to discuss a deal.'

'We were going to go to Trev's Toilets, but we heard that closed down,' Clifford added, watching for any kind of reaction from the toilet mogul. 'Very strange how he just went out of business like that, don't you think?'

'Not really,' Crapp replied bluntly, before turning back to Jean and speaking in a well-rehearsed tone that didn't suit him. 'I'm sure we can do you a good deal.'

'Also, do you have any toilets?' asked Clifford. 'As in… you know… I know you've got toilets, because you make them… I mean ones my wife can use.'

'I need to spend a penny,' HyJean added with a faux embarrassed shrug.

Crapp slowly looked at Clifford suspiciously and then turned back to Jean. Sensing his tone, Jean gave a smile that begged for sympathy.

'Of course. Downstairs, end of the corridor,' he said with the faintest hint of… it wasn't a smile, but more of a patronising look of contentment.

Jean thanked him and swiftly left. But she wasn't going to the toilet. She carried on down the stairs, back down to the factory floor to investigate the secret door. She snuck into the production line room and scanned for any signs of employees. There were a few dotted around, but the big, noisy machinery meant she was able to sneak over to the door unnoticed. She got a little tool out of her pocket to pick the locks. Within seconds she was in. Back in the office, Clifford sat nervously trying to expand on the hotel story, talking Crapp through their made-up plans for the fictional rooms in the unbuilt hotel and what sort of coffee machines they planned to install. After a while, Crapp gave up the pretence. He sat up from his slouched position and addressed his guest with a menacing stare.

'That's very interesting,' he said in a calm but sinister voice. 'Because you see, while you've been sitting there wittering on, I've worked something out.'

He leant in a little closer and lowered his voice to a threatening whisper.

'I know who you are… Captain.'

Clifford was stunned. The game was up. Crapp had somehow seen through his incredible disguise and figured out who he was. He said nothing. Crapp's mouth twisted into a smirk as he reached forwards and slowly took the captain's old glasses off and crushed them with one hand.

'Now, I don't know what you and your friend are doing here,' he said, pausing to turn his computer screen around to show CCTV footage of Jean being escorted off the premises by one of his men, 'but I don't want to see you or any of your cleaning crew around here again. Understand?'

Clifford got the message, but he had a message of his own and he wasn't afraid to deliver it. He leaned in himself to get closer to Crapp's face.

'I understand,' he said. 'But know this: I will find out what you're up to, and if I don't like it, then I will stop you.'

Crapp leaned in further, 'No you won't.'

Clifford leaned in a little bit more, 'Yes I will.'

Crapp leaned in again, so their faces were almost touching. 'No,' he said and spat in his face, 'you won't.'

'Yes, I will,' said Clifford, and then, unsure what to do he licked Crapp's face.

Crapp banged his fists down on the desk with an almighty crash, causing Clifford to fall back in his chair and stumble to his feet in panic.

'Lew, get in here!' Crapp called out.

A short, skinny man came running into the office. Lew Roll, to give him his full name, looked rather timid, like he used to be an accountant and had somehow been forced into working for Walter Crapp unwillingly. Around his neck he wore a tie that appeared to be made of toilet roll paper.

'See our friend here out, will ya,' Crapp said, relaxing back in his chair that let out a little creak at the weight being put on it.

Lew grabbed Captain Clean by the arm. He was surprisingly strong for such a short, amiable looking man, and locked the captain's arm in a position that he couldn't escape from.

'Ooh, a friend,' Lew remarked as he led the captain out of the room and down the corridor. 'He doesn't have many of those.'

'I can't imagine why,' Clifford said with a roll of his eyes. 'Nice tie by the way.'

'Thanks, I made it myself,' Lew replied. 'It's just toilet paper with some PVA glue to make it firmer, but I could do with something better.'

'I've got some micro-fibre material you could use, it's anti-tear and anti-stain,' Clifford replied, almost giving away the secret nature of his mask. 'I could drop some round if you like.'

'That would be brilliant, thank you,' said Lew.

'Stop flirting and just get rid of him!' Bog shouted after them.

💧💧

Captain Clean, HyJean and Sergeant Suds gathered back at the base to swap stories, sat on the big table in the middle of the main room of their base. A few strands of synthetic blonde hair poked out of Suds's pocket. Whether he had brought the wig in case they needed to roleplay again, or he had been wearing it again while he was out, none of the other grime fighters would ever know.

'What was that Crapp guy like?' asked Suds as he sipped a cup of tea. He'd had quite an easy afternoon with little action and was enjoying a nice rest.

'I'm not gonna lie, he was a bit scary,' admitted the captain.

'He's also very rude and unpleasant,' added HyJean, cupping her coffee like it was an emotional support object. 'And so tall! I swear he was like a giant.'

'Sounds lovely,' said Suds.

'Oh, and he goes by the name Bog as well,' said the captain.

'Why? 'Cause he's so full of crap?' asked Suds.

HyJean spat out some of her coffee and wiped her mouth as she laughed. 'Sorry, that was a good one.'

She spotted Captain Clean's wide eyes staring at the drops of coffee on the table and quickly wiped them up before he could tell her off. They all shared some more insults about Walter "Bog" Crapp and then moved on to what they'd discovered in his factory.

'So, what was behind that door?' Captain Clean asked HyJean.

'It was pretty surprising, actually,' she said with a little dramatic pause. 'It was toilets. Loads and loads of toilets.'

'What's so surprising about that?' asked Suds. 'I mean it is a toilet factory.'

'Yeah, but why keep them behind such a heavily guarded door?' she replied, drumming her fingers on the coffee cup as she thought. 'Does he think someone's going to steal them? Are they special toilets? He's not exactly known for making great toilets.'

'Maybe he's got a big order with an important client?' suggested Suds. 'That would explain why he's not bidding for the council tender, if he's too busy.'

'Hm, I don't think so. He's definitely up to something dodgy, I can feel it. But what? What could it be?' said the captain, staring off into the distance as he wracked his brain. He let out a sigh of defeat and shook his head. 'I need to get a closer look at those toilets, find out what's so special about them.'

'I doubt he's going to let you anywhere near his factory again,' said HyJean. 'Let alone give you a tour of his secret stash.'

'I wasn't planning on asking for an invite,' the captain explained. 'I'll have to break in while he's not there. Lure him out somehow.'

'No, we're not doing a break in,' HyJean protested loudly with a slight whine to her voice. This was another of his plans that she knew would not have a good ending, and she was fed up with going along with them by now. 'This guy's clearly dangerous and he already hates us, we'll find another way. Let's get some sleep and we'll come up with a plan tomorrow.'

'Fine,' the captain agreed, although he had no intention of waiting till morning. They said their goodbyes and Captain Clean waited until the others had left and he was alone. Then he went to his office to get a toilet-roll mask from his dispenser and pick up his toilet brush themed mace.

💧💧

Filtham by night wasn't much different to Filtham by day, except the darkness hid some of the dirty walls of the buildings that lined its usually busy streets. But in other areas, lampposts shone a spotlight on them, as if to highlight particularly grubby patches like a criminal under scrutiny. The walls were unable to plead their case, due to the unfortunate fact that they couldn't speak, and even if they could, they'd probably have more pressing issues to discuss, such as the dogs urinating on them or people covering them with posters for sickeningly twee pop stars that contrasted against the wall's bad boy image. Still, it was a good job that there were no sentient bricks around this night, as Captain Clean was trying to remain as hidden as he could. In the dark shadows of the night, the captain slowly made his way over the metal fence surrounding the Crapp Toilet factory. He managed the ascent with some ease, but he wasn't so good at the getting down part, landing with a thud like a sack of overweight potatoes falling off a truck.

'Ow, my back,' he muttered as he stood up.

He crept up to a door at the back of the factory, glancing around as he went to keep an eye out for any guards or security cameras. It was pretty hard to see anything in the darkness, so even if there was any kind of security, he wouldn't have noticed anyway. He successfully arrived at the back entrance door without being spotted, and pulled out HyJean's lock-picking tools, which he'd "borrowed" when she wasn't looking. He didn't often take her things, as she was very possessive of them and he sometimes broke them accidentally, but he felt this was important enough to warrant risking it. After a long while of fiddling around, jabbing and twirling the tools with no idea what he was doing, he finally gave up and resorted to plan B. He took out his toilet brush with the mace on the end and gave the lock a good whack. It smashed and crumbled, falling helplessly to the ground like a slightly smaller sack of potatoes – like those baby new potatoes, which sell a lot better than the baby old potatoes, despite the fact that people are still eating something with baby in the name – allowing the door to swing open a little. The captain opened the door with a self-assured grin. He slipped inside, closing the door after himself. Inside, the lights were out and the whole factory was filled with an eerie silence. If there had been a violinist nearby, they would have definitely been playing quietly to accentuate the tension in the moment. Though he'd only been there once, the captain managed to find his way around, wandering in and out of rooms until he recognised the factory floor. He slowly made his way through the room, but stopped when he heard a noise. Nearby, he spotted a figure coming out of the very door he'd been planning to go through himself. He hid behind a large metal machine and watched as another figure walked over and met his shadowy companion. As they walked away from the door, they passed a window that illuminated them briefly, and the captain immediately recognised one of them as Lew, Bog's assistant – he'd know that toilet paper tie anywhere. He listened intently as they spoke.

'Alright Jon,' Lew said as he saw his colleague.

'Everything ready?' the other man asked. His full name was Jon Lavvy, the other half of Bog's trusted duo of personal assistants. Captain Clean recognised him as the one from the computer screen who had ejected HyJean from the building earlier that day.

'Yep,' Lew nodded. 'Bombs in every toilet ready. Did you put the trigger in his office?'

'Sure did, locked away in his drawer,' Jon said proudly. 'I wonder why there's only one trigger. There should really be a series of them so you can't accidentally set them off.'

'Good point,' Lew nodded. 'You'll have to tell them at the lab. Hey, they might give you a job there.'

'Doubt it,' chuckled Jon. 'Anyway, wanna grab a beer?'

'Sure, I think we've earned it.'

Their voices trailed off as they left the room. Captain Clean kept his eyes on the mysterious door.

'Bombs?' he whispered nervously to himself. 'Oh crap. Oh crap oh crap oh crap.'

This was all getting a bit much now. The intimidating toilet manufacturer was one thing, but the thought of explosives made him feel like he was in way over his head. He decided to abandon his mission and follow HyJean's suggestion of concocting a plan of action together in the morning. He slipped back through the factory, now with a more urgent gait, still repeating his new chant of "oh crap" quietly as he went, and made his way back out of the door. He closed it and tried to piece the broken handle back together. He managed to slot it back in, and tried it to check it worked. As he did so, he heard a loud clunking sound.

'That's odd,' he thought. He pressed the handle down again and another booming thud rung out. He tried the handle a few more times, but then noticed the wall in front become darker as a large shadow loomed over him. He span around and was greeted by a huge, hulking figure, towering over him like a very tall tower. At least 7ft in height and glimmering in the moonlight, the monstrous being slowly leaned down. As he moved into the brightness of the security light, the captain saw that it was in fact Bog, wearing a suit that appeared to be made of the same material as his toilets, including some familiar parts, like a seat that was attached to the helmet and framed his face. The porcelain armour glistened, lighting up the face of the very tall man. The light did nothing to accentuate his features, but merely showed how very angry the very tall man was.

'I told you I didn't want to see you here again,' said Bog.

'I uh... I left my pen in there... thought I'd retrieve it without bothering you,' the captain lied pathetically.

'You were snooping,' Bog replied. 'I don't like snoops. They make me get all… punchy.'

At which Bog lunged forwards and punched Captain Clean in the face with his hard, porcelain glove. The captain fell back against the wall. He quickly pulled out his toilet brush mace and swung it at Bog's suit, but it merely bounced off with a clang. Bog snatched it off him and snapped it in two, throwing the pieces behind him. The captain tried to escape, but Bog reached out and grabbed the grime fighter by his cape, swinging him around and flinging him like an old ragdoll into a large row of metal bins on the wall opposite. Bog was not only very tall and very angry, but he was also very strong. Captain Clean had gone up against many strong fighters in his time, but Bog's strength was like nothing he'd come across.

As Bog lumbered towards him menacingly, the captain looked around, surveying his surroundings for any slight advantage. There were the bins; he could hide in one of them. There was the metal fence all around; he doubted he'd be able to climb it quick enough. There were a few trucks, most with Crapp's Toilets printed on the side, but one with Bathrooms R Us 4 U graphics instead. That seemed odd. Why was his competitor's truck parked amongst his own? His thoughts were interrupted as Bog swung his porcelain-clad leg and gave him an almighty kick, thrusting him back and denting the bin with an almost too perfect impression of the captain's torso.

The ever-resilient captain managed to compose himself, pulling himself up slightly and mumbling with a feeble attempt to sound confident, 'Is that… is that all you've got?'

Bog gave a little chuckle. 'O Captain my Captain, you ain't seen nothing yet. After Wednesday you'll see what I'm really capable of.'

'Why? What's happening Wednesday?'

'Uh…. Nothing. Forget I said that,' said Bog, realising he'd let a bit of important information slip. This was a habit of criminal masterminds that the captain was grateful for, as he was often able to get them to reveal information just by getting them talking. But Bog was not about to give up any more information quite so easily. 'In fact, let me help you forget.'

Bog then threw another porcelain punch at the captain's face, and in an instant, everything went black. Captain Clean lay on the ground, unconscious, unaware of Bog carrying his body down the road to dispose of him in a ditch like a broken vacuum cleaner.

💧💧

Captain Clean stumbled into the base the next morning, covered in blood stains and bruises. Sergeant Suds and HyJean had already arrived for work and rushed over to help the captain over to a chair, into which he slumped down.

'Looks like someone had a fun night out,' said Suds, trying to lighten the mood a little. He could see how sore the captain was and hoped, like many do, that a light-hearted remark would somehow ease his discomfort. Which it didn't. Because it rarely does.

'What the hell happened to you?' asked a more bluntly concerned HyJean. 'You look awful.'

'I had a bit of a run in with our new friend Bog last night,' Captain Clean admitted with a sore twinge in his voice. 'He must've known I'd go back.'

'What?' cried HyJean. 'What did I say about not breaking into his factory alone? I swear you never listen to me!'

'Jesus, what did he do to you?' asked Suds as he inspected the captain's wounds closer.

'Well, he punched me. Then he kicked me. Then he punched me some more,' explained the captain. 'I think there was some more kicking at some point, it all went a bit fuzzy after a while.'

'And did you actually get anything out of your ridiculous adventure?' asked HyJean, adding, 'Other than a severe beating.'

The captain nodded weakly, 'He's got bombs… I heard that… Lew guy talking… and he's planning something on Wednesday.'

'Wednesday? That's tomorrow,' said HyJean.

'Which is why we need to be ready,' said Cap, standing up determinedly and then instantly collapsing back down into the chair again.

'Cap, you're in no state to go up against him again,' said HyJean.

'Ah, I'll be fine,' he replied, waving away her concern. 'I just need a few hours is all. Some of my scars will probably heal up by then too so they won't be visible anymore; it's amazing what a bit of rest can do for you.'

He pulled himself up once again and limped across the room to head to his office, but as he reached the desk in the centre, he could no longer hold himself up and collapsed down into a chair with a breathy grunt.

'Ugh… it doesn't make sense though,' he mused aloud. 'Why would he make a ton of toilets with bombs in? If he's going to blow up his own factory, that seems a ridiculous waste of materials.'

'Maybe he thought he was going to win the council contract and he was planning to blow them up then?' suggested Suds.

'But he didn't put a bid in,' HyJean reminded him. 'He knew there was no way he'd win it.'

'Or maybe he didn't want to win it,' the captain said, a weak lightbulb flickering on hopefully in his battered brain. 'Think about it, he knew the other company would win. In fact, he made sure of it by taking that other company out of the race.'

'Maybe he's setting them up?' suggested HyJean. 'He's going to frame them?'

'Of course!' the captain said, banging his hand down on the desk and then immediately wincing in pain and rubbing his hand. 'The lorry. The competitor's lorry at his factory. It all makes sense now.'

The assembled squad members turned to their captain, waiting for him to explain his sudden revelation. He sat grinning at them while they waited, until eventually HyJean gave a little shrug to prompt him to explain and he remembered the others hadn't been with him when he saw the lorry.

'There was a Bathrooms R Us lorry in with his lorries at the factory. I bet he's going to drive the lorry into his factory, which will set off the bombs and destroy his factory. Then he can claim on the insurance!' the captain said excitedly, holding his hands up with a look of total pride, like he'd just announced a mind-blowing scientific theory.

'What?' asked Suds. 'What would be the point in that?'

HyJean shook her head. 'I think the more likely plan is that he's going to interrupt the shipment, delivering his booby-trapped bogs in the other lorry instead. They get installed, he sets them off, takes out the competition and causes chaos for the council.'

'Pffft, don't be ridiculous Jean,' the captain chuckled. His laugh soon died down though as HyJean folded her arms and raised an eyebrow. There was no confusing what this facial gesture meant. 'Okay, so maybe that plan does sound more plausible. I still prefer my idea though. Have Mary call all the insurance companies in Filtham to warn them just in case. And call me a doctor, I think I've got a ruptured spleen.'

💧💧

A few hours later, Faucet returned to the base and informed the rest of the squad about what had happened with the Commode Dragon. Captain Clean had been cleaned up, had a shower and changed into his everyday clothes. The ruptured spleen turned out to be cramp, but he still looked the worse for wear.

'They said it was just a small stroke and he'll be alright in a few days. I would've been back sooner, but one of the doctors saw me use my powers and asked if I'd go to the children's ward and entertain the kids,' he said as he entered the base and took off his mask. 'Oh, and you may get a letter saying they're suing us for water damage, sorry.'

In the background, a loud groan came from Mary's office. A familiar groan that she'd recorded and had Flush save as a message alert on her phone for when HyJean messaged her – it was always bad news.

'What?' asked HyJean. 'Why? What happened?'

'It totally wasn't my fault,' said Faucet, using a phrase that is very rarely true. 'This annoying little kid said I couldn't hit the sign next to the alarm system from the other side of the room, and –'

'Alright, I can see where this is going,' said HyJean. 'Anyway, we've got more important things to discuss.'

'Oh yeah, the Crappy guy,' said Faucet as he took a seat at the central table. 'How did that go?'

HyJean and Suds filled Faucet in on their encounter with the evil businessman, from the Blockbusters-themed undercover story, to being thrown out by a man named after toilet paper, to being beaten up by a man in a porcelain suit. Once Faucet was caught up and convinced several times that the story was in fact a hundred percent true, they then moved on to their plan of attack.

'He already knows we're on to him, but hopefully he doesn't know how much we know,' HyJean explained. 'In any case, we need to get in there before he has chance to move the bombs.'

'Wait, us?' asked Faucet. 'What about the police, can't they get involved?'

'Not really, we've got no evidence, other than our word on what we saw when Cap here illegally broke into a factory. I don't think that'd go down to well,' she explained.

'Yeah, fair point,' Faucet replied.

'I spoke to Dovedale and the council are expecting the first delivery at lunchtime tomorrow,' she continued. 'So that gives us a small window of opportunity to stop him tomorrow morning.'

'Today,' said Captain Clean wearily.

'What? We can't go today, you can barely stand,' HyJean pointed out.

'No, I'm fine, look,' said the captain as he pulled himself up and started doing star jumps, although he only managed one before wincing in agony and falling back down into his seat whilst clutching his ribs. 'On second second thoughts, I think we'll go tomorrow morning.'

'Thank you,' said HyJean, throwing her hands in the air in frustration. 'So, here's the plan: Cap, Suds and I will go to confront Bog. Faucet, you and Flush will need to get everybody out of the factory, just in case.'

'I can do that,' Faucet nodded.

'And how exactly are we going to stop Bog from detonating the bombs?' Suds asked with a concerned tone in his voice.

'I'll talk to him,' said the captain, raising a hand.

'You'll talk to him?' said Suds with a hint of frustration in his voice. He'd heard this plan many times before and it rarely worked. The captain was convinced that he had an ability to talk criminals round, but the linguistically challenged captain generally struggled with speeches and, more often than not, only made things worse by provoking the very people he was trying to win over.

'Trust me, I know his type. He's got a tough exterior, but it's all just a front,' the captain explained. 'He's a typical misguided soul desperate to succeed. He's probably an orphan as well or suffered some sort of tragedy or abuse as a child. You just need to find out where it went wrong and help them to see that they can be better.'

'Yeah, he doesn't look like the kind of guy who just needs a cup of tea and a nice chat,' said HyJean.

'Look, I know what I'm doing and when we go there, you'll see,' the captain insisted.

'Hang on,' interrupted Faucet. 'How do we know that's where he'll be?'

'Oh, don't you start,' groaned the captain as he slumped down onto the table face first, the conversation wearing him out almost as much as his injuries.

'He'll need witnesses that he wasn't around when the bombs go off,' explained HyJean. 'It makes sense that he'd stay in his factory to give him a good alibi.'

HyJean asked Mary to book The Driver to escort them to factory in the morning and provide a quick getaway should they need one. She also asked her to call Flush and ask him to be in early so that they'd have time to explain and prepare for the mission. Captain Clean, meanwhile, retired to his office to rest and prepare himself both physically and mentally. The captain had faced many mutated monsters, crazy criminals and barbaric businessmen in his time as a grime fighter, but Bog seemed more intimating and scarier than any of them. He didn't like to admit it, neither to the team nor himself, but he wasn't sure how the afternoon would go, and hoped his years of experience and loyal squad would help him succeed.

'So let me get this straight,' said Flush, pinching the bridge of his nose and bowing his head. 'You want me to go into a building that we know will be full of bombs, with a lunatic ready to press the trigger at any moment, and risk my life to save a bunch of strangers?'

The captain hesitated for a moment, only now realising what he was asking of his fellow hero. With a tentative sigh, he replied, 'Yes.'

'Bostin!' Flush grinned. 'Let's go then.'

The Sanitary Squad suited up and gathered their weapons, heading out to The Driver to try and squeeze 5 people into his car that seated 4 passengers. It was tricky, but eventually they all clambered in, and then they were off. After years of using the Driver's services, it still amazed the Squad how he could get anywhere in seconds. He didn't even seem to drive particularly fast; the world outside just seemed to slow down around them, allowing him to spot all the gaps that he could whizz through. They never questioned how he did it; they were just grateful he did, today more than ever. They arrived at the end of the road, away from the factory so they didn't draw any attention to themselves. As they fell out of the car like clowns in a circus, they all stood and stretched their limbs, which were sore and squished after the uncomfortable ride. Captain Clean was now in much better shape – the rest had done him the world of good, and his scars were remarkably well healed, with just a few stitches to reassure people that he definitely had been involved in a fight recently. As they walked down the road together, they gradually separated into their two groups, each with their own mission.

They climbed the fence and slipped into the front entrance of the factory. The two grime fighters walked up to the reception desk, where sat the receptionist whose real beauty was buried deep beneath layers of make-up. She looked like she had been put there as a punishment, as she scrolled through an article about her favourite reality TV show on her computer whilst pretending to greet the visitors in a professional manner. Flush went to speak, but Faucet pushed him to one side. Flush rolled his eyes and picked up a pamphlet off the counter to browse while his colleague took charge of the conversation.

'Uh... hi,' Faucet said, leaning in a little to try and catch her attention.

'Hello, welcome to Crapp Toilets, can I help you?' she said in a well-rehearsed monotone friendly voice.

'Yeah, I'm here to save your life and possibly take you out for a drink after,' Faucet said, leaning on the counter and giving her his most charming smile. After his recent encounter with the nurse, he found himself even more determined to prove to himself that he could still win the ladies round.

'Have you got an appointment?' the girl said in the same monotone voice, as if she'd not even listened to Faucet and was just reading off a script.

'Of course I don't have an appointment,' Faucet said, waving to try and get her attention. 'This is a rescue mission, you're in serious danger and we're here to save your life.'

'Then I'm afraid you'll have to ring up and book an appointment sir,' she continued, unphased.

'Ah, forget this. You can keep your appointment,' said Faucet, knocking the little cardboard stand on her desk over and walking away in frustration. He called back to her, 'And that drink's off as well!'

The receptionist finally looked up from her screen to see Faucet walking off and Flush still reading the pamphlet, surprisingly engrossed in the list of toilet specifications.

'Gee, what's his problem?' she asked.

'He was trying to warn you that the building is going to be blown up in about 20 minutes,' Flush said casually as he looked at the photos of the various models of toilets.

'What? Oh my god, you're terrorists? Security!' she cried, and before Flush could stop her, she lunged for the phone to call security.

'No!' shouted Flush, leaning over the counter trying to wrestle the phone from her hands. 'We're not terrorists, we're superheroes!'

'You don't look like superheroes,' the girl argued, still trying to get the phone.

'We can't afford proper suits… look, just put the phone down and listen will you!'

After much persuading, the girl eventually relented and put an announcement out on the tannoy system to start an evacuation. Meanwhile, Faucet had found a staff room full of people working at computers. He ran inside and shouted 'The building is in danger! Quick, everybody out!'

A few people jumped up from their seats and ran out of the room, but others were not so easily convinced. Faucet was a little confused, as this wasn't how it usually happened in the films that he'd seen.

'Who are you?' asked a balding man in thick glasses and a tie with cats printed on it. His name was probably something like Gerald or Gordon. He was the office know-it-all who thought he was superior to everybody else because he knew how to change the password on the photocopier, though he was totally oblivious to the fact that the girls who sometimes made him tea often added sugar instead of sweetener like he requested.

'I'm the guy who's trying to save your life,' said Faucet, 'now move!'

'What's your name?' the man asked.

'Faucet,' he said proudly.

The man chuckled, 'No, what's your real name?'

'I'm a grime fighter,' Faucet explained. 'I'm not supposed to tell you my name.'

'A grime fighter?' the man snorted. 'A load of rubbish. Come on, what's your name? I'll report you to HR.'

'I don't work here. And like I said, I'm not allowed to tell you,' Faucet said, rolling his eyes, 'Look, why does it matter anyway?'

'Well how can I trust you if you won't even tell me your real name?' the man replied, crossing his arms confidently like he'd somehow won the argument.

Faucet was beginning to get fed up of these people refusing to co-operate. 'I'm a grime fighter, trying to help people. You're supposed to just trust me, that's how this works.'

'Well then, I'm not going. I've got work to do,' he said, turning back to his computer.

'For Christ's sake,' sighed Faucet. 'I haven't got time for this.'

Faucet aimed his arm at the man's computer and sprayed a jet of water straight at it. The computer was sent crashing back into the wall, where it smashed and erupted in sparks as the screen glitched and turned itself off. The man in the cat tie jumped back in his chair and almost fell out of it, letting out the wimpiest of squeals.

'There, now you can't do your work,' said Faucet, grabbing him by the sleeve and pulling him up off his chair. 'Anyone else want to stay here?'

Nobody did.

💧💧

'Sir, you can't go in without an appointment!' called a timid young woman as she chased after Captain Clean, HyJean and Sergeant Suds, who were all quickly striding towards Bog's office.

'Sergeant!' called the captain without taking his eyes off the door to the office.

Suds lifted his gun, apologised to the receptionist, and shot a small pink blob at her feet, which fixed her to the ground. She struggled and stumbled over, clawing at the blob of goo, but the unique substance that had come from Suds' gun was too strong for her to break free. They reached Bog's office and knocked on the door.

'Go away!' came a disgruntled voice from inside.

'What do we do now?' asked HyJean.

Suds swiftly stomped his foot on the door, his heavy boots smashing it open and almost off its hinges.

'That,' said the captain with a smirk.

Inside the office, Bog was midway through assembling his porcelain suit, with only the legs and torso piece on so far. Evidently, he had heard the tannoy announcement and was preparing himself for battle, with the help of his two henchmen Lew Roll and Jon Lavvy

'I thought you might show up,' grunted Bog with a sneer.

'You know you're really taking the phrase "dress for the job you want" a little too seriously,' said the captain as the three heroes strode confidently into the office.

'I warned you before -'

'And I didn't listen, never do,' the captain interrupted. 'Hello again, Lew. Another great tie.'

'Thanks,' said Lew with a little smile that was clearly a rarity in his life. 'It's double quilted.'

'Shut up and pass me my helmet,' grunted Bog, smacking his henchman on the back of his head.

'I know what you're planning Bog,' continued the captain. 'But you don't need to do this. Blowing up your factory for insurance purposes or blowing up toilets in council buildings will kill lots of innocent people.'

'Innocent? Ha!' laughed Bog. 'Nobody's innocent, Captain. Especially not the council. Those scumbags almost ruined me. They made up lies about the toilets being faulty and put it all over the news. My reputation was ruined. I nearly went out of business. I had to diversify into… bidets.' He shuddered at that last word, as if it were a disrespectful word that he dared not speak. He shook his head and sneered. 'It's time they got what was coming to them.'

'Mr Crapp, just stop and think about this, please,' the captain begged. 'We can speak to the council, explain your frustrations. You don't need to hurt anybody else.'

'Enough talk,' Bog grunted. 'Lew, Jon, restrain them.'

Lew Roll and Jon Lavvy stepped out from behind the desk and rushed quickly over to the heroes. Lew grabbed HyJean while Jon grabbed Sergeant Suds.

'The captain!' Lew called over to his fellow henchperson. Jon let go of Suds and grabbed hold of Cap who was stood in the middle.

'What about the army guy?' asked Jon.

'I'll get him,' said Lew, who let go of HyJean and ran across to grab Suds.

'They're really not the brightest are they?' Suds whispered to the captain.

'Nope,' Suds replied.

HyJean quickly grabbed one of her spray bottles and sprayed Jon Lavvy in the face, causing him to stumble back and rub his eyes. This distracted Lew Roll enough for Sergeant Suds to be able to give him a whack and temporarily knock him out. Now free of henchmen, the three grime fighters marched towards Bog, HyJean and Suds flanking him either side while Captain Clean approached him face on.

'You just don't learn, do ya?' Bog sneered as he finished putting his helmet on and adjusted it. He stepped forward and swung at the captain, who managed to dodge his attack. Suds took the opportunity to get a punch in, but his fist merely bounced off the porcelain armour, doing more damage to his hand than it did to Bog, who kicked him out of the way. Captain Clean grabbed a tall lamp from the corner of the, swinging it at the armour but doing little more than leaving a few small dents. Bog needed no weapons other than his fists, which he swung in carefully considered paths to deal blows to both men.

While the men fought, HyJean took the opportunity to sneak behind Bog's desk to a safe she'd spotted on the wall. She sprayed one of her acidic sprays on the door and made a hole in it big enough for her to fit her hand through. She felt around and finally felt what she was looking for. From the small safe, she pulled out a small rectangular box that had a little clear plastic case covering a red button in the centre. She looked around and saw the captain had been thrown back a good distance from Bog.

'Cap, catch!' she shouted as she tossed the device over to the captain.

'What's this?' he called back, holding it up with a confused look.

'It's the trigger for the bombs!' she replied.

This caught the attention of Bog, who threw Sergeant Suds down on the ground and turned to them, his face a mixture of worry and anger.

'Gimme that,' he roared and started to walk towards Captain Clean, though his movements were slow, as his suit weighed his already hefty bulk of a body down.

'Ah ah aaaah,' the captain teased, flipping the clear case up and revealing the button. 'Lots of bombs down there, all in one place and ready to blow, I'd stay back if I was you.'

As the captain paced around the room backwards, avoiding Bog, the two henchmen slowly came round and stood up.

'Hey boss, he's got the trigger,' pointed out Jon.

'I'm well aware of that,' grunted Bog as he continued to edge towards the captain.

'Shall we get him?' asked Lew.

'No!' snapped Bog.

The porcelain giant knew he had to do something, but he couldn't risk lunging for the trigger in case the captain dropped it and it went off. He decided instead to try and talk Captain Clean into giving it to him instead by using his one weakness against him.

'Be careful Captain, there's a lotta germs on that trigger,' he said with a slight smirk. 'It's very dirty. Give it to me, I'll look after it.'

Suds and HyJean both looked at each other with wide eyes, knowing that Bog's words would trigger a reaction from the captain. And it did. He looked down at the trigger and gasped. There were indeed a few specs of dust and dirt on it, which Captain Clean could not stand.

'You're right,' he said, pulling out a wet wipe from his utility belt and giving it a quick wipe. It should have been obvious to him what would happen, but his obsession about cleanliness often masked everything else in his mind.

'Noooo!' shouted everyone in the room as the captain rubbed the trigger with the wipe. And sure enough, within a few rubs, the wipe hit the red button, which glowed red and started a beeping noise in the device. The captain just looked up with wide eyes and a worried look. 'Oops.'

The room shook as the toilets below exploded in unison, sending a raging blast throughout the whole factory. Windows smashed and walls collapsed as balls of fire burst out in every direction. The machinery in the factory floors below joined in the explosive action as they exploded and flung metal everywhere. Carefully stored chemicals added to the chaos, fuelling the fires even more. As the whole lower ground burned and crumbled in the fiery blaze, the floors above began to give way. On the third floor, Bog's office – which was thankfully one of the farthest away from the source of the blast – began to shake and give way.

'You idiot!' shouted Bog as he ceased keeping his distance and lunged towards the captain, his arms flailing around.

'Run!' shouted HyJean, running over to help Suds up.

Lew Roll and Jon Lavvy, who were nearest to the door, quickly escaped, fleeing the office as swiftly as they could. Captain Clean, HyJean and Sergeant Suds followed, rushing to the exit with a furious Bog stomping behind them. The two henchmen ran through the door at the end of the corridor, but the staircase was engulfed in flames. They were trapped.

💧💧

'We've got to go in and help them,' Faucet cried over the roar of the flames as he ushered the workers away from the blaze.

'We can't,' Flush replied, squinting from the bright red glow of the burning building. 'We'll be burnt to a crisp.'

Faucet shook his head and held up his arms, 'I can clear us a path.'

'No, I can't, I…' Flush replied, looking uncharacteristically nervous. Until this point, Flush had always seemed to relish the idea of a bit of danger, but as the fire burned its red glow on his face, it was clear this was too much. 'I can't go in there, I'm sorry, I just can't.'

'Why not?' asked Faucet.

'I don't like fire, okay!' Flush growled.

'Dude, it's okay, I'll be with you,' said Faucet, trying to reassure him.

'No, it's not that… you don't understand,' said Flush, wrestling with his emotions. 'My brother… he burned down our house. Almost killed me and my parents. We survived and he was arrested, but since then…'

'Oh jeez. No wonder you don't like fire,' said Faucet. 'But dude, you can do this. I know you can.'

'What? Based on what? We've only known each other a week,' Flush snapped back.

'Well yeah, but y'know, you seem pretty cool,' Faucet shrugged. 'I mean you took down that dragon guy with just a pun.'

'He had a stroke, Faucet,' Flush replied, his usually light-hearted tone now more serious, the jokes gone in favour of a realistic view.

'Because of your pun!' said Faucet, desperately trying to reassure him. 'Look, we can't stand around here debating it all day, our friends are in there and they need us. I can't do it on my own, I'll have enough trouble keeping the flames back. So, are you gonna come and help me or are you gonna stand here like a wimp and be scared?'

'I'm not being a wimp,' Flush replied. 'It's a rational fear based on genuine childhood trauma.'

'And the only way you're ever gonna overcome that fear is to face it head on in a high-pressure environment with a friend by your side,' said Faucet.

'Alright, fine,' said Flush with a heavy sigh. 'But if we die in there, I'll kill you.'

They made their way cautiously towards the building and Faucet raised his arms. As they got to the fiery entrance, he set off two jets with his hands. It blasted through the fire and created a hole in the flames. He turned back to Flush and nodded, and his fellow grime fighter simply nodded back.

'Stay close,' Faucet warned as they took a few small steps into the building.

'Yeah, like I'm gonna wander off,' Flush replied, but Faucet didn't hear his words over the noise around them. The flames crackled and roared, while machinery hissed and roared all around them in a cacophony of clangs and crashes.

As they walked a little farther inside, Faucet suddenly started to feel hot. Not just from the flames. He felt hot inside. Like his insides were burning. And then he realised, he was boiling. Literally boiling. With so much water in his body, it was being heated and was starting to boil. His body felt weak, and his head was spinning. His jets faltered and started to die down as he stumbled on his feet.

'Faucet? What's going on? What's happening?' asked Flush, speaking quickly and moving in closer as the flames began to reform around them. 'Faucet? Oh crap. Come on, mate, we've gotta get out of here.'

He pulled at Faucet, who understood what was going on and what they needed to do. As much as he wanted to continue to try and save his fellow grime fighters, there was no way they'd make it through reception, let alone up to the office. He focused his energy on keeping the jets of water going so that they could turn around and make it out safely. Once they were out of the door, Faucet let out a pained groan and fell forward. Flush caught him and wrapped one of Faucet's arms around his shoulders, carrying him away from the building.

'Cap… the others,' Faucet whimpered, glancing back at the crumbling factory.

'They'll be okay,' Flush replied, though his words sounded uncertain.

As if on cue, there was a faint smashing sound from high up, and then a stream of pink goo came pouring out of the broken window, like a bubblegum waterfall. It landed on the floor and built up into a large, bubbly mound of goo.

💧💧

'Okay, I think that should be a thick enough cushion to land on,' said Suds, looking down from the window above at the pillow of goo below.

The captain looked back and saw Bog getting closer. He was advancing towards them with a rage almost as fiery as the flames around them. The porcelain armour was his undoing though, as he moved slowly, and his heavy footsteps stomped down on an already weakening floor. Within a few steps, the floor gave way, and Bog was dragged down into a hole as the floor crumbled away. He dropped down, clinging onto the floor in desperation, the roaring flames coming up through the floor around him as he roared out himself. Captain Clean wrestled with his conscience and then made a decision.

'We have to go back for him,' he said.

'What?' said a surprised Suds.

'If he dies, that's on us,' said the captain. 'You two get out, I'll follow you once I've got the big guy.'

Suds paused, wanting to protest, but knowing it would only be wasted on the stubborn captain. He just nodded and said, 'Good luck.'

Suds jumped out the window and HyJean looked from Bog to the captain.

'Please try not to die,' she said as she swiftly followed suit and jumped out of the window.

'Gee, I thought at least one of them might have tried to stop me, or at least offered to help,' said the captain. 'Still, no time to monologue.'

He ran back to where Bog was still struggling to hold on. He had slipped down further and was now barely visible; only his arms and head poking up out of the hole. The captain held out his hand.

'Grab my hand,' he shouted over the roaring flames and crumbling structure.

Bog stared at him for a few seconds, weighing up his options. Should he fall to his fiery death or give in to his enemy? Or should he try and pull the captain down with him? What would the captain do if he did survive? Would he be arrested, or could he still complete his plan? He probably should have spent less time thinking all of this, because the floor finally gave way and he didn't have chance to make the choice. He fell. The flames pulled him down to his doom.

'Nooooooo!' the captain screamed out as he watched the giant bulk of a man fall, almost in slow motion it seemed, and disappear into the red light below. He paused for a few seconds, trying to think of something he could do but too stunned to move. The rising flames quickly brought him back to reality. He stood up, ran back to the window and jumped out, landing safely on the big pile of pink goo. He regrouped with HyJean and Suds and the three heroes watched on with the crowd of employees as the factory gave in and finally went up in smoke.

💧💧

In the noisy bustle of the employees discussing what had happened and the fire engines and police arriving, the squad managed to slip away, reuniting as they walked back to the taxi. The squad didn't usually stick around for the aftermath of their victories, mainly because there was usually a lot of damage and chaos that they'd be blamed for.

'You didn't even think to check we were out safely?' asked a disgruntled Flush.

'I knew you'd be out,' the captain said, confidently.

'No, you didn't,' argued Flush.

'Okay, I didn't, but I wasn't planning to set the bombs off,' the captain admitted. 'I was just going to use it to keep him back and talk.'

As they reached the taxi, one thought lingered in all of their minds.

'Do you reckon he survived?' HyJean finally asked.

'I doubt it,' said the captain with a defeated sigh. 'Nobody could've survived that. The fall alone would've killed him if the fire didn't.'

'You tried to save him though,' HyJean said, touching his arm comfortingly. 'There's nothing more you could've done.'

'Except y'know, not blowing his factory up,' Flush pointed out.

The next day in the roof of the community centre, Faucet was sat scrubbing an old toilet with so much force that he almost scraped the shine off the porcelain. He'd been quiet since their epic showdown with Bog, not really saying much to the rest of the squad the following day, instead retreating to the roof to be alone with his thoughts and a toilet. He was so focused on cleaning that he didn't even notice HyJean come out onto the roof.

'Hey, how are you doing?' she asked, causing him to jump a little. She quickly added, 'Sorry, I didn't mean to scare you.'

'No, it's all good,' he said, glancing up at her briefly before returning to the toilet. 'I'm okay, thanks.'

'This one of Cap's training exercises?' she asked, moving an empty box over to where he was working and sitting on it.

'Nah, I just… I need to do this,' he replied, quietly.

'Nelson, whatever you do, please don't resort to cleaning instead of talking to people,' said HyJean. 'We have enough of that with Cap.'

Faucet slowed down scrubbing and then stopped, putting the sponge in the bucket and letting out a heavy sigh.

'I failed, Jean,' he said, finally looking up at her. 'I couldn't get past the fire to get in and save you guys or Bog. It was boiling me up inside and I thought I was gonna die, so I ran. I'm the only one who could've helped put it out and I couldn't do it. I won't let that happen again. I need to train. I need to get better.'

'And you think scrubbing a toilet is going to make you impervious to fire?' HyJean replied.

'I... I dunno... I just had to do something,' he said quietly.

'Nelson, being vulnerable to fire isn't something you can overcome,' said HyJean, leaning in a little and placing a hand on his shoulder. 'You can't help what they did to you. But it's okay to not be able to do things. You can do so many things that nobody else can. You've just got to play to your strengths and if you can't do something, that's why we're here, to help. And the fact that you tried, despite it nearly killing you, shows what a hero you are.'

'I just... I just don't know if I'm cut out for this,' Faucet sighed. 'I mean, I like beating up bad guys and spraying things and stuff, but I'm not a cleaning expert. I don't know all the chemicals and cleaning techniques. I didn't even know what a scourer was. I'll never be at Mr Cane's level.'

HyJean let out a loud laugh. 'And you think we are? Nelson, nobody's going to be as OCD about cleaning as Captain Clean, especially not us. But that's not what it's about. Clifford isn't trying to get people to be as anal as he is. He just wants people to have a good basic level of hygiene. Washing their hands after the toilet, wiping up if they spill something and putting litter in the bin. If people did basic things like that, there'd be less germs about and the world would be a cleaner place. You don't have to be Captain Clean Junior, just be you, do what you can and inspire others.'

'Really?' asked Faucet. 'But what about you guys?'

'We're the same. We're not super clean people, we're just more experienced,' HyJean replied. 'Suds worked as a cleaner, I studied science and Flush – god knows what he does, but he seems to know his stuff. So yeah, we want to help make the world a cleaner place and we know our stuff, but we still eat sticky ribs with our hands and open doors without wiping the handle. Anyway, you'll get there. Hell, it's still only your first week. I think you're doing great, and so does Cap.'

'Aww, thanks Jean. I appreciate that,' he replied, a smile now forming on his face as the weight on his shoulders became lighter. But another thought that had been weighing heavy on his mind returned, and his smile dropped again. It clearly showed on his face, as HyJean continued to look concerned.

'It's not just about the fire, is it?' she asked.

'No,' he replied, returning to a quiet state. 'A nurse in the hospital saw my powers and called me a freak. I mean, I don't blame her or nothing, but it's just… am I ever gonna have a normal life like this? What woman's gonna want a man with this condition?'

'Nelson, trust me, there will be someone out there who will love you for who you are,' said HyJean. 'And I don't just mean that in a cliché sentimental way, I mean there's girls out there who would love to date a superhero. Yeah, some of them will be messed up fans thinking it's cool, but there will be some who see past it and love you for a fact that you've dedicated your life to helping people. If Spider-Man and Superman can get a girlfriend, I'm sure you can too.'

'Yeah, I guess you're right,' said Faucet, his smile returning once more. 'Can I… can I give you a hug?'

HyJean passed for a moment, then nodded. 'Okay, but try not to leak on me. This is a new top.'

The two grime fighters hugged, a little awkwardly at first, but melting into a friendly embrace of support. As the hug lingered a little too long, HyJean patted him on the back. 'Come on, Cap wants us downstairs.'

They broke the hug and HyJean returned her box as she made her way to the door.

'What for?' asked Faucet as he gathered up his sponge and bucket, knowing that Captain Clean wouldn't be happy if he left them lying around upstairs.

'I don't know, just come on,' said HyJean impatiently.

Faucet followed her down and put his sponge and bucket away before joining the others. Unusually, they weren't sat at the central table, they were standing in a line, all looking like they knew something he didn't. He looked at them curiously, but each one just smiled back at him.

'What's going on here?' he asked with a hint of trepidation in his voice.

'Nelson Spigot, you have completed your initial training to a satisfactory standard,' said Captain Clean.

'Oh, okay' said Faucet, tilting his head a little. 'Just satisfactory?

'Yes,' the captain replied, unwilling to elaborate, for the sake of time, into the many errors that Faucet had made during his training. 'The only thing left now is to take the pledge.'

'Okay. What does that involve?' he asked.

From behind his back, the captain pulled out a bottle of Pledge surface cleaner and handed it to Faucet, whispering, 'Other brands of surface cleaner are available.'

Faucet held up the bottle and looked at it curiously, then back up at the captain.

'I ain't gotta polish the whole base, have I?' asked Faucet, the trepidation returning to his voice.

'No, no. Nothing like that,' said the captain, motioning for Faucet to put one arm across his chest. 'On the back of the bottle is the pledge - the code that we live by. Please read it out loud.'

'Um, okay let's see,' said Faucet, holding the bottle up and reading from it. 'Hydrochloride benzodiazepines, polysulphate...'

'No, no, below that,' the captain snapped.

'Oh, sorry,' he said as he cleared his throat. 'I promise to make the world a cleaner place and fight against those that attempt to soil it with evil. Clean is clever. Clean is kind. Clean is good.'

Captain took the bottle and presented Faucet with a belt, featuring a buckle in the shape of a teal circle with a blue water droplet in the middle – the insignia of the squad that all of them wore on their belts.

'Congratulations, you are now officially a grime fighter,' said the captain proudly.

'That ain't a very glamorous job title,' Faucet replied as he took off his belt and replaced it with the new one.

'It's not a very glamorous job,' said the captain.

As Faucet put his belt on, he smiled for many reasons. He was happy that he had found a bunch of people whom he could consider friends, or at least acquaintances. He was happy that he'd completed his training and joined their ranks. He was happy that the colours of the badge happened to compliment his suit. But most of all he was happy that he'd found an exciting and interesting job that allowed him to do some real good. The belt buckle may have been cheaply made, but it stood for something special: a promise to keep the city clean, not only of germs, but of crime and evil. And that's just what he intended to do.

For more good, clean fun
go to sanitarysquad.com

Printed in Great Britain
by Amazon